THE BLACK CHIP

Chuck Royston

Praise for 'The Black Chip' by Amazon® customer reviewers:

"Wow! This book was referred to us by a friend, and we are super glad they did!
Move over Michael Connelly, David Baldacci, Lee Child, Stuart Woods and Brad Thor . . . There's a new author in town!"

* * *

"I loved this novel!!! It was a very fast-paced and intrigue-filled thriller. I loved the fact that Chuck Royston had a career at NASA in Mission Control during the Apollo flight. It gave him insight into the technology featured in this thriller."

* * *

"I thoroughly enjoyed the book and found it very hard to put down."

* * *

"I thoroughly enjoyed reading 'The Black Chip'. It's a fast paced suspense/thriller with lots of moving parts and a collection of well-developed characters. Set in 1999, the story revolves around a young doctor and his friends as they discover and become entangled in a deadly plot to use newly developed GPS technology for evil purposes. I was completely entertained by the author's highly imaginative narrative."

* * *

"Terrific thriller! I could not put the book down! I really loved Chuck's introduction to his book; Wow! what a professional life he has led and what a unique perspective he has on the ever-changing world of technology! I really enjoyed the premise and the look-back to 1999 to all of the then-possibilities in technology and have a new appreciation of how quickly things continue to progress! The story & characters were well-developed making for a very fast read! Well done Chuck!!"

* * *

"Chuck captures the personalities and culture of Central Texas in the early nineties. The unique vernacular of the locals is spot on. The presumed privilege and preferential regard of medical doctors is accurate."

* * *

"This book was EXCELLENT. I could NOT put it down!!!! Highly recommend! Exciting from the first chapter to the last!!!"

* * *

"Awesome book if you like suspense. Very hard to put down 'till the end and then you wish it were longer."

* * *

"The book was recommended by a dear friend and I was not disappointed. It was a chilling, thrilling read. Who knows where technology will take us in this fast changing world."

* * *

"Very entertaining - interesting story line that had me hooked from the first few pages. Nice job Chuck!"

* * *

"Royston's 'The Black Chip' is a real page turner and difficult to put down. It carried me to reading into the night. Royston has hit upon a genre that is very suspenseful, realistic, and put me right there. The twists and turns will make you want to read more. As his first mystery novel Royston certainly will be inspired and challenged to bring us his next effort."

* * *

"To be written by an engineer, the 'The Black Chip' is a big surprise. His attention to detail in describing characters leaves you with the feeling you really know them. And the descriptions of locations are such that it is like being there watching events unfold. The plot develops nicely and it didn't take long for me to be hooked. And yes, it happened – I couldn't put it down! Much to my surprise, the main characters are doctors, not engineers."

Disclaimer

Disclaimer: This novel is a work of fiction. All characters and organizations portrayed in this novel are either products of the author's imagination or are used fictionally and any resemblance to actual persons, living or dead, business establishments, events, or locales is entirely coincidental or used fictionally.

THE BLACK CHIP

by

Chuck Royston

Prologue

Early Fall 1999

The ambulance moved slowly up Lawther Drive with its headlights off and dropped to a crawl when it came within a hundred yards of the jogger, staying around the curve and just out of sight. It was a cool, crisp Fall night—perfect for an evening run. The jogger's feet rhythmically drummed the asphalt on the winding twelve-mile jogging track that paralleled the road and encircled the lake. Shadows and the full moon took turns illuminating and obscuring the emergency vehicle as it passed beneath the spreading oak trees near the road's edge. The spillway across the road was visible in the moonlight. Willow trees leaned toward the water's edge and gentle waves lapped through the reeds and against the soggy bank.

Inside the ambulance, two paramedics watched in tense silence, both hunched over the dashboard like cats set to pounce on unsuspecting prey. The driver's tense knuckles seemed to glow an eerie yellowish white each time the moon peered through the branches. Whenever a car approached from behind, the paramedic tapped his brakes to alert the upcoming driver. No one appeared to think it odd that an emergency vehicle was driving less than ten miles an hour after dark with its lights off. They didn't even look back.

The ambulance, created for one specific purpose, maintained its distance. Larger than a typical emergency medical van, its back area housed a complete state-of-the-art life support system, much like that found in a well-equipped intensive care unit. An electronic package that could pass for a compact stereo receiver rested on the dashboard. But, it was much more. The black anodized aluminum box contained a display screen, a small speaker, and a hand-held microphone that sat perched on a simple chrome holder. The two-inch-square screen emitted a soft green glow behind a detailed map of the area, clearly showing the road and two dots, one red and one blue. The blue dot followed the red dot as it made its way up the winding path next to the road. Each time the red dot neared the upper edge of the square, the picture automatically adjusted downward to keep both dots within the viewing area.

As if responding to a sudden ethereal mandate, the driver—the older of the two, his long, straight hair secured in back with a rubber band—nodded, snatched the microphone from its chrome perch, and stretched the coiled cord until the microphone pressed against his lips. With deliberate, dramatic flair, he squeezed the transmit button and whispered, "Okay, Chicago. We're on his tail. He's right where you said he was gonna be. We'll keep you posted." Once, an unfortunate punk had called this skinny and deceptively frail-looking karate expert, "Ponytail." He quickly found himself spitting out his front teeth and staring at a concrete sidewalk. "The name's Pony to you, not Ponytail," the punk had been informed. The name had stuck. The word on Pony's now legendary quick temper had also stuck.

Pony released the button and replaced the mike on its holder. He looked at his younger partner, whose signature diamond stud earring reflected the moonlight, and smiled with one corner of his thin mouth.

"Now, listen, Stud-muffin and you might learn something," Pony said, alternating his focus between the target and the screen. "In a half a block, we're gonna run out of traffic—"

"How in the hell do you know that?" Pony's apprentice interrupted. "And don't call me Stud-muffin. It makes me sound like a damn wimp, of which I ain't."

Pony, face red and nostrils flaring, whirled and shot his partner a look designed to intimidate the young rookie. It had the desired effect. "Shut up and maybe I'll tell you," Pony shouted. He turned to study the screen and then slowly looked back at his partner. "I know that because I know White Rock Lake. And I know White Rock Lake because while you been wasting your free time chasing snatch, I been poking around the area. It's called surveillance in case you've never heard the term." Pony turned back to check on the jogger. "A little ways up the road, the jogging trail goes off to a place where there ain't no homes. That's where it'll happen. And I'll call you anything I damn well please, Stud-muffin. I'm in charge of this here assignment and what I say goes. And if you don't like it, I'll be only too happy to tell Chicago that you're being a royal pain in the ass and you'll be replaced in about one microsecond with someone that probably has a hellova sight more brains than you do."

Tony Aretti—now with the alias Stud-muffin—was not used to having someone get the best of him. A lifetime punk with a long record of minor offenses, he had landed this job because of his "clean" record. Using a concocted story about his runaway father and his drug addict mother, he had conned a naive judge into having his record expunged of all criminal offenses. But this time he had met his match. Aretti finally figured out that he had gone too far mouthing off to his foul-tempered boss and decided to soften his approach and appeal to Pony's overgrown ego. "How did they know all the way from Chicago that the guy was out jogging? And how did they know where he was?"

Aretti briefly glanced over at his partner to see if the new approach had worked. Even in the shadows, he could watch Pony's rage slowly work its way into an all-knowing smirk. It had worked. "Technology, man, technology. They got him outfitted with some kind of invisible tracking device. They know where he is twenty-four hours a day. They even know when he takes a leak. It's too complicated for the likes of you to understand. Just take my word for it. The less you know, the better off you'll be," Pony said with a smug glance. "Besides, if I told you, I'd have to kill you."

It irritated Aretti to see a fleeting smile at the corner of Pony's razor thin lips. Know-it-all son of a bitch, he thought. Aretti shifted uncomfortably in his seat. Pony was enjoying a joke at his expense. "If we got such all-fired great technology, why don't we use a cell phone instead of this black contraption that looks like some high school science project?"

Although Pony kept his eyes on the jogger, he was grinning. It was obvious to Aretti that Pony delighted, even reveled, in the one-upmanship. "What we got here is a hellova sight better than cellular. Never mind what it looks like. With this setup, we got a direct satellite hookup with Chicago all the time. That means we never lose contact with them no matter where we go. Besides, anybody can listen in on a cellular call. This here call's coded so's no one but us can understand it. They call it encryption. I'll let you in on something else." Pony leaned over and whispered, "They even got the U.S. Department of Defense working with them on this one. Ain't that a kick in the ass?" Pony slapped Aretti on the shoulder and laughed. It sounded to Aretti more like a choking cackle.

"I don't believe it."

"Believe it. Who do you think's tracking our mark for us and putting that little red dot on the screen? James Bond? Hell no, DOD. Chicago's using a bunch of DOD spy satellites to follow his every step. And that's the god's truth."

"Okay, okay. I believe you. But how do we take him? All you told me was we're gonna pick him up and drive him to the clinic. How we gonna get his permission?"

Pony grinned and said, "That's the easy part. All we gotta do is load him in the back and take off. We won't need his permission."

Aretti looked over at Pony and sneered. "Yeah, like he's gonna volunteer to climb inside the ambulance? Right."

Pony returned the sneer. That know-it-all smirk again. "Now pay close attention 'cause you're gonna watch him drop dead before your very eyes and that's when we stop and pick him up. After that, all's you have to do is take over the wheel, turn on the headlights, and drive quick but real careful-like to the clinic looking straight ahead. Don't attract no attention. I'll hook him up to the equipment and take care of everything else."

"Why do you have to hook—?"

The speaker on the small black box crackled. "How we doing?"

Pony snatched the mike again. "We're almost to Winfrey Point. It's a deserted area except for a clubhouse and there's nobody there this time of night. It won't be long now. Stay on the line."

"Good. The clinic can't wait much longer. Things are getting tight."

* * *

Kevin Laidlaw, totally unaware that he was the subject of intense observation, checked his watch and smiled as he neared the end of his run and turned right onto a well-landscaped entrance to Winfrey Point. This would be his fastest time ever around White Rock Lake. A fanatic about keeping in the best possible shape, Kevin ran at least four times a week and more often when he could manage it. An admitted exercise addict, three straight days without a good run made him edgy. He slowed his pace to a cool-down trot as he neared the impressive stone clubhouse, creatively designed by a talented architect to provide club members with a panoramic view of both White Rock Lake and the impressive Dallas skyline. Getting ready for the wedding would be hectic, he thought. He would be lucky to get in even one more good run over the next week or two. Even so, Kevin smiled anew as he thought about Becki. Fragile Becki. This wonderful girl, who takes everything so seriously, was the best thing that had ever happened to this formerly confirmed bachelor. Given time, he'd loosen her up and make her quit worrying so much about every little thing that came along. Heart rate coming down now. Time to head home, take a quick shower, work on a couple of short briefs, and then go check on his ladylove. He couldn't seem to get enough of her.

* * *

"Two-to-one that's his car up there waiting for him in the parking lot," Aretti boasted.

"Duh. Brilliant deduction, Einstein. It's the only car in the lot, it's parked way at the back, and all the lights are out in the clubhouse. Good, really good."

With calculated movements, Pony—all the while watching the jogger—lifted the microphone from its chrome holder and stretched it to his mouth. He poised his forefinger over the black transmit button before pushing it. "Okay, Chicago. We're ready. Do it now," Pony barked and then lifted his finger off the button. He turned to Aretti. "Watch close Stud-muffin, and don't take your eyes off the mark."

Aretti had no time to react to the insult. "Son of a bitch," he said under his breath as he watched Kevin Laidlaw falter and then drop to the asphalt where he lay motionless in the dark.

The ambulance stopped and the two paramedics jumped out. Looking around to make certain they hadn't been seen, they loaded the lifeless form into the back of the ambulance.

"Quick, get to the clinic," Pony snapped, climbing into the rear of the vehicle.

Aretti slammed the rear door and rushed to the driver's side. As the ambulance sped toward the clinic, the paramedic, knowing he had only four minutes, connected the life-support system to the still form with swift and expert precision. That done, he picked up a scalpel, felt around on the jogger's scalp, and then carefully made a small incision on his forehead, just above the hairline.

* * *

Three hours later, the tall, lean doctor smiled to himself as he peeled surgical gloves off his manicured hands. He tossed them into the waste bin and began washing up. After donning fresh whites, he looked around with pride at the best medical equipment available anywhere in the world. Finally, after thirty years in practice, money had not been a factor when he had ordered and personally supervised the installation of the special organ transplant facility in the small clinic. No hospital in the world was as well equipped. With a glance back, he pushed open the swinging doors and, humming to himself, left the operating room. Another day . . . another quarter million transferred to my personal account, he thought. The surgeon strode down the narrow but gleaming hall toward his patient's anxious wife.

* * *

As she paced, Carolyn Harrison, a stately woman of obvious good breeding and schooling, took little note of the luxurious waiting room. She passed by a majestic antique eighteenth-century armoire that stood at attention against the pearl white wall. She turned away from the window and walked over to the plush hunter green sofa with its perfectly arranged cinnabar tapestry throw pillows. The patient's refined wife gazed at the mahogany coffee table with its plethora of current news magazines arranged on either side of an ivory figurine of Rodin's The Thinker. Carolyn Harrison enjoyed the advantages of being from a wealthy family with many generations of business success. Her designer dress had been created to enhance her statuesque form. Unaware she was doing so, she stroked her flawless three-carat, emerald-cut diamond pendant. Her nerves were raw. Startled by the sudden noise of a door opening, she gasped when the doctor entered the small, elegant room.

"Mrs. Harrison, your husband is fine. The operation went extremely well and he should be out of surgical recovery soon. You'll be able to see him then," the eminent surgeon said as he took her hand and patted it. "I know it's been a long day for you."

A rush of relief left her weak and she sank onto the couch. She sent up a prayer of thanks and covered her face with her hands. The relief was momentary, however. It wasn't over yet. She looked up at the doctor, her face mirroring contrasting emotions. "What about rejection?" the woman implored. "I've heard so much about it and I'm still scared for Douglas."

"His chances are excellent for retaining his new heart. As you know, we gave him his first dose of cyclosporine prior to his surgery. We will continue him on that antirejection medication as long as he's in the clinic. After he leaves the clinic, he'll be given a different antirejection medication in pill form that he will have to take on a daily basis. Patients who continue with their medications have done well. You must keep him away from all alcohol, however, as that will counteract the benefits of the medication. If you don't, he will likely develop serious liver and kidney problems. You can help him in this. Don't let him skip any doses and see that he doesn't drink.

Also . . ." The doctor didn't finish his thought.

"Also what?" Carolyn asked, eager to cooperate.

"Also—above all else—you must remember the need for absolute secrecy. That's why we brought him here where he's not well known—to be a thousand miles away from his typical media scrutiny. You must tell all of your family and friends that your husband's 'bypass' surgery went well. I cannot stress this enough and he understands this, too. Mr. Harrison's heart transplant would not have been possible this soon under normal circumstances. Your husband would have died before the system was able to cut through the red tape and find him a donor heart. He had very little time left, Mrs. Harrison. I know you understand that and I know I can trust both you and Mr. Harrison to be completely discreet."

"Oh, yes, of course," was her soft response.

The dignified surgeon smiled at Carolyn and took her by the elbow. "Well, in that case, the Governor will see you now. Shall we go?"

Chapter 1

"Mr. Thompson has returned to the office for follow-up after his cervical X-rays were completed. The fifty-two-year-old white male is still complaining of slight pain in the cervical region. No history of previous back pain or trauma to the back. X-rays reveal early degenerative disc disease. Probably Osteoarthritis. Otherwise, patient appears in good health. Physical exam shows—"

"Excuse me, Dr. Young," his nurse said, peering through the doorway into his well-appointed office strewn with medical books, journals and reports stacked at random around the room, an inevitable consequence of the young physician's continual self-education to stay abreast of medical advances. "Sorry to interrupt but you asked me to let you know when B.J. arrived." She stared at the fresh coffee ring on his mahogany desk and frowned.

"Have her come on in, Debbie. I'm almost through dictating my notes on Mr. Thompson," Stuart said. He snuffed out his cigarette and swiveled around to face her. He hated it when anyone caught him smoking. He'd been trying to quit for years.

Dr. Stuart Hopkins Young had been practicing general medicine in Dallas for only four years but had built a substantial practice in that short time. He appeared older than his thirty-three years—his dark hair beginning to gray at the temples, adding to an already distinguished appearance—and had a compelling bedside manner that calmed even his most nervous patients. After Debbie left, he resumed his dictation but not the cigarette.

"—no decrease in range of motion from prior exam. Patient given muscle relaxant and Tylenol III for pain every four hours PRN. Is to return in two weeks. If patient shows no improvement in management of pain, will consider referring him for physical therapy."

Stuart clicked off the recorder, glanced in the mirror, combed his thick hair with his fingers and stood to greet his fiancée. Stuart's height dwarfed hers. At six foot four, he was exactly one foot taller than B.J. His perky blond girlfriend had none of his "ideal woman" attributes, but her zest for life was intoxicating and contagious. He couldn't be around her enough. She came strolling through the door and straight into his arms, looking pleased with herself.

"Hi, Stu-pendous one," B.J. said, straining to look up into his eyes. Beatrice Joyce Welborn, known to everybody as B.J., was a pretty, twenty-seven-year-old electrical engineer with Texas Instruments. When B.J. smiled, which was often, she was almost beautiful. "You'll never believe what I just did."

"Hon, with you, I'd believe practically anything. What have you done now? Please don't tell me you found another mongrel stray," he pleaded, trying to look pitiful.

"No. What I did today will save us a bunch of money." B.J. pressed her head against Stuart's broad chest. "You'll be proud of me. Thanks to the fact that I don't smoke," she said, tilting her head up to shoot him an accusing look, "I got a new medical insurance policy that saves 25 percent over that Mutual of Omaha policy we were looking at."

"Twenty-five percent? Wow, I'm impressed," Stuart said as he laid his chin on the top of B.J.'s head. He reached over and pushed the door closed before sitting down in his leather and mahogany executive chair and pulling her onto his lap.

"It gets better." She paused and grinned.

"Hon, quit playing around," Stuart said. "I don't have all day. Give me the bottom line. I have to get back to my patients."

"Okay, but you're taking all the fun out of it, doctor. All right. Bottom line. I got an additional 25 percent discount because I signed this, wherever it is," B.J. said with obvious pride. She rifled through her purse, pulled out what appeared to be a credit card and thrust it in his face.

Leaning back to read the card, he said, "What's this, an organ donor card? They gave you 25 percent off for signing an organ donor card? That's really weird. Why would they do that?"

"I wouldn't know about that, but weird or not, they did it," she said with a shrug, "but while I was there, I really pulled a stunt. It was the most embarrassing thing I ever did. You'll never believe what happened. I was mortified and may never be able to show my face in that clinic again."

"What happened, hon? Did somebody walk in when you were undressing? That's nothing to be ashamed of, not with a body like yours," Stuart said, pulling her close and getting rewarded with a jab in the stomach.

"Worse. Much worse. I fell totally asleep in the waiting room after the exam. I can't believe it. And I can't believe they didn't wake me up. I was out for over two hours and I'm still groggy. I don't understand it. They didn't give me anything and I got plenty of sleep last night, but even now, I'm still woozy."

Stuart reached down and tilted her chin back until she was looking straight into his eyes. "Hey, don't worry about it. You got the insurance coverage and that's what matters. Why would you ever have to go back there anyway?"

"Oops, look at the time. I gotta run. I'm due back at the office. Actually, I'm quite late because of my nap. I was gone a lot longer than I expected. I'm sorry, Doc. What did you say? I can't concentrate when you look at me that way. It must be those eyes. They're the exact color of the water at Virgin Gorda. And those eyes don't match the rest of you. They're such a light shade of blue that they're almost transparent. I can see straight into your soul," B.J. said. "I love you, Dr. Stuart Hopkins Young. Will you marry me?"

Stuart shook his head and smiled. "How many times do I have to say yes? Doesn't that rock on your finger convince you of anything? Now get out of here and let me finish what I was doing. You're way too much of a distraction."

* * *

"Dr. Young's office. May I help you?" Debbie answered the phone in her usual cheerful way. She waited while a man on the other end of the line explained that he was new in town and needed a general physician. He went on to tell her that he wanted no young wet-behind-the-ears whippersnapper practicing medicine on him. As Debbie listened, her teeth clinched and her back stiffened. She had the proverbial temper that went along with her fiery red hair and wouldn't hesitate to stand up to Godzilla himself to defend her doctor.

"Pardon me, sir," she interrupted, trying her best not to shout, "Dr. Young, while he may be a young man, is definitely not inexperienced and certainly no whippersnapper. He graduated summa cum laude from the University of Texas Health Science Center in Dallas. You could not find a better general practitioner in the entire state of Texas. Believe me, I know. I've worked with some of Dallas' finest doctors and Dr. Young is one of the best. Would you like for me to make you an appointment?"

Debbie's frown morphed into a satisfied nod as she reached for her appointment book. Debbie Smith had been Dr.

Young's nurse since he opened his practice. She never once regretted leaving the nursing staff at the hospital to come to work for him. Debbie had been a registered nurse since she was twenty-two and no nurse loved her work more. Although she was short and overweight, she was content with herself and comfortable with her life. If anybody had a problem with her appearance, it was their problem, not hers. She began writing.

* * *

Billowing steam fogged the clear glass shower doors in the spacious bathroom rendering them quite opaque. The hot water felt soothing on her back and it had even begun to dissipate her wooziness. B.J. had taken a nap when she'd gotten home—the first one in years—and still didn't feel quite done. She reached for the shampoo, poured a capful in her hand and began to massage the liquid into her wet scalp. She winced when she reached a spot in her hairline above her right eyebrow. "Ouch. That hurt," she exclaimed, gingerly feeling the area and discovering a small bump that was tender to the touch. Something must have bit me, she thought.

After her shower, she reached for the towel, dried herself and wrapped it around her wet head. As usual, she

29

couldn't see her reflection in the fogged mirror because she had forgotten to turn on the exhaust fan again. She grabbed a hand towel, took a couple of swipes at the mirror and glanced at her reflection. Dissatisfied, she eased herself onto the scales. Damn . . . 116 pounds. Back to the diet. A constant dieter, B.J. felt fat at any weight over 115 pounds. She despised fat and consistently exercised, running at least five miles a day. Her large breasts were a problem to her as a runner. Stuart shouldn't be so against her having a breast reduction operation. It's a real problem. Those things hurt when they bounce. As she brushed her teeth, she leaned over and peered into the gold-framed mirror and again longed for real eyelashes like everyone else had. As a true blond, B.J.'s lashes were nearly invisible. She might sometimes go out without other makeup but she would never step out of the house without having applied her mascara. She opened the bathroom door and almost tripped over Fred, her latest adopted stray. When she bent down to scratch his ear, two cats ran over and demanded equal attention.

As she lay in bed that night and rested her arm on her forehead, she again felt the sore spot in her scalp. It was still tender, like the incision after her biopsy.

"I swear it won't kill you, Mitch," Stuart said as he drove his silver Lexus into the North Dallas Athletic Club complex with its beautiful, expensive landscaping. The early morning dew glistened in the sun. He avoided running over Jerry Jones, who was jogging around the trail as if he owned the world as well as the Dallas Cowboys. Stuart waved, easing into a parking place. His gesture was ignored.

"You cannot guarantee that. You have no idea what bad shape I'm in. I'll probably have a coronary occlusion right there on the court," his best friend complained, heaving his bulk out of the vehicle.

"The worst thing that can happen is that you'll suffer accelerated arrhythmia. Don't worry, I'll be right there with you to administer CPR," Stuart said. He popped the trunk lid and slipped around back to retrieve his rackets.

"Promise me you won't do any mouth-to-mouth. You're not my type. But that cute little nurse of yours could have her way with me," Mitch said.

"Debbie? Are you serious? She's a gem and I wouldn't trade her for a Mercedes, but somehow I never thought of her as your type," Stuart said as his trunk closed and locked itself.

* * *

B.J. entered the briefing room after a short search through an unfamiliar building at the Texas Instruments facility on Central Expressway at Interstate 635. She looked around. No one else was in the room. She wondered again about the hush-hush meeting. She had been told only that she should attend. Twenty burgundy leather executive chairs surrounded the polished inlaid mahogany conference table in the middle of the large and impressive conference room. The room looked to be twenty feet by thirty feet with a ceiling height of at least twelve feet. Floor to ceiling picture frame paneling covered the walls and the room was bright although no light fixtures showed. The room was lit by dozens of indirect fixtures hidden in the paneling. B.J. looked around. She had never seen one of Texas Instruments' executive briefing rooms before, much less been in one. Large portraits of executives important to T.I.'s success hung prominently in the room. She recognized most of them. They gave the room a decided aura of power.

A man she had not met but recognized as Ralph Sanderson, President of New Products Development Division, strolled into the room. "Miss Welborn. Glad you could make it on such short notice. The others will be here shortly. I actually asked you to come a few minutes early so we could talk a bit before the meeting begins. I need to cover a couple of things with you before they show up." He sat in the chair at the head of the massive table and gestured to the chair next to his.

B.J. selected a spot one down from his and pulled back on the chair. It rolled with ease on the tightly woven carpet. She made herself comfortable. So did he. "Of course, Mr. Sanderson," B.J. said, "but please, call me B.J. I prefer it."

"I prefer that myself. So you must call me Ralph. Deal, B.J.?"

"Thank you, Ralph. I must admit, I'm a bit curious about the reason for the meeting. I've been told nothing. So I'm hoping you can shed a little light on the mystery."

"Glad to. In fact, the meeting was my brainchild." Sanderson leaned forward. "To come straight to the point, the work you've been doing in our scientific calculator business has come to my attention and I have asked Dr. Westbrook's permission to offer you the lead role on a very important joint venture that Texas Instruments has in the works right now. It may well be our most important and far-reaching undertaking since the late '50s when Jack Kilby did his first work for us experimenting with silicon as a potential semiconductor material. Right here in Dallas on this very site. I believe this may have that kind of potential." Sanderson stopped talking and looked at B.J. as though he wanted an immediate answer. The intensity of the man made her uncomfortable. He added one more comment. "I've never been wrong."

"Wrong about what?"

"In my choice of a person to head up a project."

"Well, the project would have to be pretty important to even come close to the one you mentioned. You've piqued my interest. Go on."

"B.J., what do you know about the GPS?"

"The Global Positioning System?"

"Exactly. What do you know about it?"

B.J. shifted in her chair, not sure what Sanderson wanted to hear. "I know a little. Only what I've read in technical magazines, though."

"Such as?"

"Oh, let's see, that it's a system comprised of several, 24 if I remember right, navigational satellites in several orbital planes—six I think—that were put up by the Department of Defense to guide missiles to their targets. That it was used extensively in the Gulf War with amazing accuracy to take out Iraqi ammunition bunkers. That—"

Sanderson, more excited now, interrupted. "That it could be used in a hundred useful ways that we haven't even thought of yet. B.J., do you remember about six months ago when we announced a breakthrough in chip technology? It was covered by all the national magazines."

"Of course. It concerned our new smaller, faster chips made of silicon germanium."

Sanderson stood and began to pace. "Right. With silicon germanium, chips can be made smaller by orders of magnitude and will use far less power than the standard silicon chips. Now, are you familiar with all the ways that GPS is currently being used?"

B.J. followed Sanderson with her eyes. "I know of some. It's used by hunters and campers to keep track of where they are so they don't get lost. I've seen those handheld navigation devices advertised in magazines. They're also used on boats to pinpoint the boat's position on the water. A lot of cars have them now."

Sanderson returned to his chair but stood behind it, his eyes darting between B.J. and something on the wall behind her. "Cars, yes. General Motors started the ball rolling in '97 by offering it on the Cadillac DeVille. It's called the OnStar system."

"I've heard of it. I know a couple people who've bought cars with it."

"Thousand-dollar option. Twenty-something a month. What does it do? A lot. You get in a wreck bad enough to blow the airbags and your car notifies General Motors that you're in trouble. They call you on your cell phone. If they can't get hold of you, they send out the nearest emergency service provider. Bingo, an ambulance arrives in the nick of time. How do they know where you are? Right. GPS. GM is tracking your car twenty-four hours a day. They know where it is all the time. If it's stolen, just call them and ask where your car is. They can tell you the exact intersection to look for it. Locked your keys in the car? Guess what?"

It was all B.J. could do to keep from laughing at this top business executive bubbling like an excited adolescent. "I'll bite. What?"

"Call them. They push a button at OnStar Center and zap. They unlock your car from two thousand miles away."

* * *

Mitch followed Stuart into the main building. "What do you mean . . . not my type? Debbie's the woman I've been looking for my whole life. Haven't you ever noticed how pretty her face is? And those killer cerulean eyes . . . not to mention that red hair and those dimples the size of moon craters."

Stuart held the door open for Mitch. "Cerulean?"

"Yes. You know. *Deep* blue. Not light blue like yours."

"Well, if that's the way you feel, why don't you ask her out?"

"No way. Look at me. Fifty pounds overweight. Short. Ugly. Not like you. You could pass for a tall Tom Cruise. Me? A short Dom DeLuise. You can't really think she'd go out with me. The only way I can get a date these days is to point out the medical emblem on my license plate. And that's only good until they get to know me. And there's no way Debbie would be impressed by my medical degree. I know too many doctors who call *her* for advice," Mitch said. "The woman's an acknowledged medical guru."

After an exhausting round, the two sat in the corner of the racquetball court on its glistening new wood floor while Mitch recovered. Stuart noticed that his friend had been unusually quiet. "Hey, Buddy, are you okay? Is something bothering you? You haven't said much. Is it Debbie this time or is something else bugging you?"

"Stuart," he said, after a time, "Have you ever had a perfectly healthy patient die . . . for no apparent reason?"

* * *

"From two thousand miles away?" B.J. began to relax with the hyper man whose fingers tightly clinched the leather at the top of his executive chair as he stood behind it. Maybe this kind of intensity was what it took to land a department head position. Whatever it was, Sanderson had it in spades. "What if you can't afford a Cadillac?"

"What? Oh, you're kidding, of course. It's available on most cars nowadays. In fact, you can even get aftermarket units. I haven't heard how good they are, but there's at least one system that someone makes. Now, where do we go from here?" Sanderson looked at B.J. as if he expected an immediate answer. "B.J., it's 1999. We're on the cusp of a new century. Don't you see? We've got to take maximum advantage of this new technology. If we don't, our competition will."

B.J. shook her head. "Ralph, can you be more specific?" she asked.

When Sanderson relaxed the grip on his chair, he left finger impressions on the backrest. He then circled the chair and sat back down. "I'm not making much sense, am I? Picture this. An old man wanders away from his home. He has

Alzheimer's and his family has no idea where he may have gone."

"Go on."

"Okay. Let's say he's signed up with our locator service. The family calls our operator and reports the old man missing. Our operator looks on his screen and tells the caller that the missing gent is standing at the corner of First and Main and that he's been there for the last ten minutes."

"Pretty impressive."

"Wait. Get this. What if all children are equipped with a GPS device? And what if we equip all newborns with it? How much would that help toward solving kidnapping cases? How would that affect the missing children problem? What if all we had to do was look at a screen and tell exactly where a missing child was?"

B.J. was beginning to see where the conversation was going. "There are some problems that are going to have to be solved before that can happen," she said.

Sanderson beamed as if he knew what B.J. was going to say. "What would you say if I told you that all infants could be vaccinated against kidnapping with our new technology in microchips?"

B.J. raised her eyebrows and was about to say something when someone entered the room. She looked up and recognized the man from his pictures. Dexter Manning was the inventor of the silicon germanium microchip. Although he looked like his pictures, he wasn't at all what she expected. The man looked more like a con artist than a genius, his jaw muscles working, his eyes scanning the room as though he expected to see spies in every corner.

"Ah, Dexter. Glad you're here. We were just getting to the good part."

* * *

"A perfectly healthy patient die for no apparent reason? Weird you should ask. I've had two in the last two months. Why?" Stuart asked. "Did that happen to you?"

Mitch frowned and looked down at the court. "Last night, this young, healthy guy with a terrific law practice, everything going for him, about to be married, fell dead while he was jogging. Stuart, the man was as healthy as a horse."

"I know what you mean. I double-checked the autopsy reports on my two and couldn't find any reason whatsoever. Both were listed as death by natural causes and yet there was nothing wrong with either one that I knew about. I talked with Hawkins about them and he couldn't come up with anything. And if the Deputy Medical Examiner for Dallas County can't find a cause, then I don't know who can."

"Jeez. You've got to be kidding. That makes three in the last two months for the two of us. That's incredible. Is it possible there's some new type of mutated virus that Hawkins doesn't know to check for?" Mitch asked. He lifted himself off the floor and groaned.

"I asked him that very question," Stuart said as he followed Mitch to the exit. "He didn't think so. Hawkins is well up on the latest outbreaks. That's his job. I'd sure like to look at your autopsy report when it comes in."

"Well, about a half hour ago I was sure you'd be getting *my* autopsy report tomorrow."

Stuart laughed. "You know what I mean."

"I know what you mean. I'm kidding. I'll fax you a copy. Maybe Hawkins will be more successful when he looks at my patient," Mitch said as he lumbered from the court. "If he isn't, I'll talk to my patient's fiancée—see what I can learn. I don't like this."

* * *

Dexter Manning slipped into the chair between B.J. and Sanderson and focused his gaze on the wall. He said nothing. Sanderson grinned and stuck out his hand. Manning gave Sanderson a weak handshake and quickly looked away. Sanderson seemed not to notice anything unusual. Maybe she was wrong. Maybe this is the way geniuses are, she thought.

"Dexter, meet B.J. Welborn. If I can talk her into the job, she'll be heading up the expansion program for your new chip. B.J., ask Dexter anything you want to. Believe me, he has all the answers."

B.J. jumped in. "I do have some questions if you don't mind." Manning said nothing. "Like how you plan to put this device on newborn babies?"

Manning managed a weak smile. "The breakthrough with silicon germanium has allowed us to make the device so tiny that we'll be able to inject it under the infant's skin with a sterile hypodermic syringe. It will use so little energy that the chip will be able to contain an integrated microscopic battery that should last for at least ten years. And we're working on a recharging circuit. If the chip is placed under the skin in an area where the skin temperature fluctuates, we can generate enough of a charge to keep the battery level up. This would increase the chip life to twenty years or more. What do you think about that?"

Now, *that* would be truly a vaccination against kidnapping. "Tell me more," she said.

* * *

When he walked past the reception counter after returning to his office, Stuart shot Debbie a knowing glance.

Debbie paused in her conversation. "Can you hold for a moment, Dr. Cooper? My boss just came in. Great. I won't be but a second." She covered the mouthpiece with her hand. "What was that look supposed to mean?" she asked. "You know something I don't?"

"Dr. Cooper? Dr. Kenneth Cooper? The father of aerobics? That Dr. Cooper?"

"Of course. Who else?"

"Why is he calling this office?"

"To let me know about a problem that I can help him with. What was that look all about?"

Stuart lifted his eyebrows in response and stepped into his office. After Debbie hung up the phone, Stuart returned to her desk with a skull. Holding it as a fortune teller would a crystal ball, Stuart said, "Poor Yorick here tells me that he sees romance in your future."

"Yeah, right," Debbie sneered. "And your invitation to the Pope's wedding came in the mail today. There's an RSVP. Are you going?"

Chuckling, Stuart returned to his office and closed the door. After replacing the skull in the cabinet, he dialed the Medical Examiner's Office. "Dr. Hawkins, please. Dr. Young calling." After a short wait, he heard, "Hey, Stuart, what's up?"

Stretching the phone's 25-foot handset cord to its limit as he paced, Stuart asked, "Hey, buddy. Gotta quick question for you. That young attorney patient of Mitch's that was brought in last night . . . is the autopsy done yet?"

"Quick answer. Yep. The death has been listed as natural causes slash undetermined. The one thing I couldn't check was his heart but obviously it was good or it wouldn't have been accepted as a donor heart."

"The body came in without a heart?" Stuart asked.

"Yep. Just like your two," Hawkins replied.

* * *

Stuart climbed the stairs to B.J.'s second floor apartment on Plano Parkway. He marveled again at the thorough security check he had to undergo each time he came to see B.J. There was no way to surprise her since they always called her for authorization. He smiled when her door opened. Before he could brace for what he knew was coming, he found himself holding her in his arms.

Stuart carried B.J. back into her apartment and she pushed the door shut behind them with her foot. He failed to notice Fred. As he crossed to the leather couch, he managed to step on Fred's tail. Fred let out a yelp and Stuart almost dropped B.J. "Your damned animals," he said. "When are you gonna get rid of these things? They always look at me like I don't belong here."

"Forget the animals for a minute. Sit, Stu, and let me explain what your future wife is going to be doing." He obligingly collapsed onto the couch with her on his lap. The furniture creaked in protest under the extra stress.

"You finally told them when you were getting married," he said with a grin and pulled her close.

"Yes, I did . . . and only then did they tell me what they had planned for me after we get back from our honeymoon. I am so excited. They are about to hand me the plum job of my life," she said, moving closer.

"No kidding? What?"

"You're not going to believe it. TI, Motorola and the federal government have collaborated on the most incredible new communications technology to come along in decades. I've been looking into the progress. It's a worldwide positioning network and it's already in place for certain applications. And . . . guess what?"

"I give up."

B.J. shoved Stuart's head back to full arm's length and frowned. "Oh, don't give up so easily. Guess."

"Okay, let's see. They are going to create a sitcom about it and you are going to play the lead role. It will be called 'B.J. and her Wonderful Worldwide Positions.'"

B.J. sighed. "Come on, Stu. Be serious. This is important to me. TI is going to put me in charge of the expansion program," she bragged and looked up at him.

"B.J., honey, that sounds wonderful but you'll have to be more specific. I have no idea what you're talking about," Stuart said, nuzzling her neck.

"Okay. Now, pay attention," B.J. said. She scrambled from his lap and gripped his shoulders. "About a year ago, one of our brilliant senior engineers developed a self-contained microchip that is both transmitter and receiver. He made it out of a new semiconductor material called silicon germanium. With it, we can make electronics far smaller and cheaper than we even can today. And we make them pretty small now. Best of all, silicon germanium uses a fraction of the power of today's chips so batteries can be smaller, too. And talk about fast. They're ten times faster than anything we have today so they use less power because they spend a lot less time computing. The whole thing, including the receiver, transmitter, antennas, battery and everything is smaller than the head of a pin."

"Are you serious? The head of a pin?" Stuart would rather talk to B.J. concerning anything but technology but he knew how excited she got about her work. It was a small price to pay to spend time with the most fascinating person he had ever known. Her eyes blazed with excitement as she continued.

"Yeah, believe it or not, and we're going to use it in conjunction with an existing constellation of twenty-four synchronous satellites in six earth orbital planes that were launched by the Department of Defense. They also maintain them. It's called the Global Positioning System, GPS."

"I think I follow that. I've heard of the GPS. How will it be used?"

"To generate twenty-four-hour three-dimensional position, velocity and time data anywhere on earth. The basic system is already being used commercially in quite a few applications. But we've only scratched the surface."

"Yeah, I read about that. Like for hikers and hunters. To keep track of where they are so they won't get lost."

B.J. cocked her head and looked up at the ceiling as if to recall something. "They briefed me on some of them today if I can remember it all. From what I heard, you couldn't get lost in the mountains of Tibet with one of those new gadgets. Magellan makes one for hikers. So does Trimble and Lowrance."

"Sounds like a good thing for people who like to live on the edge."

"Sure, but they've also got ships and planes equipped with it, too. How many ships and planes have gotten lost over the years and never been found like in the Bermuda Triangle? Garman makes one for boats that can grab you a fix in 15 seconds. With that kind of utility, you'd think the things would be huge. But some of these gadgets are so small you carry them in your pocket. And if you travel a lot, BMW's got an optional system with a six-inch screen that lays out both your position and destination on a map. Shows you how to get there and where to turn. A bunch of new cars are coming out with some version of it. GM got the ball rolling back in '97 with the Cadillac Deville model. In '98 they came out with it on most all their cars. At least fifteen vehicles as I recall them saying. Matter of fact, Ralph Sanderson told me they had over fifteen thousand GPS customers within the first year with very little fanfare. And it wasn't cheap, either. Something like a thousand-dollar option and twenty or twenty-five dollars a month. Guess they wanted to perfect it before they put the big push on. It's called the OnStar system."

"OnStar? I thought that was what they called their engine. You know, the one that goes a hundred thousand miles before the first tune-up?"

"You're thinking of North Star. The engine is North Star. This is the OnStar system. With OnStar, the GPS satellites constantly track each car that's equipped with the option and General Motors knows where it is at all times. Within a few yards, anyway."

Stuart frowned. This was taking a sinister detour. What at first sounded like a genuine technological marvel had begun to seem more like an Orwellian prediction come true. "Why? So the car won't get very far if it's stolen?" he asked, hoping that's all she meant.

"Much more than that," B.J. answered. "Okay, say the car is in an accident and the airbags go off. The car itself notifies GM and an operator calls the car's cell phone to see if the people are all right. If there's no answer, an ambulance is immediately dispatched to the scene."

"Because they know exactly where the car is."

"Right. They can tell the emergency operator which intersection to go to."

Stuart pursed his lips, mumbling. "Because they've been following it."

B.J. looked at Stuart with a puzzled countenance. "Yeah. What's the problem? You look like you have a bad case of indigestion."

Stuart sighed. "I don't like the idea of being followed around. It spooks me."

"You're missing the whole point," B.J. argued. "This is progress, real progress. GPS is the system the Air Force used in the Gulf War to get such incredible accuracy with their bombs. That's how they could send those rockets through the front doors of the ammunition bunkers. That's why they called them 'smart bombs.'"

"I see."

"*My* system will eventually be accurate to within a few inches, no more than three feet. Three feet," B.J. repeated, her eyes widening. "And they want me to take the project over and expand it. Can you believe it?"

"Three feet? Is that possible?"

"Not only is it possible, we'll do even better when we learn to work with DOD's Selective Availability Errors. That's the term for artificial errors introduced by DOD for all but certain authorized users to keep them from having the kind of accuracy that could be dangerous to the United States."

"Like terrorists?"

"Like terrorists."

"And just how selective is DOD going to be? Who will they let use the system?" Stuart was fighting hard not to squash B.J.'s enthusiasm, but he didn't at all like what he was hearing. "You're serious, aren't you? You mean you could pinpoint the whereabouts of anyone on earth to within thirty-six inches?" Stuart asked.

"Right, or even less. Anyone or anything."

Stuart was beginning to feel claustrophobic. "So someone in, say, China with this technology could theoretically know that we are together right now in your apartment?"

"Right."

"Then it doesn't take much of a leap to add some clever computer software and be able to figure out what we're doing at any given moment. What if it falls in the wrong hands? What if I don't want anyone to know what I'm doing?"

"Well, then don't buy one, if you want to keep your whereabouts to yourself. Not everyone will have one, you know. Hey, now. Don't get paranoid on me. It's damn useful technology. And don't worry. It's under tight military control. They're planning to use it on very dangerous and very valuable animals. There's one right here in Dallas that'll be one of the first to be implanted with a microchip. Remember when we went to the zoo and I showed you that beautiful white Bengal tiger? He's the one. Once he's implanted, if he ever escapes, they'll be able to track him down."

"Well, what if he slips out of his collar? How do you track him then?"

"That's the beauty of it. It won't be in the collar. It'll be placed under the skin in a spot where the tiger's skin temperature fluctuates."

"Why's that important?" Stuart asked, his knit brows belying his attempted calm.

"Because the microchip will contain a tiny, rechargeable battery that's kept charged by temperature fluctuations. They're even considering using it on the most dangerous Federal criminals. And that's not all. Once we perfect it, we can use it on all newborn babies. Think about it. No more kidnappings." B.J.'s voice rose with excitement.

Stuart let out a low whistle. "I don't know. It's one thing for a Bengal tiger to earn his freedom, and I'd rather not have murderers and rapists on the loose. But babies?"

"Of course. Why not? They could never get lost if they were implanted."

Stuart frowned. "I don't know."

"I can see you're underwhelmed. Anyhow . . . that's the program I'll be heading up." B.J. leaned over and kissed his cheek. "Hey, I'm getting hungry. Why don't we continue this discussion over dinner? Before you go, though, let's rehearse feeding the animals and walking the dog."

"That sounds like a real blast to me. But I guess if I have to, I have to. After we rehearse I'll go pick up the steaks and get them started while you finish packing. Come on over as soon as you're done. One thing's for certain, though. Even though I'm skeptical, that new TI program couldn't be in better hands. It'll be done right if you're in charge."

* * *

As he signed out of the apartment complex, Stuart looked up at the guard and said, "You know, even though it's a bummer to get in and out of this place, I appreciate everything I have to go through. The love of my life lives here, and it's comforting to know how safe she is."

* * *

Back at his apartment, Stuart decided to call Mitch before B.J. showed up. Since Hawkins hadn't been able to shed any light on the jogger's death, maybe Mitch could come up with something when he talked to the jogger's fiancée. He caught Mitch at home in his kitchen. "Hey, buddy. Guess what?"

"Hi, Stuart. Hang on a minute. I'm taking a masterpiece out of the oven as we speak. Oh man, that looks good. Smells good, too. Okay, I'm done. What's up?"

"I won't take long. I don't want to keep your dinner waiting, but—"

"Oh, this isn't dinner. It's dessert. Peach cobbler . . . a family recipe. It's magnificent but it has to cool down a bit. So, no hurry."

"I called Hawkins about your jogger. He couldn't add any more to what you told me except for one thing."

"Oh? What's that?"

"He was an organ donor. Did you know that?"

There was a pause at the other end of the line. Stuart pictured Mitch blowing on a spoonful of cobbler to cool it down. "No, but why? Is that important?"

"Not in and of itself. But Hawkins also told me that both of mine were, too."

"Really. What are the odds against that?"

Stuart sighed. "No idea, but the strangest thing about it was that all three came into the Medical Examiner's office sans heart."

"No joke? That *is* odd. I don't know what to think of it. Well, that settles it. I'll for sure get with his fiancée and see what I can find out. Thanks, buddy. I'll let you know what I come up with. Gotta go now. My cobbler's calling me. Bye."

Chapter 2

B.J. moved closer to Stuart's side, reveling in the quiet period following their lovemaking. They had whispered and held each other until Stuart drifted off to sleep. She admired how Stuart had decorated the masculine bedroom but was looking forward to adding her own touches. That picture of the red Ferrari hanging over the bed would have to be the first to go. A tasteful tapestry would look much better in its place. The exercise machine that Stuart seldom used and kept bumping his shin on was definitely headed for the garage. She glanced over at the vertical blinds on the picture window. They were okay but a delicate lace swag curtain would be much nicer.

She turned to study Stuart. In sleep, his features were relaxed and the pressures of his practice were erased. She studied his high cheekbones and his square jaw, then traced the outline of his Roman nose with her finger. In his sleep, Stuart swiped at her hand. She withdrew and then retraced the outline of his nose. Her efforts were rewarded when his eyelids opened and he smiled that dazzling smile and looked into her eyes.

"Come here, you," Stuart mumbled as he pulled B.J. even tighter into his arms. "I know what you're up to. You can't stand for me to sleep when we're together. Don't you realize that the human body requires sleep? Don't you know that people can die from sleep deprivation?"

B.J. molded her body to his. "Maybe I'll get so used to you after we're married that I'll want you to sleep all the time."

"Like hell you will," he growled. "Seriously, I'm gonna miss you. Do you really have to go?"

"We've been over this a thousand times, Stuart. You know perfectly well that Cathy and I made a pact when we were seniors at—"

"I know," Stuart inserted. "At the Hockaday School for Girls. And you vowed to take this trip before either one of you got married. I've heard all this so many times that I can recite it from memory, but it doesn't make me like it any better. Two weeks is a long time. What other vows have you made that are going to affect our lives? And how am I going to reach you when you have no route, no schedule and no destination?"

"That's the way we planned it way back when. The only thing Cathy and I are missing is a convertible. Oh, and we'll need a gun, too." B.J. grinned and propped her head up against her hand to look into his eyes. "We don't plan to kill anybody, rob any stores or drive off any cliffs."

"It's a shame they didn't call that movie *Cathy and Beatrice*," he said, smiling, and brushed the back of his hand against her soft cheek.

"You promised you would never call me Beatrice *or* Joyce. My great-aunts were wonderful ladies but they had horrible names. We are not doing that to any of our kids. You hear me?"

"But what about Uncle Beauregard? He'd be hurt if we didn't name our first son after him," Stuart said, grinning. He reached for the cigarettes on his nightstand. Catching B.J.'s frown, he said, "There are certain times when a man needs a cigarette. Just one, Hon. Don't worry. I'm gonna quit soon."

"Right. Anyway, Cathy's going to pick me up here in about two hours so we can pack for the trip. Then, first thing in the morning, we'll head north, destination unknown, like we've always planned. After we first stop by TI for a few minutes, that is. Shouldn't take long. I have one last meeting on my new assignment and then we're off. Stu, please don't forget to feed Fred and the cats," she implored.

Stuart groaned. "I'll take care of them. Did you say they needed to be fed every Monday? I think I can fit that into my schedule. Ouch. That hurt."

"Well, you deserved it."

"Why don't you put your mongrels in one of those fancy kennels? An article in the *Dallas Morning News* yesterday mentioned a place out by the airport that keeps the animals in luxurious quarters. Clowns painted on the wall and stuff," Stuart said, rubbing his shoulder where B.J. had tried her best to pinch a hunk out of his flesh.

"But that would cost an arm and a leg . . . or a vital organ. We're supposed to be saving money for our wedding." B.J. kissed his shoulder.

"Are you certain you'll be safe? At least take my cell phone with you," Stuart said. "Maybe getting you a gun wouldn't be such a bad idea either." He hadn't been worried before. Now, he felt unsettled.

"Stuart Young, you know perfectly good and well how I feel about cell phones. I don't trust them. Too much radiation danger."

"I think that's overblown. There's no proof."

"How long have cell phones been in common use now?"

"I don't know . . . maybe ten, fifteen years."

"My point exactly. Not nearly enough time to get any meaningful data. I know what's being emitted from those things. It's my field, okay?"

"But you won't even call me on *my* cell phone. That wouldn't give you any radiation."

"No, but I sure would be radiating *you* the whole time we talk."

"Okay, I give up on the cell phone, but what about a gun?"

"There's not enough time for me to get trained and issued a gun permit. Besides, it would only allow me to carry a weapon in Texas and we'll be out of Texas the first day," she replied. "And as for the phone, Cathy and I agreed. It's a girl thing. No phone, no interruptions. Sweetheart, nothing's going to happen. I'll be fine."

He wasn't convinced. "What if you run out of gas? What if you have a flat tire? What if you're in an accident?"

"First of all, I know when to fill a gas tank. Second, either one of us can change a flat all by ourselves—and have. And last, don't worry about an accident. Cathy and I are both excellent drivers. Besides, I'll have my new insurance card with me to cover a trip to the ER for minor cuts and bruises. And if I get killed, I still won't leave you totally. You can marry my donor recipient and we'll still be together," she said with an unconvincing laugh.

"That's enough, Beatrice Joyce. That wasn't funny at all. And I'm just about ready to forbid you to go," he said.

"Forbid? *Forbid*? I have never been forbade anything in my life. We have to get something straight right now, Stuart Young. This is going to be a partnership if it is to be anything. I don't lay down the law for you and you don't lay down the law for me," she yelled through clinched teeth. She jerked herself out of the bed, grabbed her robe and stormed out of the bedroom to the bathroom, slamming the door behind her.

* * *

Stuart lay in bed for a time raking his hair with his fingers. "What'd I do now?" he mumbled. This was a side of B.J. he'd never seen before. He got up, crossed over to the bathroom door and knocked softly. "B.J.?"

* * *

Early the next morning, Stuart sat in a booth at The International House of Pancakes and watched Hawkins lumber toward the entrance. He grinned as he was reminded of why

Hawkins always wanted to meet here. The "all you can eat" breakfast places always lost big time on Hawkins. Chuckling to himself, Stuart waved as his friend wound through the crowded room and made his way to Stuart's booth. Dr. G.P. Hawkins, a physically imposing, six foot four, two-hundred-eighty-pound black man without an ounce of fat, looked as though he could go ten rounds with Evander Holyfield. A kid from South Oak Cliff, the eldest of twelve children, Hawkins had had to work his way through college and medical school. He was forty-three when he finally got his medical degree, graduating in the same class with Stuart and Mitch.

"'Bout time you got here. Trouble kicking some beautiful young thing out of your bed?" Stuart asked with as straight a face as he could muster.

Hawkins' laughter rippled like distant thunder. His booming James Earl Jones voice matched his physique. "You got that right," he said, grinning and revealing flawless teeth. "I almost couldn't get that woman to leave." Hawkins slid effortlessly into the booth despite his size.

Stuart motioned to the waitress who filled both their cups with steaming hot coffee. He automatically reached for a cigarette, then withdrew his hand. Gotta quit, he thought.

"To tell the truth, I was up all night reading. Have you read Robin Cook's latest novel?" Hawkins asked, his eyes brightening. "Couldn't put it down."

Stuart shook his head. "You do love a good mystery, don't you, buddy? When we were interning together, if you didn't have your nose in a medical journal, it was in a medical mystery. I'll bet you read everything the library had to offer. But, no, I haven't read it. What's it about?" He watched his friend get more excited by the moment.

"My specialty. Forensic medicine. There was this doctor that had all these unexplained deaths, much like you and Mitch. I thought I might find a clue that would help me but as it turned out, it was the hospital administrator killing patients with a nearly undetectable poison. The only reason he got caught is that he was seen administering the poison. They had set up a video camera to catch whoever was doing it. This doesn't help us though. We're pretty advanced in forensic medicine here in Dallas and we can detect even the most undetectable substances. Back to square one. I've got to figure this out. Maybe when I go to—hey, I didn't tell you. Dr. Perwani, the Chief Medical Examiner, has a schedule conflict and asked me to go in his place to represent Dallas at the Annual Medical Examiner's convention. I'm Chicago bound," Hawkins boomed as he high-fived Stuart. Several customers turned to look.

"Hey, that's great. Congratulations. Maybe you'll learn some new technology that will help you solve our mysteries." The two of them headed to the breakfast buffet. Stuart saw the manager wince when Hawkins started piling food on his plate.

* * *

Ralph Sanderson stood when B.J. entered the conference room. "B.J. Good of you to come by. Sorry to interrupt the start of your vacation like this. Last minute details. You know. A primer on GPS, a briefing on our progress to date and what'll be happening in your absence. It should give you something to think on for the next two weeks. Exactly what you wanted on your first day of vacation, right?"

B.J. laughed and glanced around at the people seated at the table. "Right. Keep your seats everybody. Hello Dr.

Westbrook. Ralph. Dexter. I . . . don't think I've met the rest of you folks." She smiled at the unfamiliar faces and sat in the nearest chair.

Sanderson remained standing. "Miss Welborn, Dr. Westbrook and I would like to welcome you to the program and introduce you to your new staff. They'll be keeping the home fires burning for the next two weeks while you're gone. And there will be plenty for them to do. You know Dexter Manning, of course. To your immediate right is Shirley Massey. She's your personal assistant."

B.J. turned to shake hands with her new assistant, a pleasant looking older lady with gray hair tied in a bun. Looks reliable, she thought. "Good to meet you, Shirley."

"Next to Shirley is Dr. Bill Bass. Bill is your lead design engineer. His doctorate thesis was on satellite communications. He knows more about the possibilities for exploiting GPS than probably anybody on the planet. Next to Bill is the best breadboard technician in the business, Roy Tallman. These are the key players in this ball game. There are others that you'll meet when you get back."

Bass looked the part of a stereotypical engineer with his sandy brown flattop haircut, skinny tie, pants that fell two inches above his shoe tops because of the way they were hiked up on his slender waist and a shirt two sizes too small. Tallman, partially balding, was more presentable in a conservative pinstripe suit that fit his bulky frame, up-to-date tie, and polished shoes.

Sanderson pressed a small button in front of him on the table's edge. A panel slid open behind him revealing a backlit projection screen. "What you see here, B.J., is a diagram of DOD's GPS satellite system. I'll sit down and let Bill explain it." Bill Bass picked up a chrome laser pointer and held it in both hands.

* * *

Mitch hesitated before ringing the doorbell. He'd never had occasion to visit the family of a deceased patient before. It was more than a little unsettling. They never told me about this part of it in medical school, he thought. While he waited, he admired the North Dallas house, a red brick colonial with massive two-story-high pillars that seemed overlarge when he stood close to them. Meticulously trimmed bushes lined the brick walk leading from the brick driveway to the raised front porch. Almost too soon, the door opened. She stood there smiling and yet looking sad at the same time. She was beautiful.

"Dr. Mitchell?"

"Yes. Are you Becki?"

"Yes, I'm Becki Rogers. I'm pleased to meet you, Dr. Mitchell. Do come in. Kevin spoke highly of you." She stepped to the side and gestured for Mitch to enter. Mitch looked up as he stepped into the foyer and was treated to a ceiling profile that seemed to explode upward and outward into the rest of the house. He had never seen such architecture. The house appeared much larger on the inside than he had expected from standing on the front porch. "May I fix you something to drink, Dr. Mitchell? Some hot tea, perhaps."

Mitch stepped into the den and sat on a leather sofa, turning to face the young woman. "Thank you, Becki, but I don't have much time. I was hoping to learn something from you that would help me determine the cause of Kevin's death."

Mitch waited until Becki sat in a nearby chair before continuing. "I know how you and your family are suffering over your loss. You should know that it can also be devastating for a physician to lose a patient. It's even more difficult if the death is unexpected, like Kevin's. In cases like his, we don't have several years of watching the patient grow old to prepare for the inevitable. We wonder what we could have done differently. What we should do differently next time. Next year. How we can be better prepared."

Becki looked up, her eyes wet. "Thank you for telling me that, Dr. Mitchell. It was kind of you. How can I help?"

"Maybe some family history? There was nothing in my records that offered any possibilities and I talked to the Medical Examiner's office. The autopsy report showed nothing either."

Becki sat on a matching leather chair facing Mitch. A tear glistened on her cheek. She shook her head. After composing herself, she said, "The whole family has discussed it. Kevin's parents are both very healthy and three of his grandparents are still alive and well. There have been no problems on either side of his family with premature death or serious illness of any kind. We're completely baffled."

Mitch looked at Becki to get her reaction to his next question. "Did you know that Kevin was an organ donor?"

Becki smiled. "Yes," she said. "He signed up only a couple of months ago. It wasn't something that he was fanatical about or anything. He just did it. I don't know why. I didn't press him about it. Is it important?"

"Probably not. What else can you tell me about Kevin?" Mitch leaned back. So did Becki.

Her eyes darted around, looking at nothing in particular. "He would tell me over and over how perfect his life had become. He would say that life was too good to be true. His law practice was thriving. It kept him so busy that he was planning to take on a partner. He said his love life was remarkable and he told me every day I was the best thing that had ever happened to him. Kevin was a very happy and fun-loving person. The day before he died, he laughed himself silly when I spilled red wine all down the front of my white blouse and nearly ruined it. And he loved to jog. He told me that it was very addicting in a good sort of way. He especially loved jogging in the evening. The cool air invigorated him and cleared his thinking. He was forever telling me about a record run—some new personal best. Twelve miles in under an hour or something like that. He wanted me to be proud of him. He . . ." Becki began sobbing silently.

Mitch had an almost overwhelming urge to rush over to this woman and throw his arms around her. Instead, he rose, crossed the short distance between them and placed his hand on her shoulder. "I'm sorry." He looked at the woman. She'd almost married a man who had everything to live for but, instead, had been struck down by some strange malady. But what?

* * *

B.J. watched as Bass clicked on the laser pointer and aimed the red dot at the display. He spoke in a rich baritone voice. "What you see here is a navigational system of 24 satellites in six orbital planes developed by the U.S. Department of Defense to precisely guide missiles and smart bombs to enemy targets. We call a group of satellites like this a constellation. It was quietly put in place during the cold war and it was used extensively for the first time during the Gulf War. That's how we were able to get such incredible accuracy when we took out those Iraqi ammo bunkers. It works by transmitting precise 3-dimensional position, velocity, and time 24 hours a day. These satellites know exactly where they are and they tell you. By getting a fix on several of the satellites and doing a few simple calculations, you can triangulate your exact position anywhere on earth to within a few inches. In other words, since you know precisely where the satellites are, if you have the right receiver and the right software, you can know exactly where you are. Velocity is calculated much the same as your typical highway patrolman does it, by measuring Doppler shifts using the satellites' velocity vector. All you—"

B.J. spoke up. "Bill, can I stop you and ask a question at this point?"

"Of course. You're the boss."

"Thank you. We seem to be focusing this whole discussion around GPS uses for the chip. Are there not many other uses we can put the chip to?"

"Yes. TI has set up a similar department to this one to study the possible non-GPS uses of the chip. We know that we could use it for identification and to store large amounts of data. For instance, if we implanted a chip in your hand that's unique to you, we could use it for security to allow you access to buildings and the like. It would be permanent. A scanner would verify your identity and give you access. You couldn't open the door if you weren't the right person. I'll mention one other non-GPS item we're working on and then we'll continue. We're putting a lot of effort into the smart card. We think it has enormous potential."

"Smart card?"

"Right. It's like a credit card but much more, although people will tend to think of it as a credit card. Smart cards will come with a thumbnail-size computer chip embedded in the plastic. The chip will store many thousands of times more information than the little magnetic strips on credit cards ever could. Theoretically, a single smart card could replace a billfold full of cash and credit cards. Using a cell phone or a computer with a card reader, you could download money from your bank account directly onto your card. Then spend it just like you would money. Parking meters will be set up to accept the cards, vending machines, laundromats, virtually everything. It'll make ATM's a thing of the past. It's already happening in Europe. We're a little behind here. But, mark my words. They'll replace cash in this country someday."

"I see. Fascinating, thank you. Our emphasis, then, will be strictly on GPS uses. Okay, back to the basics. I understand that a lot of companies are using GPS now. I know hikers can buy handheld devices that use it and I know some cars have it now, some boats, airplanes and the like. How many companies use it?"

"Dozens, at least. Maybe hundreds. I'd have to do some research to find out."

"Can you do that?"

"Of course. I know General Motors uses it. And I have a friend with an Acura that's equipped with it. He paid $2,000 for their navigation system option that's linked to the GPS. I've looked at his system. It has an onboard gyroscope and a 340-meg hard drive that work together to display the car's location on a 6-inch color LCD screen and keypad located just above his radio. He punches in his destination and hits 'direct route,' 'easy route,' 'minimize freeways,' or 'minimize tolls.' The system maps his route, guides him there visually and, if he wants, with voice commands. It's great."

"What about the handheld units?"

"Okay, let's say for the sake of argument that you're lost in Afghanistan. No problem. Reach in your pocket and pull out your Magellan NAV DLX-10—or a similar unit made by Lowrance or Trimble—press a button, a screen lights up and a map appears. On the map, a blinking dot flashes, along with the words 'You Are Here.' It's that simple."

B.J. was impressed. "I've heard that animals are now being chipped to identify them. What is that? Is it associated with GPS?"

"What you have there are implanted, self-contained microchips that are used with handheld scanners to identify pets and valuable animals. Right now, it isn't being used with GPS. Not to say that it can't be. For a price of around $25 anyone can have their veterinarian implant a microchip in their beloved pet using a needle that looks like those used for vaccinations. It won't locate the pet but it will identify the animal once it's found. They're even implanting them in the trunks of valuable trees to aid in their recovery if you can believe it. Evidently they get stolen too."

B.J. carefully considered how to phrase the next question. "A friend of mine is quite paranoid about this technology. He doesn't even like to talk about it. One of his concerns is the number of people who can receive the signals. Who can and who can't use the technology? In other words, who's minding the shop?"

Bass clicked off the laser pointer and slipped it into his clear plastic shirt pocket protector. "Fair question. Fairly simple answer. Each satellite broadcasts around the clock at a frequency of 1575.42 Megahertz using Pseudo Random Noise codes and Non Return to Zero modulation at 50 bits per second. Anyone with the right receiver and computer software can pick up on the signals and demodulate them. There's nothing to stop them. There's a big caveat, however. DOD has introduced artificial errors in the satellite transmissions called Selective Availability Errors for strategic reasons. This stops just anybody from getting the precision that's possible with the system."

"But anybody can use the service."

"Correct. But only DOD-authorized users have access to keys that enable them to calculate out the DOD-induced errors and get the maximum precision and accuracy."

"What's DOD's criteria for authorization?"

"I have no idea. I'll look into it and have an update for you by the time you get back."

"Fine. Bill, what accuracy do non-authorized users have since they don't have access to the keys that allow them to calculate out the Selective Availability Errors?"

"Good question. Not very accurate. We're talking maybe within 150 feet or so."

B.J. was relieved when it became apparent that Sanderson was about to call an end to the briefing. She had run out of questions and she knew Cathy would be getting antsy to leave. It had taken longer than she had expected. "Okay, everybody," he said. "Good job, but let's wrap up this meeting so B.J. can get on the road. We've given her enough to think about for a while. We'll meet back here again in two weeks. B.J., you have all our phone numbers. If you think of any questions while you're gone, call us."

* * *

The blackjack dealer gave a nearly imperceptible nod to the man standing at the far corner of the casino. The administrator, at the signal, worked his way through the maze of slot machines and the zombie-like customers that sat stone faced in the crowded Las Vegas establishment. From the looks on their faces, no one was having any fun but all were looking for the big payoff. When he reached the blackjack table, he tapped the distinguished-looking gentleman on the shoulder and whispered, "May I speak with you in private for a moment, Dr. Nation?"

Annoyed at the interruption, Conrad Nation checked his hole card and threw down his hand. "Okay," he grumbled. "What is it this time?" Nation followed the administrator to his office. Once inside, the administrator closed the door. Instantly the din subsided. Nation took a moment to let his senses adjust from the casino cacophony to the eerie quiet of the soundproofed office.

"Please. Have a seat. May I offer you a drink? Absolut straight, isn't it?" he said as he reached for a glass.

"What's this? My last meal?" Nation snarled.

The man laughed politely and handed the doctor his drink. "Nothing like that. We have a slight problem in that you've reached your credit limit again. Would you like to use my phone to call your bank?"

"How about raising my limit?" he asked and took a sip of vodka. This time it didn't have its usual calming effect.

"You know we can't do that again, unless you can put up some collateral. We've gone as far out on a limb as we can with you," he responded and walked around his desk to refill the doctor's glass.

"Damn it, man. You know I clear over five million a year. I'm certainly good for whatever losses I may have," he said. Nation held his glass out for the refill and nodded.

"Yes, that's true. But we also know that you spend it as fast as you make it, don't we? We've discussed this before."

"Look. I have a lot of expenses. Besides, how I make my money and how I spend it is none of your damn business." Nation slammed his glass on the hand-carved teakwood desk, spun around and stormed out.

Chapter 3

Stuart turned south from Highway 635 onto the north entrance of Dallas/Fort Worth International Airport. Hawkins pored over his travel itinerary in the passenger seat. Stuart drove up to the multi-lane control plaza, lowered his window and punched the button. The machine spat out a timed parking pass and the bar lifted allowing him into the airport complex. DFW Airport confused most travelers with its eight separate terminals.

"Pull out your ticket and tell me what airline you're on," Stuart said as he began easing his way to the far left lane that led to the terminal entrances.

Hawkins studied his ticket and then thrust it at Stuart's face. "Hot damn," he boomed, nearly causing Stuart to stomp on the brake pedal. "Look at this, man. They forgot to change Perwani's tickets. I'm flying first class."

Stuart laughed. "I'm happy for you but we're approaching the entrance to Terminal 2E. Are you flying on American Airlines?"

Hawkins glanced at his ticket again and nodded. "Yes, American. Exit here."

As Stuart pulled up the departure ramp, he said, "B.J.'s as apt to wind up in Chicago as anywhere. If she does, I'll have her give you a call. Since they just left this morning, they're probably somewhere in Oklahoma . . . but no telling."

"Seriously. You don't know where she's going?"

Stuart groaned. "No. And for that matter neither does she. All I know is that she and Cathy headed north with no set schedule and no destination in mind."

"Well, they're probably having a ball. I think that's a great way to go, but you've got to be worried about her," Hawkins said with a frown.

Stuart stopped the car in front of the departure entrance. "So much so that I tried to forbid her to go last night. And she flew off the handle," Stuart said. "At least now I understand that phrase."

Hawkins looked at his watch. "Hey, Stuart, I got a few minutes. You want to talk about it?"

"No, you go on ahead and check in. Enjoy that first-class treatment, buddy, and have a good time." He watched as his friend entered the escalator and waved. Several people moved aside to let the large man pass.

* * *

Hawkins was surprised by the amount of activity at the Omni O'Hare Hyatt Hotel so early in the morning. People scurried in every conceivable direction. He had arrived late enough the night before to miss most of the hassle associated with checking into a major hotel. So far, he had seen no one he recognized. Nothing unusual though since this was his first major function. Without even being aware of it, most people gave Hawkins a wide berth. He was used to it and didn't even notice. Hawkins stood in the lobby poring over the convention room map he'd picked up at the front desk. He turned it over. It still made no sense. The opening remarks were scheduled to begin in the Erie Room at eight o'clock in the morning. Appropriate for a meeting on the study of cadavers, Hawkins thought. Giving up on the convention room map, he tossed it into the nearest trash container and stepped onto the escalator. The Erie Room was on the next floor. That much he knew. As he ascended, he belched loudly. Embarrassed, he looked around for someone that he may have offended. Seeing no one, he smiled at the recollection of the mammoth breakfast he had enjoyed not thirty minutes earlier. Always in search of an all-you-can-eat buffet, he had struck the mother lode this time. Four days of all-you-can-eat. What more could a man want? Except grits. Hawkins made a mental note to speak to the manager about it and another mental note to look up his hero, Dr. Charles Ito. Dr. Ito had been the Los Angeles Chief Medical Examiner for over thirty years. In 1978, Ito was the first to identify the deadly AIDS virus in an emaciated cadaver that everyone else thought had wasted away with cancer. The feat, however, had virtually gone unnoticed outside of the forensic community. Hawkins wanted to do something as important in medicine someday. He hoped to meet Ito, whose career he had followed with interest.

After locating the meeting room, Hawkins went to the front row of the vacant auditorium. He took the agenda off the seat and eased himself onto a too-small convention chair in front of the podium, taking no notice of the pre-chilled room's temperature. As with most large men, it couldn't be too cold for Hawkins. He glanced at his watch and began to review the itinerary. His excitement grew when he saw a breakout meeting scheduled for that afternoon on the unexplained death phenomenon. And chaired by Ito himself. This was one meeting he would not miss.

* * *

B.J. would kill me if she knew, Stuart thought. He was supposed to feed her mongrels yesterday. Stuart climbed the stairs to B.J.'s second story apartment and turned the key in the door. Fred looked accusingly at Stuart as he entered the room. The smell wasn't too bad. It took him a few minutes to clean up Fred's mess. Thank goodness he chose the kitchen to do his business. Stuart mouthed a prayer of thanks that dogs can't snitch. He poured food into Fred's bowl and refilled his water. After thinking about it, he reached into the cabinet, pulled out three more bowls the size of Fred's food bowl and filled them to the brim with dog food. He absentmindedly petted one of the hungry cats while searching for the can opener. He found it and opened a can of Fancy Feast which he divided in half and placed in two saucers on the counter. Surely Fred couldn't jump high enough to get the cats' food. Might as well put out extra for the cats too just in case, he thought, and opened three more cans. Next, he filled two large mixing bowls with water and put one on the floor for Fred. Satisfied, Stuart announced, "That'll have to do you until I get back, guys. Fred, you stay off the counter." Fred's ears twitched at the sound of his name. "Oops, I forgot about taking you for a walk. You'll just have to wait 'til next time. I'm in a hurry." Stuart looked around. He pulled half a roll of paper towels from the holder and lined the kitchen floor. He then went into the laundry room and poured more litter into the cats' litter box. "There, that should do it."

As he was leaving, he saw some envelopes lying on the floor beneath the mail slot. He hadn't seen them when he came in. The fat envelope stamped "Policy Enclosed" must be her new medical policy, he thought idly. He glanced at the return addresses before tossing the mail onto the end table. After looking around, he decided he'd better lay some newspaper down to protect the carpet, too. The corner. "That's where I'd go if I were a dog. Right, Fred? Bye, guys," he yelled as he shut the door. "Let's hope I remember to feed you again."

* * *

"Dr. Ito, it is such a pleasure to meet you. I have studied your career for years and hope to be one-tenth as successful someday. I'm Dr. Hawkins from Dallas and I'm representing Dr. Perwani, who couldn't be here this week," Hawkins said. He pumped the small doctor's hand and bowed.

Dr. Ito smiled as he watched this black giant execute a near-perfect salaam. "Ah, yes, and how is the esteemed Dr. Perwani these days. Please convey my regards and tell him I'm sorry to have missed him. However, I feel certain you will prove to be a more than adequate replacement."

"Thank you, Dr. Ito. He's fine. And you can count on me being an attentive replacement. I am looking forward particularly to this breakout meeting. In Dallas County, we have had over twenty unexplained deaths within the past year," Hawkins boomed. He bowed again.

Dr. Ito's expression sobered. "Hmm. I see. Might you be available to compare notes with me after the meeting today? We too have been experiencing many, many unexplained deaths. Proportionately as many, I might add. I find myself curious and anxious to discuss these matters with you. In fact, I specifically set up this breakout meeting to find out if this was happening elsewhere in the country. I appreciate your forthrightness. Would you be so kind as to meet with me this evening at six o'clock in my suite? Shall we begin the meeting? I do believe everyone is ready."

* * *

Hawkins nervously checked his digital watch and rang the doorbell of Dr. Ito's suite at precisely six o'clock. He reached into his suit pocket, pulled out a handkerchief and mopped his brow. He shoved it back into his pocket, straightened his tie and stood at attention. After a few moments, the door opened. Dr. Ito smiled and bowed slightly. "Nice to see you again, Dr. Hawkins. Good of you to accept my invitation. Please come in. My apologies to you. I should have thought to inform you that this would be a casual get-together. Dr. Hawkins, please meet Dr. Joseph Legato. Dr. Legato is the Chief Medical Examiner for Cook County here in Chicago." Dr. Ito turned and bowed toward Dr. Legato. He then turned and bowed toward Hawkins and said, "Dr. Hawkins is most a suitable substitute for Dr. Perwani this week."

Hawkins exaggeratedly returned the gestures of politeness as he self-consciously entered the enormous suite. Ito was dressed in sweats and tennis shoes, not at all what Hawkins had expected. Legato wore jeans and a tee shirt that read "I Want Your Body." Ten-foot ceilings and a generous use of mirrors made the suite appear even larger. A glass wall separated an elegant dining area. Across the room, the Chicago skyline radiated its brilliance through the massive picture window. Yet another glass wall divided an arboretum from the living area and a hall extending from the arboretum which led into the sleeping quarters. Hawkins had never seen anything like this in his life and realized just how far he'd come from South Oak Cliff.

Dr. Legato frowned and turned to Dr. Ito. "Do you mean to tell me that this man is not the Chief Medical

Examiner? How can he possibly have enough experience and insight to be of any help?" Joseph Legato, sixty-two, an opinionated, condescending, slightly built man, disliked having to look up at someone taller. Legato much preferred the company of men shorter than himself, such as Dr. Ito. He also disliked conversing with anyone he deemed his intellectual inferior.

"Look, pipsqueak," Hawkins boomed and stepped forward menacingly, "I don't know who you think you are, but I don't take that crap off anybody. I may not have as much experience as you obviously do but at least I'm not a pompous old fart who thinks he knows everything. And I'll pit my insight and my forensic expertise against yours any day."

Legato, taken aback, said nervously, "Take it easy, young man. Nobody is accusing you of inadequacy. I expected someone with much more experience in these matters. That's all. You don't need to take it so personally."

"Well, then, how about reserving judgment until you give me a chance. You might be surprised. I may look like a dumb NFL linebacker, but I'm a damn good forensic scientist and I intend to prove it to you."

Dr. Ito stepped between the two. "Gentlemen, gentlemen . . . now is not the time to air out such differences. We have much work to do and we need to operate as a team. Please to set aside your disagreements and we will accomplish much."

Hawkins startled the two doctors when he threw back his head and guffawed. "I'm sorry, gentlemen. This suddenly struck me as funny. It's my background I'm sure. My apologies to you, Dr. Ito and to you, Dr. Legato," he said. He extended a beefy hand.

Legato reluctantly shook Hawkins' hand and said, "You may call me Joe. We almost got off to a bad start, didn't we? Let's get to work. And may I call you by your first name?"

"No."

Shocked at having his overture rebuffed, Legato said, "Well, excuse my boldness. May I ask why?"

"I have no first name and I don't use my initials. So, please, just call me Hawkins."

"Why? What are your initials?"

Hawkins shuffled his feet, looked at the floor and mumbled, "G.P."

The men broke up. After the laughter died down, Dr. Ito motioned for Hawkins and Legato to sit. "May we please to begin? As you may have noted, I asked everyone at the breakout meeting that had more than one unexplained death per hundred thousand population in the last twelve months to see me afterwards. As it turned out, only in our three esteemed cities does there appear to be an unusual number of such instances. It would be good for us to compare notes and find any similarities that may exist. May I offer you some refreshment?"

Both men declined and Ito continued, "I think it would be good from an investigative standpoint if the two of you would have the records of your dozen most recent unexplained deaths faxed in as soon as possible." Ito gestured toward a small table covered with electronic equipment and medical folders. "I have had a fax machine installed in my suite for this purpose. My records accompanied me on the plane and I have them laid out in chronological order."

* * *

Three hours, two phone calls and twenty-four faxes later, Hawkins sat cross-legged on the floor as the three men pored over the autopsy reports from the three cities. Hawkins had long ago shed his coat and tie and had unbuttoned his shirt.

"The incision shows up on this one, too," Joe said with increasing interest. He tossed aside one report and picked up another.

"Attention, gentlemen," Dr. Ito said. "Please to pardon my interruption, but I think we're ready to compare results. My office faxed to me earlier this evening the one autopsy that I didn't bring with me. It was the most recent and the only unexplained death in our collective records that does not include a small incision above the hairline. This is most unusual and warrants further investigation. I shall telephone my office and have them reexamine the unfortunate gentleman who is still residing in our morgue." He reached for the phone.

After requesting the additional investigation, Ito replaced the receiver and turned to face his colleagues. "So what we have here is a set of facts that is most unusual. All but one of the subjects sustained a mysterious cut and all, with no exceptions, were organ donors. Very suspicious, indeed. In addition, each cut was clean and fresh and appeared to have been incurred postmortem . . . with surgical precision. We shall await the final investigation results from my office before continuing. I do not expect anything before tomorrow morning, so I wish to thank you both for your patience and your help in trying to solve this dilemma and I suggest that we meet tomorrow morning for breakfast."

Hawkins grinned. "I know just the place."

* * *

Cathy negotiated the turn from Farm Road 691 onto Farm Road 120 toward the towns of Pottsboro and Fink, one of their many scenic detours. They had decided to explore Lake Texoma, a large lake dividing Texas and Oklahoma and meandering for miles along the two states' borders. The leaves had yet to begin changing to their fall colors. The late afternoon heat had dissipated enough for them to have taken the top down on their rented, fully equipped, red Cadillac El Dorado convertible with plush leather seats, Northstar engine, air suspension and wraparound stereo sound.

"Can you believe we've lived so close to Denison our whole lives and never visited Eisenhower's birthplace before?"

B.J. said, attempting in vain to keep her scarf in place. She winced when she touched the sore spot in her hairline. Susceptible to sunburn and not wanting her bare arms and legs to suffer, B.J. had covered herself with a thick layer of sun block. "With this scarf on, I do feel like Thelma."

Cathy laughed and said, "And can you believe I've lived in Dallas my whole life and have never gone to the top of Reunion Tower? Are you ever going to tell me why you're so mad at Stuart? The two of you never fight."

B.J., silent as she watched a herd of cows hurry toward a farmer throwing hay out of the back of a dilapidated pickup truck, thought about Cathy's question. Why *had* she gotten so unreasonably mad? She didn't know. Her thoughts returned to last night. She knew that Stuart wouldn't have forbade her to do anything. He was simply thinking out loud. Then why did she still have this tight knot in her stomach? Her father had manipulated her mother as long as she could remember. But that was different, wasn't it? After all, Dad was an alcoholic and he couldn't help himself. He had some demon inside that caused him to drink and precipitated his controlling personality. Stuart was no alcoholic. So, why the anger? All she knew was that she couldn't talk to Stuart. Not yet. She turned and rested her arm on the console and looked at Cathy, who, as usual, gave her time to sort out her thoughts. She wished she could.

B.J. finally spoke. "I don't know. I've gone over it and over it in my mind and I still can't figure out why I'm still so angry. It's very important to me to maintain my independence, even after we're married. I got my engineering degree for that very reason. I decided long ago that I would be dependent on no one. It's something deep-set within me and stirs the fiercest of emotions. I don't know any other way to explain it. I can't even explain it to myself and I sure can't explain it to Stuart. It's a part of me that he'll just have to accept. He will. I know he will. He knows I'm different. He's always telling me so. I guess the poor man is going to have to take the bad-different along with the good-different." B.J. laughed. "You know, even though I didn't answer your question, I feel better already just having talked about it. I'm sure I'll get over this in a few days and then I'll call him. In the meantime, it won't hurt him to stew a while . . . pun intended."

Cathy glanced over at B.J. and shook her head.

B.J. studied the map spread out across her lap. "Tell you what, Louise . . . this road that we're on looks like it goes out onto a peninsula that extends into the middle of Lake Texoma and stops. Why don't we spend the night somewhere on the peninsula and get up early in the morning? We can rent us a big motor boat and ride around all day on the lake. According to the map, we could go a hundred miles in any direction. We'll have to make an 'X' on the side of the boat so we don't get lost."

"And I'm trusting *you* with the navigation on this trip? We're liable to end up in Mexico City," Cathy said. She swerved to miss an armadillo, a little armored tank of an animal, lumbering across the road.

"Fink is coming up in about two miles. Let's find out there where to spend the night. Hey, this no-destination thing is great, isn't it? We don't have to be anywhere, anytime," B.J. said. She removed her sunglasses and grinned at Cathy. As the sun disappeared behind the tall pine trees, flickering rays remained.

"True, and what could be safer than a town named Fink, Texas? Maybe we ought to stay there."

"What was that maneuver all about?" Pony grumbled, bored out of his mind and desperate for any diversion.

Aretti cackled. "Aw, she was just trying to keep from hitting one of those stupid prehistoric animals they have down in this neck of the woods. She was trying to miss it, that's all. Those things are so dumb and so slow, it's a wonder they don't all end up as road kill.

"How long do you think it'll be before we can take her?" Pony asked.

"Hard to say. Yours is not to ask questions."

"My what is not to ask questions?"

Aretti sighed and shook his head.

"My *what?*"

* * *

"Manning here."

"Oh, good. I was afraid I might miss you. This is B.J. Welborn, Dex—"

"Yeah? Well you almost missed me. I was walking out the door when the phone rang. What is it?"

B.J. switched the phone to her other ear, frowning at the grime-encrusted receiver as she did. "You know how we talked about all the possible future uses of the chip and GPS in that last meeting?"

"Yeah?"

"A lot of ideas were thrown out that I've now had time to think through and I have a couple of questions. You're probably the best person to answer them. I've thought of an application that we didn't discuss. I think I know how we can put the chip to a good medical use."

Manning's quick answer had a sharp edge to it. "What are you talking about?"

"We never discussed medical uses. What if we implanted sick people with the chip so their doctor could monitor their condition and know where they are at all times? What if the doctor could transmit signals to the patient through the chip that could somehow restart his heart like a defibrillator? Wouldn't that—"

"Ms. Welborn, you must have missed the whole point of the program. It's about location, not medical heroics. What good would it do for your doctor to know where you were unless he needed to direct you to the nearest hospital if you got sick?"

"Wait a minute, Dexter. Are you telling me there's no way to do two-way communication with someone implanted with a chip?" There was no response. "Hello? Are you there?"

His answer was weak. She pictured Manning pale and sweating. "There are ways."

B.J., angry at the obvious put-off she was getting from Manning, raised her voice. "What ways, Dexter? Talk to me."

"I guess you could set it up like a pager system. Use FM broadcast radio stations. They have a standard for that now."

"I'm familiar with that system. It's used a lot in Europe and more recently in the states. The stations use their 57 kilohertz subcarrier to transmit alpha-numeric codes to support pagers, traffic alerts, and the like. What if—"

"I gotta go now," Manning said. B.J. heard a click and found herself staring at a dead phone. So much for genius. What was behind Manning's reluctance to discuss two-way communications with the chip?

Chapter 4

"Before we check out and take off for the boat ramp, I have to call the office."

"Again? You're on vacation, for crying out loud," Cathy complained. She finished zipping her suitcase.

"It won't take long. All I have to do this time is find out what's happening on my old project. It's got to be finished before I can move on to my new one," B.J. said.

"All right. But make it snappy," Cathy said, not trying to hide her disappointment. "We have a lot to do today and I'm ready to have some fun."

"I have to know what's going on. It won't take but a minute." B.J. carried her luggage to the door and sat it down.

"There's a phone in the lobby where we have to go to check out anyway. I'll do it for both of us. Maybe it'll go faster that way." Cathy walked down the hall to the hotel clerk, their papers between her teeth. B.J. was soon on the phone. After searching through her electronic directory, she entered her calling card number and dialed. She turned to Cathy. "It's ringing. Won't be long now."

"Sam. It's B.J.," she said after hearing his familiar twang. "How're we doing on the project wrap-up? I hated to leave before the calculation series was completed. Did we come up with the right formulas for system integration?"

"We're in luck, B.J. They were right on the nose. We'll get the exact amount of accuracy we need to take our old calculations to a whole new level. Your hunches were right on. Point of fact, they were incredible. I'm gonna miss working with you when you move on to greener pastures. Your instincts can be awesome."

"Well, I hope my communications instincts are as good."

"Speaking of communications, Ralph Sanderson has called four times since you left. I promised him I'd transfer you to him the instant you got in touch with us. Anything else we need to talk about before I do?"

"No, that's the only thing I was worried about. The rest ought to go pretty smoothly. I'll leave it in your capable hands."

"Okay, boss lady. I'll transfer you now."

B.J. was glad Ralph wanted to talk to her. The excitement of the new assignment had her itching to catch up on the latest developments. As much as she was enjoying the trip, she was—at the same time—anxious to get back and tackle this new technology. And she wanted to tell Sanderson about her strange phone conversation with Dexter Manning.

"Sanderson here."

"Ralph. It's B.J."

"Thank God you called. I've been going nuts. I tried calling your apartment but either your answering machine doesn't pick up or you don't have one."

"I do have one but I turned it off before I left. When I'm on vacation, I've found it to be more of a hassle than a help. Why? What's wrong?"

"We have a serious problem here. I know you're on vacation but I'll need for you to touch base with me periodically while you're away. Let's see. Monday's a holiday so give me a call on Tuesday. Okay?"

"Why? What could possibly be so serious? We haven't even started the basic research yet on combining the technologies. And we already know they're compatible."

"It has nothing to do with technology, I'm afraid. That would be easy. It's much more serious. We may have been compromised."

* * *

Stuart drove slowly down Preston Road toward Mitch's town house oblivious to the angry stares of commuters who zipped past him, sometimes honking and always cutting back ahead of him sharply as if to teach him a lesson. The unwritten minimum speed limit in Dallas was nine miles above the posted limit. Anyone caught driving slower got subjected to derision and scorn and deserved such abuse. Dallas. A big city in an even bigger hurry. Inside his Lexus, Stuart could hear little of the din that accompanied rush hour traffic. Noise isolation was a major reason for his choice of transportation. Had he opted to practice in a slower-paced community, such sequestering wouldn't have been necessary. Stuart always drove slowly when deep in thought and today, he couldn't shake the ominous feeling that B.J. was somehow in danger. In danger? Ridiculous. The argument? Yes, the argument . . . the stupid argument precipitated by his unintended threat to make her cancel the trip. But how could he have anticipated such a reaction? Overreaction. Realizing that he had slowed to less than twenty miles an hour, he sped up only to miss his right turn onto Spring Valley. More angry stares. He smiled and nodded in return. Okay, Dr. Young, he thought, pay attention so you can get where you're going. A right turn onto Hughes put him within three blocks of Mitch's town house and out of the heavy traffic. He admired the stately entrance to Northwood Country Club as he passed beside the manicured golf course while his senses imagined the aroma of freshly cut grass. Mitch was a member, although he seldom took advantage of his membership. He didn't play golf and the chef—in his opinion—couldn't cook. Indeed, when it came to preparing a meal, Mitch was a true gourmet that few chefs could challenge. "It's a good investment," he would tell Stuart. Never mind the monthly dues. He could sell his membership for a big profit in a few years.

Stuart parked in Mitch's private driveway, walked up the winding brick sidewalk laced with Aspidistra and strode in without knocking. He was welcomed by a heavenly blend of fragrances that foretold of yet another Mitch Mitchell culinary success. Other than medicine, cooking was Mitch's life. "Come on back here, Stuart. I'm in the kitchen," he heard above the clanging of cooking utensils. Stuart passed through the sparsely furnished living room. Mitch cared for nothing in the house except the kitchen. There, he spared no expense. Stuart entered the gleaming cooking area with its restaurant-sized refrigerator and stove. Mitch had knocked out a wall to increase the kitchen space. He hadn't used the spare bedroom anyway except to store his vast collection of gourmet pots and pans. Utensils now lined the walls and hung down over the center island. The island, designed by Mitch himself, was little more than an oversized cutting board with cabinets beneath. The cabinets held even more cooking paraphernalia. Stuart pulled one of the many bar stools over to the island where Mitch busily created his masterpiece and sat down facing his friend.

"You're gonna think you done died and gone to heaven, Dr. Young," his boastful buddy drawled as he offered a spoonful for Stuart to taste. As always, Mitch was in paradise working with food.

"Scrumptious. You outdid yourself, my friend. I've never tasted better veal," Stuart raved and handed the spoon back to Mitch.

"I guess not . . . since that's braised lamb. For a culinary expert, you make a great disposal engineer. Now, do me a favor and set the table." Mitch returned his concentration to the artful arrangement of sautéed vegetables on a silver serving tray.

Later, the two friends discussed their unexplained death cases. They hoped Hawkins would learn something at the convention that would give them a clue. Both men jumped when the phone rang. It was Hawkins.

* * *

"What do you mean compromised?" B.J. was shaken.

"Hold on a minute. I have to make sure nobody else is on the line." B.J. could hear Ralph lay the phone on his desk and pick up another extension. "Sorry. I had to go into the outer office so I could see all the extension phones. Had to make sure no one could listen in on our conversation. Can't be too careful."

Now she was getting really concerned. "Ralph, please tell me what's going on. I'm on long distance."

"Oh. Okay. Give me your number and I'll call you back."

"No. Ralph. Dammit. I'm fast losing patience. Say what's on your mind."

"Okay. I don't know how else to put it. We think Dexter Manning sold out to the competition."

The genius behind the microchip? A traitor? She didn't think so. A strange guy for sure, but no traitor. She said, "Now why would he sell out? He'll eventually get plenty of royalties with the deal TI offered him. He'd have no reason to sell out."

"That's what I thought. But maybe eventually wasn't soon enough for him. Look at the clues. Manning's report showed that he's always made good money but he's always spent more than he makes and he spends huge amounts on women."

"Report? What report?"

"I had everybody assigned to the project investigated. It's pretty much standard practice for such an important project."

"Yeah, I'd heard that. Is that it? Anything else?"

"Day before yesterday he drove to work in a new Jaguar convertible."

"So he went deeper in debt. Anybody that makes the kind of money he makes can get tons of credit. That doesn't mean he sold out."

"There's more. Lots more."

"I'm listening."

"The Jaguar wasn't suspicious in and of itself. But now we find out he bought a house last month in Willow Bend that cost over seven hundred thousand dollars."

B.J. let out a low whistle. "I don't think even Dexter could afford that much house. How do you know this?" She shifted the phone to her other ear. As she did, she noticed a dirty look from Cathy. B.J. nodded and held up a finger.

"The boss got suspicious and hired a private detective. Guess what else?"

"I'm afraid to ask. But tell me anyway."

"He paid cash for both the house and the car. *Now* what do you think?"

"Wow. I still can't believe it. How long ago did we have all that publicity about the microchip?"

"Hang on. Somebody's coming." There was a pause. "It's okay now. I believe it was six months ago. Why?"

"And covered by *Newsweek* and *Business Week*."

"Among others. The whole world knew about it. That's when any one of the competition could have approached him."

"Well, maybe he inherited it."

"We thought of that, too. It didn't check out. His parents died over ten years ago and only left him some bills to pay. He has no relatives to speak of. No rich ones, anyway."

"Ralph, look. I know Dexter is weird. When I called him to get some answers about possible medical uses, he acted strange and cut the conversation short. But he's not a stupid man. He wouldn't do something so obvious as openly spend money that he got illegally, would he?"

"No . . . unless he got assurances that it would never become public."

"Yeah. I suppose that's possible. What are you going to do?"

"It hasn't been decided yet. There has to be some kind of investigation to find out if any of the competition is working on the technology. That'll take a few days. What we do next depends on what we find out. So call in periodically. Okay? Gotta go. Somebody's coming." B.J. heard a click and some shuffling noises. She knew that Ralph had hung up the phone he had been talking on and was rushing back to hang up the phone on his desk.

Later, in the boat, B.J. tried to get her mind off the possible sellout. "I was born to be a sailor," she yelled and made a wide turn before straightening the wheel. Discovering the speeding boat to be a wonderful catharsis, she opened the throttle and the speeding craft skimmed over the water at more than forty knots. "This is awesome. Look over there. Is that an alligator?" When she turned and pointed, the wind caught her hair and blew it over her face. She laughed and brushed it back out of her eyes. Still, she couldn't help but think about Manning and the huge ramifications of his selling out to the competition. Even if they prosecuted Manning, B.J.'s assignment was in serious jeopardy. If the competition had that much lead time, TI couldn't catch up. The best they could hope for would be to win a protracted court battle against whichever company paid off Manning.

"That's a log," Cathy shouted over the wind, breaking B.J.'s train of thought. "It's only dangerous if you run over it. Watch it," she screamed as B.J. barely missed another floating log. "Slow down, B.J. You're gonna kill us both. Me, I'd like to survive this vacation." B.J. reluctantly slowed to a crawl, stopped and dropped anchor close to a scenic island.

The two basked in the late afternoon sun. The water gently rocked the boat, encircling them in serenity. The sun set and the evening cooled. Trees surrounding the lake housed multitudes of chirping birds. They could hear crickets and the croaking of frogs from the distant shoreline. They saw an occasional fish leap from the water as if to admire the beauty with them, if only for a second.

"Hopefully, we'll both survive this vacation. But if I don't, at least I've known Stuart's love. That's a lot more than some people find in a lifetime. You know something?" B.J. said pensively. "I still haven't figured out why I had such a violent reaction to what Stuart said the other night. And I still feel weird about it but there's no way I could ever love anybody else as much as I love him. And I'm lonesome for him. Can you believe that? We've only been gone two days and already I feel like a part of me is missing. I've read stuff like that in romance books before but I never experienced it 'til now."

"You're lucky. I haven't found my soul mate yet," Cathy said, her hand dangling in the cool water. She was not smiling.

"Don't worry. You will." B.J. hoped she was right. Everyone should be so lucky. "I'd better call Stuart tonight. I think I've let him worry long enough. Besides, I have to remind him to feed Fred and the cats. If I don't, the poor things will starve." B.J. brushed back her hair and again noticed the soreness at her hairline. "Hey, Cathy, how about looking at this," she said, leaning over to show Cathy the spot. "This thing doesn't feel like it's going away. Is it infected?"

"What is it?" Cathy asked. She parted B.J.'s hair to peer at the bump.

"I don't know. Maybe it's a mosquito bite. I found it before we took off. What do you think?" she asked, holding still so Cathy could get a better look.

"Well, maybe it is some kind of insect bite. But then again, maybe not. It's just a little raised area but there's nothing in the center of it. It's a little red but it looks like it's healing okay. If you want, we can put some hydrogen peroxide on it to be on the safe side. Couldn't hurt," she said. Cathy leaned back in her swivel chair. "Speaking of being on the safe side, we'd better head back. The sun's gone and I don't think we can find the boat dock in the dark."

* * *

"Hold it, Hawkins," Mitch said. "Slow down. What are you saying? You'll have to start over." Mitch shot Stuart a glance and gestured to the phone on the far wall of the kitchen. "Stuart, get on the line. This sounds important." Stuart hurried over to the extension phone. "Okay, Hawkins, Stuart's on now. Start over and talk slower this time."

Mitch and Stuart listened while Hawkins related the events of the past several hours. He told them about the excessive number of unexplained deaths in Los Angeles and Chicago. Per capita, Dallas had had as many as those cities. Apparently these three metropolitan areas were the only ones so affected. He went on to explain about the small incision on the scalp of all but one of the cases. It was still being investigated. The two looked at each other and frowned. "I don't remember seeing anything about cuts," Mitch said. "Do you?"

Stuart shook his head.

"Listen to me guys," Hawkins said, his voice even louder than normal. "I had the autopsy reports faxed to me from my office. There was a similar notation in each record. We just didn't notice the coincidence before." Stuart held the phone away from his ear. He could have heard everything without even being on an extension telephone.

Stuart paced and stared at the wall. "Were there any other commonalities?" he asked.

"Other than all being organ donors, we didn't notice any. That doesn't mean similarities don't exist. We're still looking. Now, I need for you two guys to look in your patient files for things that would not show up in my records. Anything at all that is common to the three . . . anything you can come up with. Let me know immediately, no matter what time it is. If I'm not in my room, have me paged."

After hanging up the phone, Stuart said as he turned and headed to the front door, "I'm sure you must have outdone yourself on the desert, but we'll have to forgo it for now. Let's get going. My office is closest. We'll go there first. Mitch, something's wrong here. I don't know what it is but we've got to find out. I can't shake this weird feeling, this . . .

foreboding. Something is bothering me and I can't put my finger on it."

* * *

As Hawkins replaced the receiver, he noticed his call light. He dialed the operator. The call turned out to be from Dr. Legato. He asked the operator to ring Legato's room.

"What can I do for you, Joe?" Hawkins asked in a monotone, still bristling at the recollection of the insult.

"You and I got off on the wrong foot and I'd like to apologize again. I think I misjudged you. You're a lot sharper than I gave you credit for. Tell you what. To make up for it, how about going out for a late meal with me and my wife? How does the best Italian restaurant in Chicago sound? It's called Alfredo's. My treat."

"Well, I'll have to admit. I'm so hungry I could eat an Italian horse. You're on. I'll meet you in the lobby in five minutes." Hawkins hung up smiling and said to himself, "Maybe I was wrong about the old fart." He went into the bedroom of his small two-room suite and slipped out of his suit and tie. He rummaged around until he found his favorite sweatshirt and jeans. When he reached the lobby, he spotted Legato in a blue pinstripe suit. They both laughed. "I refuse to go back and change," Hawkins boomed as he walked toward Legato, who stood next to a petite dark-haired woman.

Legato grinned. "No need. I know the owner. It'll be okay. Hawkins, I'd like you to meet my wife, Rose. Rose, this is the Hawkins I've been telling you about."

"A pleasure to meet you, ma'am," Hawkins said. Her eyes twinkled and she shook Hawkins hand firmly. He immediately liked this woman. She didn't appear intimidated by him like most women he had met.

Legato turned toward the exit. "Okay. Let's get out of here. Hawkins, you're gonna love this place. We do. It's on the edge of a forest preserve and it looks like wilderness all around."

"Pretty unusual for a big city, I would think," Hawkins commented as he followed the Legatos to their vehicle.

"You'd be surprised at all the forest preserves in the Chicago area. This way. The car's parked over here. You'll have to excuse the tight fit. Rose wanted to have her little Fiat here for running around while I'm in meetings. The restaurant is less than thirty minutes away."

Rose laughed as she watched Hawkins trying his best to squeeze into the back seat. "Hawkins, I don't think you're going to fit. I didn't know they grew them that big in Texas. Let me take the back seat. I'll sit behind Joseph and you can move the passenger seat as far back as it will go."

Hawkins grinned. "Thank you, ma'am. I think you're right. If I had managed to get in, I doubt that I could have gotten back out."

"Did you hear that, Joseph? Why don't the young men around here talk like that? We don't have many southern gentlemen in Chicago. Hawkins, as nice as it sounds, you don't have to call me 'ma'am.' Please call me Rose. I'm much more used to that."

"Okay, you two. Let's get situated. The restaurant is still thirty minutes away and I'm hungry," Legato said.

* * *

"Well, I see the forest, but there's no sign of an Italian restaurant," Hawkins said peering out the window. "All I see is a huge place called the Windy City Restaurant. And look at all the cars in the parking lot. Quite a few for this time of night. They must get a bunch of traffic from both interstates."

"This *is* the intersection of Interstate 57 and Interstate 80, isn't it? Look at the signs," Legato said in disbelief. "Honey, isn't this the right place?"

"I'm certain of it, dear. Your mother and I came here not six months ago."

"Well, we're headed south on I-57 and the sign says exit Interstate 80 but all I see is the Windy City Restaurant. It's big enough that we could move the convention there," Hawkins quipped.

"Well, I'm gonna pull off here anyway and we'll ask for directions." Legato pulled the Fiat close to the restaurant and parked. "I'll run in and ask," he said opening his door.

"I'll walk in with you," Hawkins said. He unfolded himself from the small car. "I need to stretch anyway."

Once inside, Legato and Hawkins strolled up to the counter. "Could you give me some directions here, please?" Legato asked.

"Why, certainly, sir. How may I help you?" the well-trained animated brunette asked with a broad smile.

"Could you tell us how to get to Alfredo's? I thought it was here," Legato said. Hawkins glanced around inside the large restaurant.

"It was, sir . . . up until about six months ago. They moved to Skokie, thirty minutes north of downtown Chicago."

Legato glanced at Hawkins, who looked like a cop stopping traffic when he threw up his hand. "No way. I'd starve. How about let's grab a few cheeseburgers while we're here. I'll go get Rose. You pick us out a choice table." Hawkins turned to the waitress and asked, "Y'all aren't fixing to close anytime soon, are you?"

"We're not fixing to . . . oh, no, sir. We're open twenty-four hours a day."

* * *

"Here they are," Stuart said, pulling the records out of the wall file. "Let's go in my office and see if we can make heads or tails of this. You take the Fredrickson file and I'll take the Williams file. We'll compare each entry and then look for clues in the notes." Mitch nodded and the two reviewed the files, line-by-line.

"Okay, let's see what have here," Stuart said after they finished. He held up his scratch pad and studied it. "Both were in exceptional health. That we already knew. Both were nonsmokers. We knew that, too. So, there's only one other relevant similarity between them. It's not much but it's all we've got. Both were insured by the same medical insurance company."

"Nothing strange about that," Mitch said. "If you picked any two folders at random, you'd have a fifty-fifty chance that both would have the same insurance company. Try it. See what you get."

"Okay, Einstein. We'll check out your theory." Stuart walked over to a wall stacked to the ceiling with files, closed his eyes and felt for two files four feet apart and opened them.

Mitch shot Stuart a questioning glance and asked, "Do we place all these files in plain sight of our patients for our convenience or to impress them?"

Stuart shrugged but didn't answer. "Okay, here's two files picked at random and both have Blue Cross. You win, Einstein."

Mitch stood and moved toward the door. "What can I say? I'm a genius. Well, it's not much but it's all we got. Let's make a quick trip to *my* office and see what we can turn up."

* * *

Mitch sat at his receptionist's desk studying the chart on his "unexplained death" patient. He was silent for a time before saying, "Let's see. Single. Non-smoker. Good health. I don't see anything unusual. What was the name of that health insurance company again?" He watched while Stuart fished through his pockets.

"It's . . . hang on." Stuart flipped through a small spiral notebook. "I got it. It's Chicago Christian Insurance Corporation.

* * *

Stuart sank into his overstuffed recliner and pushed back. He closed his eyes. It had been a long day and he felt emotionally drained. At least they had something to report to Hawkins. Not much, but something. The nagging apprehension that had been with him since early in the day continued unabated, even increasing in intensity. He reached for the answering machine on the end table. With his eyes still closed, he jabbed for the "play messages" button. He hit it on the third try and the machine rewound to the beginning of the messages and then started playing them. "Dr. Young, this is Debbie. You asked me to leave you a reminder that you have a seven o'clock appointment tomorrow morning with Mr. Henson. He's the gentleman who doesn't want any whippersnapper practicing medicine on him. See you tomorrow." He could hear the smile of self-satisfaction in Debbie's voice. He chuckled as he waited for the next message.

"Stuart, I'm sorry I missed you. It's ten o'clock . . . thought you'd be in by now. Where are you and who are you out with? It better be Mitch or you're in deep trouble. Anyway, I wanted to say I love you and I miss you. We're having a blast. I drove a speedboat all day today and didn't wreck it a single time, although I think I scared Cathy half to death. We're at an Exxon Station somewhere in Oklahoma on

Highway 70. And, Stuart, you'll never believe what I found. Come here, Okie. Say hello." Stuart grimaced when he heard a faint mew. Might have known, he thought. "She's so cute and I know you're going to love her. Oh, by the way, we decided to go to Chicago and walk the Magnificent Mile. Gotta go, Stu. I'll call you next chance I get. Don't worry. I'm fine. Love you." Stuart heard a click followed by five beeps. No more messages.

"Highway 70. Did I hear that right? She must have said Highway 75," he mumbled as he pushed replay. B.J.'s message repeated. No, she said 70. He ran out to his car, pulled his road atlas out of the glove box and returned to the house. He found the Oklahoma map and discovered that Highway 70 was an east-west road. She must have meant Highway 75. Oh well, at least she didn't sound mad.

Stuart reached for the phone and dialed Hawkins' hotel number in Chicago. When the operator told him there was no answer in Hawkins' room, Stuart left a message. "Tell him we uncovered an odd coincidence. He'll understand."

Stuart again replayed B.J.'s message. "Chicago. Chicago. Why does that bother me?"

Chapter 5

Stuart tossed in his sleep, furrows lining his forehead. He groped for B.J . . . his arms enveloping her pillow. The frown deepened. His jaw clinched. Fragmented pieces of disconnected events now assail him. B.J. is in a boat. A huge alligator is swimming straight toward her. A jogger falls dead. Hawkins is performing the autopsy. B.J. is in Chicago, walking the Magnificent Mile. A car careens out of control and crashes into her. Her body lies bloody and still on an autopsy table. Stuart walks closer to look at the body. Hawkins is working at a furious rate, sweat pouring off his face. A phone is ringing. Hawkins looks up with an evil grin that can be seen through his surgical mask. He's holding up something for Stuart to see. Stuart moves closer. It's B.J.'s heart . . . still beating.

"*No!*" Stuart's own scream jerked him back to consciousness. Dazed, his head pounding, Stuart looked frantically around, slowly sinking back in relief after realizing that it was only a dream. The phone continued to ring. It hadn't been part of the dream. Shaky, he reached for the receiver. "This is Dr. Young."

"What odd coincidence did you uncover?" Stuart winced as Hawkins' voice boomed over the telephone. It took him a moment to realize what Hawkins meant.

"Oh, yes. We went over the three files like you asked." Stuart leaned forward to look at the digital readout on his alarm clock. "What time is it, anyway?" he asked.

"It's one o'clock," Hawkins replied. "Sorry to call so late but we're meeting for breakfast in the morning before the scheduled agenda. I need to know what you found out."

"Well . . . not much. It may be a coincidence and I don't know if it means anything but all three were healthy nonsmokers and the only other similarity we could find was that they all had the same medical insurance company," Stuart said as he guiltily lit a cigarette.

"I heard your Bic click. Put that cigarette out, man. I'm not looking forward to your autopsy. Don't you know what your lungs must look like by now?" Hawkins admonished.

"Can the lecture. I went to medical school. I know what smokers' lungs look like. Besides, it's my first one today," Stuart said, before taking a long drag and then snuffing out the cigarette.

"Back to the subject at hand. You certain the only similarity was the medical insurance?" Hawkins asked.

"We scrubbed the files as much as possible—entry by entry—and it's all we found. All different ages. One married. One divorced. One single. Different family histories. Different educations. All three males if that means anything," Stuart said, leaning back on his pillow.

"No, we've got almost as many women as men. Okay, if that's all you've got. What's the name of the company?"

"Chicago," Stuart replied. "Chicago Christian Insurance Corporation. I'm not familiar with the company."

"Neither am I but that doesn't mean a lot because I don't deal much with insurance. Sweet dreams, buddy. Talk to you tomorrow." Click.

"Thanks." Stuart hung the phone up and stared at the ceiling, his hands intertwined beneath his head. The uneasiness remained, although he still couldn't quantify it.

* * *

Hawkins returned to the table, his plate piled high with bacon, eggs, sausage and biscuits. He glanced again at the restaurant entrance and was rewarded by seeing Ito and Legato entering. Hawkins motioned for them to join him. He stood to shake hands with the Chicago and Los Angeles medical examiners. "Good morning, gentlemen. Seems I've got a head start on you. The buffet looks great. Grab a plate and join me. I'll order you some coffee and juice."

Hawkins sat back down and gestured for the server to bring more coffee. He wondered if there was any significance to the three patients having the same insurance company. Probably not uncommon. He stood again as Ito and Legato approached the table with their food. Ito returned the courtesy with a slight bow.

After getting settled, Legato turned to Ito. "By the way, I took Hawkins out to eat last night at Alfredo's. Remember? I took you there last year when you were in Chicago for the AMA convention."

"Ah, yes. Alfredo's. I remember it well. Most delicious as I recall. And a most beautiful forest setting, too. Nothing like that in Los Angeles at the intersection of two major freeways. Only gas stations. How could I forget?" Ito flashed a faint smile at the recollection. As a lifelong bachelor, he had long ago learned the pleasures of dining at finer restaurants.

"Only we didn't make it to Alfredo's," Legato said.

"Oh?"

"They had moved Alfredo's to a little town north of Chicago."

"Yeah," Hawkins said, "and it was too late to try and find it then. So we opted to eat at the new hamburger place where Alfredo's used to be. It's a huge truck-stop operation now that's open twenty-four hours a day. Reminds me of many in the Dallas area."

"Perhaps you can go to the new Alfredo's the next time you're in this fine city. Alfredo creates exquisite Italian masterpieces. Please allow me to change the subject. Much interesting news this morning," Ito said. Legato and Hawkins looked at Ito with expectation. He continued. "I received a call from my office about an hour ago. You will recall that I requested further examination of the unexplained death case which had no incision. My esteemed co-worker has now completed the reexamination and has a tenable theory."

Hawkins fidgeted while he watched Ito take a sip of coffee and dab his mouth with a napkin before continuing. "After examining the body, they observed a small bump under the skin at the hairline, an almost imperceptible protuberance. You will recall that all of the postmortem cuts were noted in the same area. After excising the mass, they discovered a foreign body imbedded in the flesh. Upon microscopic examination, they found it to be fabricated." Ito paused and looked at his colleagues. "Manmade."

* * *

Stuart stuck the key in the lock, opened the door a crack, and saw Fred's nose poke through the opening. "Back off, Fred. I can't let you out. I know you're itching for a walk and I promised B.J. I'd take you but not this morning. Sorry, pal." Stuart slipped into the apartment and slammed the door shut before any of the animals could escape. The stench assailed him. "What the hell?" He glanced around and spotted Fred's piles. They weren't anywhere near the newspaper he had laid out.

"Stupid mutt," he said and headed for the kitchen, where he yanked four paper towels from the roll. Holding his nose, he went back into the living room and cleaned up the mess. He flushed the whole thing down the toilet, which almost caused it to overflow. He returned to the kitchen and discovered that Fred had vomited all over the floor.

"Fred, did you eat all that food the first day?" After cleaning up that mess, Stuart emptied a can of air freshener. The extra cat food that Stuart had put out was now rancid and remained mostly untouched. As he sprayed, he noticed the overflowing cat litter box, grabbed another paper towel and began picking out the pieces, which he flushed down a different toilet and watched as *it* almost overflowed. "How the hell do you get rid of this stuff without screwing up the plumbing?" he said aloud making a mental note to ask B.J. about it the next time he talked to her. Stuart looked at his watch. Six forty-five. He might make it to his first appointment.

"Can't fix this now, guys. Be back as soon as I can. Honest." He refilled the animals' regular food and water bowls as fast as he dared and started for the door. On his way out, he spotted several days' deliveries lying under the mail slot. He picked it all up, tossed it onto the coffee table, and started to leave when something makes him pause. That fat envelope stamped "Policy Enclosed" that had come the day before. With unexplained dread rising in his throat, he picked up the envelope and stared at the return address. The words Chicago Christian Insurance Corporation leapt out at him. He opened the envelope and scanned the policy. "Beatrice Joyce Welborn.

Non-smoker discount - 25 percent. Organ donor discount - 25 percent." Feeling increasing uneasy, he laid the policy back on the table and left.

* * *

"Manmade? What was it?" Legato asked, his voice rising in anticipation. Both Legato and Hawkins leaned forward, their meal forgotten.

"This may be hard to comprehend and I had them explain it several times. They're not certain of its makeup, but it appears to be some sort of electronic device. They described it to me as a miniature computer chip with what looks like two tiny hairlike antennas protruding from it."

"My God," Hawkins said in an uncharacteristic low voice. "Do you mean to tell us that these victims were like robots or androids?"

"No, no, nothing quite so dramatic. Just a microchip inserted under the skin . . . for what purpose, we do not know. My competent staff had already contacted the UCLA Computer Center and the head systems manager has agreed to study the device and determine its function."

"How long do they expect this to take?" Legato interrupted.

"Such matters cannot be rushed," Ito admonished with a stern look. "We cannot afford to damage the device or we'll never determine its function."

Legato looked as though his teacher had scolded him. Hawkins repressed a smirk, glad that he hadn't asked the same question. He was about to, but Legato beat him to the punch.

"Remember, it is our only clue and we cannot risk destroying it, so we selected non-destructive testing, commonly known as NDT," Ito explained before taking another spoonful of his bran flakes and strawberries.

Hawkins hesitated before asking, "How can you do nondestructive testing on something that small?"

Ito thought for a moment and said, "May I please submit an example. When a pregnant woman offers herself for an ultrasound examination, they are able to obtain much information with no harm to the woman or the fetus. NDT is much the same. They obtain images of the circuitry components and wiring and have them enlarged. From the enlargements, they will ascertain much about the function of the chip. One thing has me very puzzled, however."

"What's that?"

One of the tiny wires had been inserted into the victim's brain through a microscopic hole drilled in the victim's skull."

* * *

"Thank goodness you're here," Debbie exclaimed when she spotted Stuart entering through the back door of his clinic. "Mr. Henson is waiting in Room 2. Here's his chart." Debbie looked at him with a hint of a grin before adding, "First, let me get you a paper towel."

Stuart reached for the chart. "Whatever for?" he asked.

"To dry behind your ears before you go in," she quipped.

Stuart groaned. "I had to go and hire Joan Rivers as my office nurse. But there is something I want you to do while I'm in with Mr. Henson. Off the top of your head, how many of our patients have their medical insurance through Chicago Christian?" Stuart turned to walk toward the examining room.

"Why do you want to know?" she asked after him.

Stuart jerked around. "What difference could it possibly make? I simply want the information. All right? Is that against some law?"

"Okay, okay. Maybe half a dozen or thereabouts, as best I can recall. I'll pull it up on the computer if you insist. Don't blow a gasket." Debbie whirled around and marched to her reception area.

* * *

"I can't believe you're making me get up this early," B.J. complained. She pulled the pillow over her eyes. "We didn't get to bed 'til after one."

"Stop your whining," Cathy said. She pulled B.J.'s pillow away. "Get up, sleepyhead. We need to take off for Hot Springs. The geothermal waters beckon. Besides, your kitten is hungry."

"Okay, okay. I'm awake. I just need some coffee," B.J. muttered.

"So, you better get up. There's no coffee in this fine establishment. We'll have to find a truck stop for coffee and breakfast," Cathy said. She threw her nightgown into her overnight case and said, "I've studied the map and it's only seventy-five miles to Hot Springs. Our road atlas says the 'world famous bathhouse row' is a must-visit. You can soak your head and heal your bite."

"Why don't you go soak yours?" B.J. retorted as she climbed out of bed. "I thought we were on vacation."

"And, my fellow vagabond," Cathy continued, her voice charged with excitement, "we can go to the horse races there before taking off for Little Rock. And you know how much I love thoroughbreds." Cathy had a longstanding love affair with horses. A passable equestrian in her own right, she had brought home several trophies. Her father, Kenneth Nix, district attorney of Dallas County, had access to some of the area's finest riding stables. With no compunctions at all, Cathy took full advantage of her father's standing in the community.

By eight o'clock, B.J., Cathy and the kitten, Okie, had piled into the car to begin their search for coffee. They headed east toward Hot Springs. One minute later, an ambulance pulled out of the motel parking lot and onto Highway 70. Both paramedics lowered their sun visors to shield their eyes from the bright morning sun.

* * *

"Where the hell do you suppose they'll go today?" Aretti asked. "If I didn't know better, I'd say they were trying to shake us. 'Cept they ain't going fast enough."

"And they don't know we're following them," Pony added.

"Well, I wish Chicago would make up their minds. I'm getting tired of this."

Pony groaned. "You don't know nothing. I told you they won't be giving us a call until everything is set up. It won't be long. Be patient, okay?"

"Yeah, yeah." Someday, Aretti thought, someday. You wait and see.

* * *

"You must come back soon so I can feed you some real Italian cooking." Rose frowned. "You're much too thin."

"What?" Hawkins said. He couldn't fathom what she was saying. No one had ever accused him of being thin.

"After I feed you, then I can take credit for fattening you up. With Joseph as my model, people think I don't know my way around the kitchen."

Hawkins laughed. The sound echoed through the large hotel lobby. "I can see why that could ruin your reputation." He slapped Legato on the back, almost knocking him over.

"Hey, wait a minute. I'm a prime specimen of manhood. Never had any complaints before," Legato said as he attempted to regain his balance.

"Hawkins could redeem me, even in the eyes of your mother," Rose said. "She's been accusing me all these years of starving you to death. I've told her a thousand times that I can only feed you when you're at home. You spend so much time at the office and in your autopsy suite that it's a miracle we ever had four children." Rose turned to Hawkins. "Seriously, Dr. Hawkins, we've enjoyed your company and would love for you to come visit again. Anytime."

"You two have made me feel right at home in your city and I appreciate it. And, Legato, I'm glad you're not an old fart after all." Hawkins grinned as he anticipated Legato's response.

"An old what? Why, you young whippersnapper, I'd take you over my knee if it wouldn't break it." Legato laughed and reached up to pat Hawkins on his broad shoulder. "But I do second what Rose said. Let's promise not to lose touch. Who knows? Maybe you could return the favor to Rose and me by showing us your fair city."

* * *

"Hold up a minute, Hank," Mitch said, gasping for breath as he lumbered to catch up with Dr. Heister. The elder doctor turned around to see who had shouted and gave Mitch a disapproving look as he ran panting up to him.

"Good morning, Mitch. I see you're as fit as ever," Dr. Heister said with a frown. "Call my office and make an appointment. We must get you on an exercise program and see that you eat the proper foods."

"But, Hank," Mitch protested. "I played racquetball just the other day . . . and I always steam my vegetables . . . well, almost always. And if I sauté them, it's without much butter. Don't worry; I'll set up an appointment. But the reason I wanted to catch you is to ask you a question."

"Shoot," Heister said, warming up. "What's the question?"

"This may sound strange but in the last few months have you had any patients die of unexplained natural causes? The reason I'm asking is that both Stuart Young and I have had this occur in recent months and we know that there have been about twenty cases in the Dallas area in the past year."

Heister listened without comment until Mitch had finished. "Sounds like an interesting mystery. To answer your question . . . yes, I have. Do you think there might be some rare pathogen responsible?"

"This is great," Mitch said with excitement as he mopped his forehead with a handkerchief.

"What do you mean . . . great?" Heister asked, offended by such a cavalier attitude.

"I'm sorry. I don't mean it's great about your patient . . . but I've been asking all morning and you're the first one I've found who has had such a case. Would you be willing to do me a big favor?" Mitch implored, tugging at his collar.

Heister hesitated before responding, "I suppose I might. What is it that you want?"

Mitch leaned over and whispered in a secretive manner, "I need to know as soon as possible what company he had medical insurance with."

Heister said, "First, the patient was a 'she' and, second, why would the name of the medical insurance company be important?"

* * *

"Dr. Young, Dr. Mitchell asked to speak with you. He's holding on line one," Debbie said after Stuart returned from the examining room.

"Thanks, Debbie. I'll get it in my office. Do we have any fresh coffee?" he asked turning toward his door.

"Sure do. I'll bring it to you."

Stuart sank into his chair, fished a spiral notebook out of his pocket and picked up the phone. "What's up, Mitch?" He listened, making notes as Mitch related his conversation with Dr. Heister.

"And guess what else?" Mitch asked before pausing.

Becoming exasperated at Mitch's dramatics, Stuart snapped, "Spit it out. What else? I don't feel like guessing."

"Steady, guy. Don't have a coronary. Hank called and told me the young lady had been insured by Chicago Christian. That's four out of four now. Don't you think that's a little more than coincidental?"

"Listen, Mitch, thanks. I'm sorry I snapped at you." Stiff with fear, Stuart lowered the phone to its cradle and picked up the phone book. He opened the yellow pages to insurance. His fingers ran down the alphabetical listing and stopped at Chicago Christian Insurance Corporation. Holding his finger on the number, he dialed and waited.

"C.C.I. How may I direct your call?"

"Is this Chicago Christian Insurance?"

"Yes, it is. May I connect you to one of our agents or does this pertain to a claim?"

"Uh, give me an agent, please."

"One moment."

"This is Chuck Green. May I help you?"

"Yes, I'm interested in some medical insurance and I heard you had a discount for people who don't smoke."

"What you heard is true. We do, however, insist that our candidates undergo a pre-insurance physical examination at no cost to the applicant. Would you have any objection to that?"

"Not at all. I'm very healthy."

"All right then. Let's get some information and I think I can set you up for an exam as early as today. How does that sound?"

"I'd like that if you can make it early in the day."

"No problem. We can make it anytime you like. The clinic is open until nine o'clock tonight if you prefer a later appointment. What time would be best for you?"

"Uh . . . how about noon? I can go on my lunch hour."

"I'll put you down for twelve. Name please?"

All he could think of was B.J.'s mongrel dog. "Fred . . ." His mind racing, Stuart glanced down at the yellow pages where his finger pointed to Chicago Christian. Below Chicago Christian's listing, a bold, blocked advertisement for Chubb Insurance Company. ". . . Chubb. Fred Chubb . . . with two b's."

"Okay, Fred Chubb with two b's, they'll be expecting you at noon. The Christian Clinic is easy to find. Preston Tower. Fourth floor. Do you know where it is?"

"Oh, yes. I pass Preston Tower every day. I'll be there." Stuart, unsettled about lying to the agent, stared at the wall. What was he getting himself into? Didn't matter. He had to get some answers. This was a good way to start.

Debbie poked her head in the doorway and said, "I've got your coffee. Are you ready for it?"

"More than you know. Thanks," Stuart said as he rounded his desk and reached for the cup. "By the way, have you finished checking the patient records for that insurance company."

"I was right . . . as usual," Debbie said, looking smug. She loved to win. "We have four. When you add the two recently deceased patients, that makes a half dozen."

* * *

"I'm sorry, sir. We don't carry dog litter boxes. As far as I know there is no such thing." The clerk looked amused.

"Well, why in the world not? Dogs have to go to the bathroom, too. Don't they? Are they too stupid to use one? Cats do it."

"Well, sir, dog owners usually—"

"Never mind. I'll take these items. Please check me out, now. I'm in a hurry. I guess I'll just buy more throw rugs."

"Yes, sir." The clerk no longer looked amused.

After ringing up two automatic dog food dispensers, two automatic cat food dispensers, three cat litter boxes with charcoal filters, three sacks of kitty litter, ten-pound bags of dry cat food and dry dog food, four large water bowls and a large can of Pet Odor Eater, the clerk helped Stuart carry his purchases to the car.

Stuart glanced at his watch. Had to hurry to get this stuff to B.J.'s apartment before his appointment. Should last them at least a week, he thought.

* * *

Stuart eased his Lexus into a parking place in a far corner of the Preston Tower parking lot near the back entrance. After making his way around to the front of the building, he slipped in, trying his best not to look furtive. The elevator bank wasn't visible as he entered but he had no trouble finding it. The elevator doors opened to disgorge a load of office workers going out to lunch. Stuart entered the now-empty elevator alone. As instructed, he pushed the button for the fourth floor. When the elevator ascended and the doors opened, Stuart saw the glass doors directly in front of him. "Christian Clinic" was stenciled in bold black letters. He pushed one of the doors and entered. The receptionist looked up and said in a bright and cheery voice, "You must be Mr. Chubb. You're right on time."

Stuart had to catch himself before an instinctive reaction took over to look behind him for a Mr. Chubb.

"Yes, ma'am." Stuart answered, feeling foolish and looking as though he suffered from a bad neck twitch.

"Please sign the register here and fill out these forms, both front and back. You'll find that our physical exams are a little different," she said, beaming as though proud of herself for something.

"What do you mean?" he asked, taken aback.

"We're the only clinic that doesn't ask you for your insurance card," she said, giggling at her own stale joke.

She must have told that a million times, Stuart thought as he forced a chuckle. He crossed over to the couch and sat in front of a coffee table strewn with back issues of various magazines, including several dog-eared copies of *People*. He made a mental note to ask Debbie about the vintage of the magazines in his office. He struggled to fill out the fake information. Occupation . . . engineer. Employer . . . Texas Instruments. Home address . . . 2600 Main Street. He hoped that 2600 was far enough from downtown to be an apartment building. He added . . . apartment 321. In case of emergency call . . . Norma Chubb, mother, Juneau, Alaska. No, I can't put that, he thought in panic as he scratched out the address. I don't know the area code for Alaska. Settling for Austin, Texas, he wrote down the phone number of an ex-girlfriend. Done at last, Stuart handed the forms to the girl, returned to the couch and absently flipped through a magazine. "The doctor will see you now, Mr. Chubb. This way, please."

* * *

The hospital administrator cleared his throat and waited for the crowd noise to subside. He looked out at the familiar faces in the briefing theater and said, "Thank you for your patience, ladies and gentlemen of the press. We apologize for the delay but Dr. Nation has now exited the surgical suite. It is my privilege to introduce the finest organ transplant surgeon in the country and who practices here at Dallas General Hospital. Dr. Conrad Crawford Nation, III." The administrator gestured toward Dr. Nation, who crossed the podium to the lectern. Dr. Nation, a trim six-footer and Paul Newman lookalike, commanded attention and respect everywhere he went. Today, in front of a roomful of news reporters, including some of the biggest names in television news casting, he appeared calm and in control. As he reached the lectern, he held up his hand to still the polite applause.

"I have completed the surgery and I'm certain you're anxious to hear the results. I'm pleased to announce that Mr. Tiger Griffin is in recovery in stable condition. His new heart is functioning completely on its own and all vital signs are strong. Mr. Griffin, as we all are aware, was a premier sportsman, having won the middleweight championship a total of three separate times, the last time being at age fifty-one. He is an inspiration to all of us in the over forty category and we all wish him well. At this time, I'd be happy to entertain any questions you might have. We'll start with Mr. Jennings. Peter, you've raised your hand . . . what is your question?"

Peter Jennings stood up before the ABC camera and faced Nation. "Thank you, Dr. Nation. Can you give us any information about the donor or the donor's family? Was the donor an athlete? Was the donor younger than Tiger?"

Dr. Nation shook his head. "I'm sorry but the identity of the donor must remain anonymous. Yes, Ms. Shriver. I believe I saw your hand."

"Do you have any statistics on the possibility of Mr. Griffin's body rejecting the donor heart?"

"I don't like to quote statistics in any type of organ transplant procedure. Each patient is unique and I do not believe there are sufficient numbers for the statisticians to formulate any meaningful statistics. I would point out that Mr. Griffin has a better than average change of compatibility due to his excellent physical condition. Mr. Brokaw, your question."

"Will Tiger be physically restricted in any way once the possibility of organ rejection is behind him?"

"He will, of course, have to remain on numerous medications for the rest of his life. He will have to avoid alcohol since alcohol would counteract his medications. Other than that, he won't be restricted any more than you or I. Don't be surprised if you see him on a tennis court within a month or so. Thank you, Mr. Brokaw. Mr. Rather, I hope you don't mind that I saved your question for last. I've been a fan of yours for years. What would you like to know?"

"Thank you, Dr. Nation. I've been following your illustrious career for years and it seems as though your number of organ transplant procedures has declined in the last two to three years.   Is this an indication of the direction of heart transplants in general or is this just a personal thing with you?"

Nation cleared his throat and straightened his tie before responding.   "While it is true that my personal number of transplant surgeries has declined, it is strictly a matter of other pressing medical demands on my time and has nothing to do with the national trend as a whole . . . which is increasing.   I'm afraid we're out of time.   I have an important appointment across town.   Mr. Patterson, our hospital administrator, will attempt to answer any further questions you may have.   Thank you."   Nation turned and exited the room.   He headed straight for his car, a black Mercedes Benz sedan.   After leaving the hospital parking lot, he turned west onto Walnut Hill.   Ten minutes later, he pulled into the back lot of Preston Tower and parked beside a silver Lexus.

* * *

"Please have a seat, Mr. Chubb.   The doctor will be with you in a moment to discuss the results of your physical examination."   Stuart entered the small but comfortable room and the nurse closed the door behind him.   Music blared from a radio that sat on a small table next to a plain, overstuffed couch. This would be the couch that B.J. fell asleep on, he thought. He sat on the couch and sunk deeply into the soft cushions. Certainly comfortable enough to lull a tired person to sleep. So far everything appeared to be normal. I would use the same procedures for a pre-insurance physical myself, he thought. Complete blood count, blood pressure check, thorough physical examination, chest x-ray and an EKG. A complete social and family history taken. Pretty thorough. The music continued to blare and the grating sound began to get on his nerves. Willie Nelson was singing *Whiskey River*. He couldn't stand that song or Willie for that matter. He stood up intending to turn off the offending music. Strange, he thought. No volume control. The thing continued to blare. Stuart grimaced and shook his head. Goodbye, Willie, he mouthed as he bent over, reached under the table and pulled the plug on the radio. Quiet now. Much better. Odd, though. He could still hear static from the radio. He walked around the small room and glanced at some books on a shelf. Hey, look at that. Robin Cook. Hawkins should be here. Stuart began to feel dizzy and shook his head to clear out the fuzziness. Bracing himself against the wall, he made his way back toward the couch. The static increased. What the hell? Thinking he somehow hadn't managed to get the radio completely unplugged, he checked under the table. The radio was definitely unplugged. It wasn't static. In fact, it was more like a hissing sound. Woozy, he looked around the room but saw nothing unusual. That infernal hissing. Coming from where? Looking up, Stuart spotted a small, clear plastic tube protruding from the ceiling and noticed a faint mist escaping from the tube. That's nitrous oxide, he suddenly realized. I've got to get out of here. Stumbling across the room, Stuart made his way to the door, opened it and took a deep breath, still feeling lightheaded. Intent upon making his escape, he lunged for a glass door that he prayed would lead into the hall. Glancing behind and still in a drunken stupor, Stuart could have sworn he caught a glimpse of Dr. Conrad Nation. Why in the world would Nation be here? He must have been mistaken. What would an organ transplant surgeon of Nation's stature be doing in this tiny clinic? The door did indeed lead into the hall where he found the stairwell. He sank down on the top step and clung to the rail. After regaining his equilibrium, he slowly descended the four flights of stairs. Making his way to his car and feeling like he'd been on a three-day binge, he opened the door and sank into the leather seat. The bastards gassed me, he thought angrily. What are they doing to people? Did they do anything to B.J.? She seemed fine. But now he was certain he knew why she fell asleep in that room. What did it all mean?

As he drove back to his office, he failed to notice that he was being followed.

* * *

"Okay, Chicago, I'm on his tail. I don't know if he headed for his job or his apartment. I'll stick with him and let you know where he ends up. I'll tell you one thing though. He's in a big hurry 'cause he's driving like a bat out of hell."

"He must have spotted you. Whatever you do, don't lose him. We don't know what he's up to. He may know more than he should and we can't take a chance. You may have to take him out."

"You got it. But he ain't driving like he's trying to shake nobody. It's like he's just in a hell of a hurry or something. That's all. Don't worry, I ain't gonna lose him. He's acting kinda goofy though. He's half hanging out the window like a dog does and he's shaking his head. Almost lost it when he passed that last car. Right now we're headed east on Forest Lane and approaching Central Expressway. Stand by."

In a desperate attempt to clear his brain, Stuart had lowered his window and driven with his head out, trying to get as much fresh air into his lungs as fast as he could. As he neared the entrance to Central Expressway, he straightened up, raised the window and turned the air conditioner on full blast with all outlets aimed at his face. Stuart began to creep out of his stupor. He shook his head again as he made a right onto Central.

"He must be going to his apartment. Texas Instruments is back the other way. That's good. It'll make it easier. Hang on. I think he's slowing down to exit and this is only Walnut Lane. Yeah. He's getting off."

* * *

Stuart glanced at his watch and accelerated. Already forty-five minutes behind schedule, he knew that Debbie would be beside herself. Almost missing the Central Expressway exit, he slammed on his brakes, barely regaining control of his Lexus before heading east on Walnut Hill. He forced himself to lower his speed as he approached the hospital district. His small clinic was across the street from Dallas General.

* * *

"Jeez. I think he's taking himself to the hospital. What do I do now? I can't take him out there."

"Back off but don't lose him. What hospital?"

"Dallas General."

"Good. We've got connections there."

"No. Wait. He turning left on Rambler. He's going to see a doctor. Sure 'nuf. He's going to see a Dr. Stuart Young. He's pulling into the parking space reserved for Dr. Young. Well, I'll be go-to-hell. He ain't no engineer. He just put on a white doctor's coat."

"We'll take it from here. You get yourself back to the clinic. Pronto. Good job."

Chapter 6

Stuart rushed through the back door of his clinic, his white coat flapping and his tie over his shoulder. In his haste, he had failed to comb his hair after the ordeal and it now stood out in all directions. Consumed by a mixture of fear and anger, his features were grim and pale. Why don't I go straight to the police? he thought. What was Conrad Nation doing at the Christian Clinic? Or did he imagine it? What did they do to B.J. during her two-hour nap? He now knew that the gas induced it. If he went to the police, the physicians at the

Christian Clinic would deny his allegations and probably had already removed the protruding gas tube he had seen. He needed more proof . . . something he could take to the authorities. If B.J. were here and he knew that she was safe from whatever threat this was, he wouldn't feel so hamstrung. Was B.J. in any danger? Would any actions on his part increase the danger for her?

"What happened to you? You look like you've been riding around at high speed in a convertible," Debbie said, handing him a patient chart.

Stuart quickly combed his hair with his fingers. "You're closer than you think. Were you able to arrange for me to have this afternoon free?"

"Yes. You only have two patients and they're both here. You're late. The other patients for this afternoon were no problem to reschedule. I'm going to go ahead and stay until five anyway because I need to catch up with your office notes and my filing," Debbie said.

"Thanks, Debbie," Stuart said with a forced smile. "I appreciate that."

"By the way, Dr. Hawkins is back from Chicago and asked that you call him at the Medical Examiner's Office as soon as you can."

After finishing with both patients, he dictated some quick notes and then called Hawkins on his direct dial number, 429-5467. Hawkins had been so proud when they agreed to give him a phone number that spelled out his name. "Hawkins, you're back early."

"Stuart, listen. I need to meet with you and Mitch as soon as possible. I've already talked to Mitch and he'll be here at four o'clock. How soon can you make it?"

"I can leave now. I'm glad you warned me ahead of time. Debbie was able to clear my schedule for the rest of the day. And you ain't gonna believe what happened to me earlier. I'll tell you as soon as I get there."

Stuart shed his white coat, ran out the back door and jumped into his Lexus. He pulled onto Walnut Hill heading west toward the Tollway. It was the quickest route through North Dallas to Parkland Memorial Hospital. Hawkins had a small office right behind Parkland. A black Lincoln Town Car pulled in unobtrusively behind him. The windows were deeply

165

tinted. The Town Car maintained a steady distance between it and Stuart's.

* * *

"Do you think it's cool enough to leave Okie in her cat cage in the car?" B.J. asked. "This is the first place we've been that wouldn't allow me to bring her in with me."

"She'll be fine. I'll leave the windows cracked. Don't worry. We're parked in the shade. It won't get hot." Cathy busied herself putting up the top on the rental convertible. "Hurry up though. I don't want to miss post time. Rapunzel Runz is running in the first race. She's the daughter of a horse Daddy used to own, Explodent. Rapunzel Runz is four years old now and she won the Atlantic City Budweiser Breeders' Cup last August."

"She sounds more like a fairy tale character than a horse," B.J. said, hurrying to catch up with her prodder. B.J. knew nothing about horses and hadn't been in favor of taking time away from more interesting pursuits. "How long does one of these races last, anyway?"

"It depends on the length of the race and, of course, on the horses running. Some run faster than others, you know," Cathy said over her shoulder.

"No duh, Shakespeare. We're a prime example of that. Because you're taller, your legs are longer than mine and you can take longer strides. Wait up. This isn't one of your horse races." B.J. trotted to keep up with Cathy.

"A fast horse can run a mile race in about a minute and a half. If the race is only four furlongs, like a lot of quarter horse races are, that's only a half mile and the time could be about three-quarters of a minute 'cause quarter horses are the fastest horses over a short distance," Cathy patiently explained to B.J. "Haven't you ever been to the races before? I thought you went to Louisiana Downs once with me and Daddy."

"No, I never did. We planned it several times but something always came up. Why don't they say a half-mile race if that's what it is . . . instead of four whatevers?" B.J. looked up at the three-story brick building housing the seating areas.

"Furlongs . . . furlongs. Never mind, just be quiet," Cathy said as they reached the ticket office. "Two on level two, please."

They entered the air-conditioned building. People scrambled to reach the escalators and elevators to take them to the second and third levels of the buildings. Many stood around studying racing forms and making occasional notes in the margins. On the second level, lines were forming in front of the betting windows. B.J. saw that one entire wall of the building was glass and overlooked the oval racing track encircling a large, lush grassy area. Tractors pulled plows in slow motion around the track. An ambulance was stationed at a distance from the starting gate. "How many races are they gonna have?" B.J. asked as she followed Cathy to their reserved table.

Cathy sighed. "Probably ten. I haven't looked at the racing form that closely yet. There may be as many as twelve."

The two reached their table and seated themselves in comfortable padded chairs. "Oh, good," B.J. said, looking around at the other patrons. "Then we can head for Little Rock in well under an hour. I'm anxious to get there. Then Branson, Missouri, will seem so much closer."

Cathy turned to look at B.J. She shook her head slowly and said, "They don't race but about every thirty minutes."

"Why not?" B.J. asked with a frown. "Can't they just line them up and send them on out when it's their turn?"

"Look," Cathy said, trying hard to control her temper, "why don't we watch them saddle the horses in the paddock between races? It'll make it more interesting."

"Oh, I guess so. Will we be able to pet them?" B.J. asked.

Cathy exploded. "Look. I've let you do whatever you wanted to so far on this trip. Remember that this is my trip, too. I put up with your boating all over Lake Texoma and it almost killed me. The least you can do is let me spend a pleasant afternoon at the races."

* * *

Accelerating to make it through a yellow light, Stuart took no notice of the black Town Car that sped through the intersection behind him. Lost in thought and trying to make sense of the recent developments, he pushed the responsive sports car far faster than his usual pace. Had there been one of Dallas' finest on Walnut Hill anywhere between Central and the Tollway, he would have had two easy targets. Hitting speeds over sixty, Stuart all but missed the entrance to the Tollway and had to slam on his brakes and swerve to the left.

Tires squealing, he raced down the ramp to the angry stares of the same drivers who usually berated him for driving too slowly. Pushing the Lexus past eighty, Stuart sped south toward Parkland Memorial. After about two miles of weaving in and out of slower traffic, he pulled into the left lane and saw a clear field ahead. Noting his speed, he slacked up a bit and leveled off to seventy. Thoughts assailed him from all directions as if he had disturbed a hornet's nest in his brain. Where was B.J.? How could he contact her? What was the significance of the gas? What had happened during B.J.'s two lost hours at the Christian Clinic? Could he prove his allegations? Who would listen? He glanced at a car pulling abreast of him in the middle lane. Too late to pull over and let him pass, Stuart thought. Oh, well, unusual for me but I'll stay in the fast lane. The Lincoln pulled ahead and maintained a distance of about three car lengths in front of Stuart's Lexus. They were fast approaching the Mockingbird Lane overpass.

When both cars approached to within three hundred feet of the overpass, the driver of the Lincoln jammed on his brakes and swerved to the left immediately in front of the Lexus. In a panic, Stuart hit the brakes with both feet. He felt a high frequency vibration through the brake pedal and the steering wheel as the Lexus' antilock brake system activated. Stuart saw that he could either hit the car or jump the guardrail and plow head-on into the concrete column and certain death. Acting on instinct and a massive surge of adrenalin, Stuart swerved hard to the right. The front bumper of his Lexus collided with the back bumper of the skidding Lincoln, throwing Stuart into an uncontrolled spin. Careening off the Lincoln and skidding backwards, Stuart saw a mass of cars barreling toward him down the Tollway and found himself staring into the paralyzed faces of a dozen panicked drivers screeching down on him in their unguidable two-ton missiles. Stuart closed his eyes and waited for the inevitable impact. After what seemed like ten minutes, the Lexus came to a stop on the far shoulder of the road, headed in the opposite direction. Miraculously, the jammed Tollway was still flowing. The Lincoln was nowhere in sight.

Stuart slumped over the wheel and tried desperately to regain his composure. He ignored the stares of the drivers that passed but didn't stop. When he at last was able to control the shaking of his hands, he waited for the next break in traffic and made a quick U-turn. Driving toward the toll booth, Stuart again had to face the angry stares of Dallas commuters, this time for going too slow. Finally reaching Harry Hines Boulevard and turning toward Parkland Memorial, he pulled into the graveled lot outside the Medical Examiner's office behind Parkland and eased into a parking space next to Mitch's BMW. After dragging himself out of the car, he glanced at the damaged bumper, shook his head, and entered the small building. He opened the door to Hawkins' office and sank into the nearest chair.

Hawkins looked up when he heard the door open and stared in astonishment at Stuart. "Good God," he said as he stood and scrambled around his desk. Mitch blanched and pulled himself out of the too-small chair. He reached Stuart's side just as Hawkins grabbed Stuart's wrist and felt his pulse. "What the hell happened to you?" Hawkins boomed.

Stuart looked up at his two friends and spoke barely above a whisper. "You'll never believe what all has happened to me today. I'm not sure I do myself." They listened intently as he related the details of his near miss with the black Town Car. Then, about almost being gassed at the Christian Clinic. After Stuart finished, they sat in silence for a time before Mitch, his face unable to hide the fear he felt, said, "What have we gotten ourselves into, guys?"

"Stuart, do you think the two events were related?" Hawkins asked.

Stuart shook his head. "I don't know what to think. Tell us what you found out in Chicago. Maybe that will shed some light."

The big man stood and started to pace. "In going over the autopsies from Chicago, Los Angeles and Dallas, we found one case in Los Angeles that had no incision. Dr. Ito requested that they re-examine the body in the area of all the other postmortem cuts. Fortunately, the body was still on site because it was the most recent case and they weren't done with it yet. When they looked closer, they found a small bump, or mass, under the skin at the hairline. If you remember, all of the postmortem cuts were noted in that area of the scalp. They almost didn't find anything. It was cleverly concealed using a subcuticular suture so that it would be virtually invisible and extremely hard to detect even under the most rigorous examination. That's why they overlooked it at first. They excised the mass and found a foreign body. Dr. Ito said something about it being manmade. At any rate, they sent it to UCLA for nondestructive testing."

Mitch finally spoke. "I'm hearing all this but what I don't understand is . . . what does that have to do with the unexplained deaths?"

Stuart rose and walked across the room. He whirled around and looked at Mitch. "I don't know, but I have an idea. Let's tell Hawkins what we found out today and get him to check with his counterparts in Los Angeles and Chicago."

"Tell me what?" Hawkins yelled, still standing. "For God's sake tell me what's going on. What did you find out?"

Stuart turned to Hawkins. "You now know what happened to me today at the Chicago Christian Insurance

Clinic." He paused. "And I told you what happened to B.J. at the same clinic. Well, you recall that Mitch and I found out that all three of our unexplained deaths were organ donors and all three had medical insurance with Chicago Christian. And if that isn't enough, Mitch talked today with Hank Heister who has had one recent unexplained death and asked him to check. Guess what?"

Hawkins let out a long whistle. "Holy Mother of God . . . Chicago Christian."

"That's four for four. What are the odds?" Mitch asked rhetorically.

Hawkins paused before saying, "Stuart, you're absolutely right. I need to get with Ito and Legato and find out if the same thing is happening in the other cities. Excuse me, guys. I'll be right back. I'm getting on the phone right now." He disappeared into his inner office, returning in five minutes. "Okay, we got the ball rolling in L.A. and Chicago. Is there anything else we can do here?"

Stuart looked at Hawkins. "Maybe there's something more in the records here. You've reviewed the autopsy reports themselves. But what about the paperwork that accompanied the victims when they were brought in? That could contain some clues."

"Good idea. I'll pull the files." Hawkins hurried down the hall and returned, his arms full of file folders. The three doctors began studying the papers.

Mitch raised his head. "Hey, guys, this is interesting. It says here that my attorney patient was transported from Dallas General Hospital. I would have thought that the ambulance would have taken him to a hospital closer to White Rock Lake. It's odd because Doctors Hospital is only a few blocks from the jogging trail."

They continued poring over the records. After a while, Stuart said, "My two patients were transported from Parkland."

Hawkins reached for a yellow pad on the far corner of his desk. "Let's make a listing. Maybe if we see it in black and white, it'll make some sense."

After their meticulous review of all twenty files, they had compiled a list showing that eight had been transported from Parkland and twelve from Dallas General. No other hospital appeared on the records.

"Does this mean anything?" Stuart asked. "Are we missing something here?"

Mitch mopped his forehead with his ever-present handkerchief and said, "In and of itself, this list doesn't mean anything. It can't hurt to confirm this with the hospitals though."

"Let's start with Dallas General," Stuart said. "Debbie used to be on staff there. She could get into the records. Can I use your phone?"

Stuart called Debbie, who was still at his clinic and related his request. He gave her the twelve names from Hawkins' list, including dates of birth and social security numbers. When he hung up, he said, "It'll take her about an hour. I told her we'd meet her back at my office. In the meantime, we can check the Parkland records."

"Okay," Hawkins said. He picked up the receiver and dialed. "I'll get Phyllis Roosevelt to check the data base over there." He told her what he needed and said he would call back. After he hung up, the three decided to go to Stuart's office while they awaited the results.

As the three walked to their cars in the parking lot, Stuart nervously glanced around, half expecting to see the black Lincoln Town Car. Satisfied, he exhaled. Only then did Stuart realize that he had been holding his breath.

Chapter 7

Debbie unlocked the back door to the small clinic, having noticed Stuart's Lexus in the parking lot. She didn't know whose BMW that was but she couldn't miss Hawkins' old '79 Oldsmobile 98 that he'd had since his undergraduate college days. As she opened the door, she heard Stuart call from the waiting room. She laid her purse down and walked through the clinic to the front.

"Debbie, you know Hawkins but I don't think you've met Mitch. This is Dr. Clarence Mitchell," Stuart said, waving from his reclining position on the couch.

Mitch shot a frown at Stuart, stood, shook hands with Debbie and said, "I'm glad to finally meet you. I've seen you around but we've never been introduced. And, please, call me Mitch."

"You don't prefer Clarence?" Debbie asked with a slight grin calculated to show Mitch her dimples. She had caught the frown Mitch aimed at Stuart at the mention of his name. Debbie noticed that Mitch's palm was still damp, even after rubbing it on his pant leg before offering it to her. She looked into Mitch's eyes after noticing that he had been staring at her but he quickly shifted his glance. Interesting, she thought. The eyes tell it all. But perhaps she was only imagining that Mitch found her attractive. I probably remind him of his sister, she thought.

"No . . . I mean . . . yes . . . I mean no. I don't prefer Clarence. I go by Mitch," he said while looking wildly around the room.

Stuart grinned and said, "Well, Debbie. What did you find out?"

"Nothing. I checked all twelve names against their social security numbers and dates of birth and came up with zilch. The twelve people were never admitted to Dallas General or treated in the emergency room. I checked all of the data bases," Debbie said, turning to face Stuart.

"Thanks, Debbie. Why don't you go on home now? I appreciate your staying late for this."

"That's okay. Glad to help. Sorry I didn't come up with anything. If I hurry, I can still catch my date at El Chico. He'll be waiting for me."

Debbie berated herself as she walked out to the parking lot and unlocked her Volvo. I can never tell a lie without blushing, she thought. I hate that.

* * *

"What do you make of that?" Hawkins boomed after Debbie had closed the door behind her.

"I think she's lying," Mitch said vehemently. "Did you notice how she couldn't look me in the eye? That's a dead giveaway."

Stuart snorted. "My guess is . . . it was the other way around. Why would you think she's lying, anyway?"

"Because falsifying medical records is a serious crime and Dallas General has too good a reputation for that to have happened." Mitch frowned and walked back to an easy chair. "The records have to be there. If she's not lying, then she doesn't know her way around a computer data base."

"No, I think it's possible. If the patients had been taken to the morgue from another location, then Dallas General would have no record," Hawkins said thoughtfully. "But . . . if not at Dallas General, where were the organs removed?"

* * *

B.J. and Cathy were jostled by the crowd exiting the racetrack. "That was more fun that I thought it was going to be," B.J. admitted. "Do you think we'll find any more horse races on our way north?"

Cathy laughed. "Don't expect to win a hundred dollars every time you go to the races. I can't believe you put two dollars on that horse because you liked his name and thought he had pretty eyes. That was pure chance. Long shots seldom win."

"Sure. You call it chance 'cause I won. Your method, with all your expertise, only lost you money." B.J. opened the car door, climbed in and rescued the kitten from its cage.

Cathy guided the Cadillac into a long line of vehicles leaving the parking lot. B.J. glanced around and said, "There's another ambulance. They had one out by the track during the races."

"Oh, that's probably some paramedics that snuck off duty to go watch the horses run. See? They're leaving, too," Cathy said. After much delay, she reached the front of the line and pulled out onto Highway 70 toward Little Rock.

* * *

"All I know is that we have to somehow get into the records at the Christian Clinic," Stuart said. He took another bite of his pizza. The three men had opted to have their meal delivered to Stuart's clinic so they could continue their discussion in private in his reception room. He seldom spent time there. It needed attention, he decided. When Stuart first opened his practice, he had had little cash to spare on furnishings for the waiting room. His parents had offered to furnish the clinic for him, but Stuart had declined, contending that they had already financed him for far too long. His undergraduate school, Southern Methodist University, hadn't been all that financially burdensome on them because of his football scholarship. His medical school, residency and internship, though, had been very expensive. Even though his practice had grown fast—and after four years, he could afford it—he never seemed to have the time to do something about the furniture. He looked at the slate blue plastic couch, durable but uncomfortable. If anyone sat on it longer than a few minutes, they were apt to wind up with a wet rear end. The scattered cloth-covered mauve easy chairs were somewhat more palatable but the cloth had worn thin. The coffee table hadn't fared well either, he thought, noting the veneer that had peeled back in several places. B.J. had issued an ultimatum that when she redecorated the reception room, the couch and coffee table had to go. She had already worked her magic in his office, insisting on it getting the first upgrade. After all, he was a successful professional and deserved only the best, she had said. He grinned briefly at the thought.

"How are we going to get into the Christian Clinic?" Mitch mumbled with his mouth full.

"I don't think we'll have any problem," Hawkins said with a booming laugh. "Don't forget that I was raised in South Oak Cliff and skills learned early in life are never lost. There's not a lock in Dallas that can keep me out. Oh . . . I almost forgot. I've got to call Dr. Ito. When I talked to him earlier today, he still hadn't heard from UCLA. He promised he'd call when he knew anything." Hawkins paused, then added sheepishly, "But I forgot to leave this number with the answering service."

"Help yourself," Stuart said, gesturing with his pizza slice. "You can use the phone in my office where it's quiet and Dr. Ito won't have to compete with the noise Mitch makes when he eats pizza. It's a mystery to me why it's the only food Mitch eats like a redneck."

Mitch glared at Stuart while pizza sauce dribbled from the corner of his mouth. Hawkins laughed and made his way down the hall to Stuart's office.

Hawkins pored over his notes as he walked back into the waiting room a few minutes later. He almost looked ashen. "Dr. Ito got the initial results from the UCLA testing. The mass turned out to contain a miniature computer chip with two tiny hairlike wires, one longer than the other. One of the wires, the longer of the two, seems to be an antenna for receiving and transmitting radio frequency signals and the shorter one is evidently for communicating something to the victim. The computer chip itself consists primarily of a high-frequency transmitter and receiver. Dr. Ito had them re-examine the area of the victim's skull directly below where the chip was implanted. They found a microscopic hole drilled into the skull at that exact point. Now the shorter wire, it seems, projects out from the underside of the chip and through to the brain. Ito consulted with a neurosurgeon friend and found that whoever designed the thing knew precisely what they were doing. The length of the short wire is such that, when the chip is resting on the skull, it's the exact length necessary for the wire to penetrate through the skull and into the dura mater but stop short of penetrating the subdural space."

Mitch frowned. "Why would that be important?"

Hawkins glanced at Mitch. "I asked the same question. Turns out, if it isn't done exactly right, the wire would penetrate and probably irritate the brain or create a leakage of the cerebrospinal fluid."

"Of course," Mitch said. "Either way, it would cause the patient—or shall I say the victim—to have some pretty serious side effects and send him scurrying to his doctor. Then the doctor might conceivably find the chip."

"Exactly."

"Like what kind of side effects?"

"Like induced seizures for one thing. Dr. Ito theorizes that the chip functions as a position tracking device with a separate circuit for delivering a brain-paralyzing energy wave through its victim's skull and directly to his brain." Hawkins shook his head and said, "So they use the transmitter to keep track of their victims and the receiver to kill them."

Stuart's head was reeling. "I know what it is," he whispered.

In unison, Mitch and Hawkins said, "What?"

"I know what it is," he repeated hoarsely.

"Man, you'd better explain yourself," Hawkins demanded. "How on earth *could* you know?"

Stuart felt the tension mount. He desperately tried to unscramble his brain so that he could make sense of it all. How do you explain the unexplainable? He looked at his two trusting longtime friends and wondered what terrible thing he had dragged them into. He longed to return to the fun days . . . the days of sweating exams, the all-night cramming sessions, the three friends snatching whatever time they could together.

"Dammit, Stuart. Say something," Hawkins roared. He stood towering over Stuart who looked lost in the leather chair.

Startled, Stuart cleared his throat and started. "I know what it is because B.J. told me about it. T.I. and Motorola developed the technology jointly. The chip is a satellite-tracking device that's implanted under the skin. It was intended for animals but if it's done right, it can track a person anywhere on earth . . . literally. She didn't tell me the part about transmitting directly to the brain."

* * *

Those idiots in Vegas don't think I'm good for it, he thought. Conrad Nation studied the sports page of the Dallas Morning News. His Leer payment due, his credit line frozen in Vegas and his mistress more demanding than ever had forced him to switch his gambling tactics. He was so intent on computing the odds on next Sunday's Dallas Cowboys game that the light rap on his door made him jump. Irritated at being interrupted, Nation barked at the nurse who stood in his office doorway, "What is it, Nancy?"

"I'm sorry to interrupt you, Dr. Nation, but there's a Mr. DeCarlo on line one for you. He said it was urgent."

"Okay, I'll take it." He reached to pick up the phone and paused. "And please shut the door behind you. Now." After she left, he put the receiver to his ear. "This had better be important, DeCarlo. I told you never to call me here at Dallas General."

"Shut up and listen, Nation. Do you think I'm stupid? Of course this is important. Turns out that engineer who ran out today before we could fix him is not an engineer at all. Everything he wrote on his new patient form was phony. He's a doctor right in your own back yard."

Nation paled. "What does he know?"

"How the hell do I know what he knows? All I know is that we can't take a chance. The goons we sent after him failed to take him out and only succeeded in putting a dent in my Town Car."

"Who is he?" Nation demanded frantically.

"Goes by the name of Dr. Stuart H. Young. He's got an office right across the street from Dallas General."

Nation stiffened. "I know who he is. I know someone who works for him. What do you plan to do about this? You shouldn't kill him. You should warn him off."

"Nation, you don't make decisions like that. I do and I'm going to put our top paramedic in charge of it. Just wanted you to be forewarned to keep a low profile at the clinic until the matter is resolved. It won't be long. I'll let you know."

His hand moved slowly as he replaced the receiver. He sighed and slumped forward. How much did Young know? There's no way he could have gotten onto the surgical floor. Too many safeguards were in place. He couldn't have learned much at the clinic. But why had he run out? He needed answers. Nation snatched up the telephone and dialed a number from memory. "Debbie, my dear. If you haven't eaten yet, how about dinner tonight?"

* * *

Stuart slammed the phone down after the eighth ring. He was desperate to leave B.J. a message but she had evidently turned off her answering machine before she left town. "What do I do? What *can* I do?" he moaned as he paced in front of the plastic couch. "Those bastards must have implanted B.J. with one of those chips. The gas jet explains why she thought she had taken a two-hour nap after her physical. It also explains why she was so groggy when she left. Two hours would have given them ample time for such a procedure. The thought of them drilling a hole into B.J.'s skull is driving me berserk. God, if I could only find her. If I just knew where she was."

"There's got to be something we can do from here," Mitch said. He walked over and put his hand on Stuart's shoulder.

"But what? She's God-knows-where with that damn chip in her head that could kill her at any second." Stuart was frantic at the thought.

"What about calling the highway patrol and giving them the license number?" Hawkins suggested.

"I'd give my life to know that number but Cathy rented a car for the trip. All I noticed when she picked B.J. up early that morning was that it was a red convertible. Damn. I don't even know what kind of car it is," Stuart shouted and slumped onto the couch.

"Okay, man. Calm down. Let's think this thing through," Hawkins said, grabbing Stuart by the shoulders and shaking him. "What about her friend . . . the one she's on the trip with? Maybe her family knows where they are? What about B.J.'s parents? Maybe they know where she is."

"I've tried . . . I've called. B.J.'s folks don't know any more than I do. It was all I could do to keep my voice calm so

I wouldn't scare them." Stuart looked at Hawkins. "Wait a minute. Cathy's dad is the Dallas County District Attorney. What the hell is his name? I'll call him right now." Stuart raced down the hall to his office with his friends straining to keep up with him. He stopped and spun around. Hawkins and Mitch almost knocked him over. "What is his name?" Seeing nothing but blank stares and shrugs in response to his question, Stuart said, "He was on the front page of this morning's paper. Something about a computer mix-up at the Lew Sterrett Criminal Justice Center. Hang on a minute. Debbie always brings the paper in." Stuart scurried to Debbie's desk. "Here it is," he said triumphantly, "in the trash. Nix. Kenneth Nix. That's his name. Get me the phone book. Hurry." After locating the number with shaking hands, Stuart picked up the phone from Debbie's reception area and dialed the number.

"Hello," he heard a woman say.

"May I speak with Kenneth Nix, please? This is Dr. Young calling." Stuart closed his eyes and prayed.

"I'm sorry but he's not in at the moment. May I help you?"

Stuart braced himself on the edge of the desk and spoke slowly. "I hope so. Is this Mrs. Nix?"

"Yes, it is."

"My fiancée, B.J. Welborn, is on a trip with your daughter, Cathy. I'm trying to get in touch with her but don't know where she is. Have you heard from them?" Stuart forced himself to maintain a calm tone.

"We've gotten several messages on our answering machine but I've not spoken with her since she left. It's my understanding that they're somewhere in Arkansas going toward Missouri." Her cultured background was evident in her voice.

"Do you happen to know the license plate number on the rental car?"

"No, I'm afraid not. Why?"

"I thought maybe I could track them that way."

"What did you say your name was, young man?" she demanded.

"Dr. Stuart Young. I'm engaged to B.J."

"Why don't you let me have Mr. Nix call you on Monday? I'm not certain what time he'll be in."

He thanked her, hung up and turned to his friends. "B.J.'s driving north. Maybe to Chicago. We've got to find out if that's the home base of Chicago Christian Insurance Corporation." He felt a chill.

Hawkins stood. "I'll call Legato in Chicago and see what he can find out. If the company is headquartered in Chicago, he'll be able to get the records from the county courthouse first thing Monday morning."

"What can I do?" Mitch asked.

"Nothing. You guys go home. There's nothing more we can do tonight. I'll be at the house if you need to call me for anything."

Mitch turned to Stuart. "Holy Cow. I almost forgot. I've got to go. I'm supposed to have a blind date tonight. My sister fixed me up with a friend of hers. But I can cancel it if you want me to stay here with you."

"No, you go ahead. I've got some heavy thinking to do, anyway. I'll talk to you in the morning." Stuart had never felt so overwhelmed.

Chapter 8

The heavy, threatening feeling wouldn't go away. If anything, it was getting worse. Stuart stared out the window as a flash of lightening illuminated his somber face. He didn't flinch. The storm reflected Stuart's turmoil and reinforced the weight that threatened to crush him. Another bolt of lightning traced the outline of the majestic Evangeline oak trees lining both sides of prestigious Loma Vista Drive. In the pandemonium, this peaceful—even complacent—neighborhood of upper middle-class homes took on the appearance of a nether world. The shadows suggested departed spirits struggling to regain their earthly form. He shook his head vigorously. Still, B.J.'s image was all he could concentrate on. All he could see. Again and again he had replayed B.J.'s message on his answering machine. Where could she be? Why had she called only once? Was she still that angry? What was the fight about, anyhow? He couldn't remember. He glanced at his watch and shook his head in resignation.

* * *

"I'll bet you don't get asked out by many doctors, do you?" Mitch asked, delighting in his gorgeous blind date as the maître d approached. Mitch's blind dates didn't usually turn out so well. For once, he was glad he'd agreed to be fixed up by his sister.

"Well, I'll say this much, doctor. The way it's raining, I'm glad you don't drive a convertible. You probably would have drowned me on the way here with the top down. I can't wait to get ahold of your sister to thank her."

Mitch roared with laughter. He loved to date a woman with a sense of humor and this woman had a wit that wouldn't stop. "Quit, please," he said wiping the tears from his eyes.

"This way, please, Dr. Mitchell. Your table is ready," the maître d said, gesturing exaggeratedly and leading them around the harpist to an elegantly set center table. Mitch held Sheree's elbow and, with his head high, he strutted to the table.

"Thank you, Dmitri. This will be fine," Mitch said with pride as he watched Dmitri pull out Sheree's chair. His date wore a conservative after-five azure blue dress which enhanced her eyes and set off her long blond hair. Mitch glanced appreciatively around the French Room. It was one of Dallas' finest eating establishments, housed in the elaborately renovated Adolphus Hotel in the downtown area.

As he sat, Mitch reached across the table and patted Sheree's hand. "Just watch me," he whispered, "and use the fork that I use. That way you won't get confused. Don't worry about it. It took me a while to catch on to this fancy living, too. I couldn't afford to come to places like this until I became a doctor."

"I'm so glad I'm with you. I just don't know what this poor little country girl would do without a big handsome sophisticated doctor like you to guide me," Sheree said through clinched teeth. "I can't wait to talk to your sister."

Mitch, flattered, raised his water glass in a silent toast of thanks. He smiled, took a sip of water and glanced around the room to make sure he was being noticed with this knockout. His scan stopped when he saw her. There she was . . . Stuart's nurse . . . sitting with someone in the corner of the room. Her date turned to catch the waiter's attention. When he saw who she was with, Mitch audibly inhaled as though he had been punched in the stomach.

"Are you okay?" Sheree asked without emotion.

"I'm fine, my dear. Thank you for inquiring. I . . . um . . . saw someone I think I know." Mitch shifted in his chair and fumbled self-consciously with the menu. My God, he thought. What if Debbie sees me with this country bumpkin? What will she think of me? I guess it's a hopeless cause anyway. I could never compete with the likes of one of the world's most famous transplant surgeons. Damn. Nation's too old for her anyway.

"Who?" Sheree asked, obviously bored.

Mitch turned to see Debbie and Nation walking out. Nation had his hand on the back of Debbie's waist.

* * *

Stuart snatched up the phone at the first ring. "B.J.," he yelled.

"It's me. You haven't talked to her yet?"

Stuart sagged back down on his pillow with a groan. "No, Mitch. She hasn't called. I thought you might have been her. What's up?"

"I just got home. Took a little cutie out to eat at the French Room. She was some stacked," Mitch said.

Stuart could hear the bragging tone in Mitch's voice and decided to indulge his friend. After all, he had "call waiting" and wouldn't miss B.J. if she called. "Okay, buddy. Tell me all about her." Stuart reached for his cigarettes on the nightstand, mentally excusing himself for backsliding. He was, after all, under tremendous pressure.

"She was gorgeous and I think she was impressed with me. I don't believe she'd ever been to a place like that before. I had to show her which fork to use. And the chef outdid himself. I could have done better, of course, but he didn't do badly at all. I even sent my congratulations to him."

That must have impressed him, Stuart thought as he took a deep drag off his cigarette and watched its tip glow in the dark.

"And guess who was there? Come on, guess. You'll never guess," Mitch said, his voice rising.

"President Bush?" Stuart said. The irritation in his voice was heavy. "Mitch, I don't feel like guessing."

"No, my friend. Not President Bush. Debbie . . . Debbie was there."

"My Debbie?"

"Right. Your nurse, Debbie. She didn't go to El Chico like she said. And another thing. You'll never guess who she was with."

"Come on, buddy. It's late and I'd rather not play twenty questions, if you don't mind. Who was Debbie there with?" Stuart asked with exasperation.

"None other than Dr. Conrad Nation. And . . . he had his hand on her waist. Boy, I saw red."

"You must be kidding," Stuart said, suddenly alert. He sat bolt upright and reached for the ashtray.

"I'm very serious. It was Debbie all right. I could never mistake that face and those dimples, and that pompous old jackass is definitely unmistakable. His face is on page one more times than not . . . what with his recent transplant on Tiger Griffin. Seriously, Stuart, do they have a thing going? Stuart? Stuart, are you still there?"

"Mitch, if you're right, we have a serious problem. With all that's been going on, I forgot to mention it but I think I saw Nation at the Christian Clinic when I went to get my insurance physical. I was pretty woozy, though. I might be wrong." Stuart winced as the implication made his head pound. "Holy hell. Maybe Nation has something to do with whatever the hell is going on. But surely not Debbie."

"But remember how she couldn't look me in the eye. Maybe she had a guilty conscience when she told us there were no records at Dallas General. Maybe she was lying," Mitch said.

"Why would she do that?" Stuart asked under his breath. "Wait a minute. I just remembered something. She told me when she came to work for me that she's from Chicago. I always wondered what she was doing down here when her whole family is up north. Single women don't normally move that far from home."

"What about that Volvo she drives? Do you pay her enough to afford something like that?" Mitch asked.

"I always thought she was just being frugal. Some people can really stretch a dollar. Maybe I was wrong. Do you think we should double-check the records at Dallas General? Damn it. I don't want to believe that Debbie could be involved in something so monstrous. If B.J. gets hurt and she has anything to do with it, I'll personally kill her," Stuart said with a growl. He jumped out of bed, unaware of the phone base hitting the floor as he paced.

"Calm down. We can't let Debbie know we're on to her. You've got to control yourself. She can't know what we suspect."

"You're right," Stuart said, flipping on the overhead light. "How soon can you get into the Dallas General database? I've got to know."

"Easy. I do it all the time. First thing in the morning, I'll check it out. I'll know something by seven at the latest. Meet you at your office then. Get some sleep, buddy. Bye."

Stuart didn't move until the dial tone had morphed into an irritating beeping noise. He slowly retrieved the base from the floor and replaced the receiver. He crossed to the window and stared out at the stormy night. After a time, Stuart turned, walked to his desk and pressed the "record greeting" button on the answering machine. "Uh, B.J., I'm not quite sure how to put this but I want you to stay right where you are until you talk to me. I know how strange this must sound to you but I have every reason to believe that you might be in grave danger. Hon, I love you and I miss you and I'm truly sorry you're mad at me but I have to talk to you. If you don't catch me at home or the office, please try my cell phone. I promise to make it very short. But call me. And please don't go any farther north. And whatever you do, do *not* go near Chicago."

Chapter 9

Cathy removed the Cadillac's gas filler cap. "Wow, would you look at that sunrise?" she called to B.J.

"Oh be quiet, miss cheerful-in-the-a.m. I've seen the sun come up before. Once I didn't get home from a date until dawn," B.J. shouted over her shoulder as she rummaged in her purse for phone change. "Sometimes I wonder how the two of us ever got to be best friends."

Cathy grinned and jabbed the 'regular' button on the gas pump. The chilly morning had prompted them to leave the top up until the day warmed. They had stopped north of Little Rock in Conway to fill the tank and give B.J. a chance to call Stuart.

"Shoot," B.J. muttered after the fourth ring began. She hung up before Stuart's machine could answer. Maybe he'd gone to work out, she thought, but it was awfully early. Oh, well. She'd try again tonight.

"Come on, B.J. Branson is beckoning," Cathy said, turning to retrieve her gas card from the automatic pay pump. The two climbed into the car and B.J. settled Okie in her lap. Cathy turned north onto Highway 65. Traffic was light.

"Look over there," B.J. said, pointing. "Another ambulance. This has to be the safest highway in the world—"

"—or the most dangerous." Cathy finished B.J.'s sentence with a laugh. "Get out the map. Make sure Highway 65 goes to Branson."

B.J. moved the kitten onto the back seat and unfolded the map. She studied it in silence for a moment, then grimaced.

"Hey, how would you like to suck on a toad?" she asked with a straight face.

"What?" Cathy asked as she glanced at B.J. "Why would you ask such a disgusting question? Have you ever known me to want to do anything like suck on a toad?"

"Seriously. With a slight detour, we can go through Toad Suck Ferry, Arkansas," B.J. said with an evil glint. "It sounds like your kind of town."

"Nope, Chicago's my kind of town. Can't wait to get there."

* * *

"Yeah, Chicago. We're on 'em." Pony replaced the mike and dropped back about a quarter mile behind the red convertible.

The radio squawked, "Stay with them. Nation should be calling soon."

"What do you think? Isn't it time yet? Let's do it and get it over with." Aretti was young, impatient and bored out of his mind. Not yet twenty, this was his first out-of-town assignment and he was antsy. They had been on the road for three days with no excitement. No action. Nada. He'd been allowed no time off for fun. Nothing but work. And the work, such as it was, was boring. Aretti was accustomed to considerable activity and was tired of having nothing exciting to do. No way could he turn down the money, though. His habit of chasing women had gotten expensive and the more money Aretti made, the more he indulged in his habit. He kept in magnificent shape by working out at the gym and he prided himself in his lean, muscular physique. His girlfriends loved it, too. Trouble was, no way to hook up with girls on the road.

Unlike Aretti, Pony had never had the slightest bit of success with women. If his dour attitude and rank sense of humor didn't turn them off, his weak chin, bony neck, hawkish nose and thin scrawny frame would. Not that he cared. He'd never had time for such things, anyway.

"No, my brain-dead friend. Things aren't set up yet or they'd have already told us." Pony shook his head in disgust. "I hate like hell breaking in rookies. They never listen. They're too careless. They always want to get on with it no matter what might go wrong. And you're no different. Hey look, man, we gotta be careful. We can't afford to screw this up. You know what would happen to us if we botched it," he added with ominous overtones.

"Yeah? Well, I don't see what difference it makes. After all, we're in an ambulance, for crissakes. And we're paramedics. Nobody's gonna think it's funny if we stop to help somebody," Aretti argued. Who did 'Ponytail' think he was giving orders like that? So he was a little older. So what? When I get to be his age, I'll be a big boss of some kind, he thought. He glanced over at Pony. Nothing worse than a punk with an exaggerated sense of importance.

Pony rolled his eyes in the semi-darkness. "Look, I already laid it out for you in plain English, didn't I? I don't know how else to put it. We ain't supposed to attract any attention. You damn well better listen. Where else you gonna make this kind of money as a paramedic? A hospital? Give me a break. No hospital is gonna give you a hundred and fifty grand a year just to plant your fat ass in their ambulance and drive around in air-conditioned comfort like a damn big shot. Besides, we usually only work two, three days a week. Look, I'm warning you. If you don't do what I tell you, you ain't gonna cut it in this business. Then what're you gonna do?"

Never happen, Aretti thought. Before long, I'm gonna be *giving* orders, not taking them. You watch, I'll be in Chicago a year from now telling *you* what to do, smart-ass. "All right, all right. Cut me some slack," Aretti retorted and turned to stare sullenly ahead. "You think you know everything." He'd bide his time and wait for his chance. Chicago would recognize his talent sooner or later. And when they did . . . look out. Katy bar the door. Then he'd show that long-haired flower child. He'd show everybody else, too.

* * *

Stuart glanced at his watch as he pulled into the vacant parking lot behind his small clinic. Good, he thought, it's almost seven. Mitch should be here before long. He parked the Lexus in his reserved space and scampered to unlock the back door. Flipping on the lights as he passed through the rooms, he entered the small kitchenette and pulled out the coffeepot. Soon the aroma of the rich brew filled the room. He heard the back door open and yelled, "I'm in here, Mitch. Come get some coffee."

"I could sure use some 'cause now I don't know what to think," Mitch said lumbering into the kitchenette. "Got to clear my head."

"What do you mean?" Stuart asked, filling two mugs with coffee.

"The damn computer system at Dallas General crashed. No one knows why. The computer engineer at the hospital told me it would take at least a week for him to retrieve the information that was lost and to reconstruct the data base." Mitch accepted the mug from Stuart, took a quick sip, swallowed and yelled. "Damn that's hot. Are you trying to scald me? I ought to sue you." He hurried to the sink, turned on the water and stuck his mouth under the running faucet.

Ignoring Mitch's histrionics, Stuart sipped his coffee, frowned and muttered, "Hmm. I was hoping to find out one way or the other about Debbie's possible involvement. Is there any other way we can find out?"

"Not today. The actual patient files are in an off-site storage facility. They don't keep records on deceased patients at the hospital. Since it's Sunday, I can't even put in a request

212

for the records' retrieval. I can do that tomorrow," Mitch said as he wiped the water off his chin and tie.

Stuart dialed his home number and queried his answering machine. No messages. "Mitch, what do we know so far?" he asked, replacing the receiver. "What do we know for a fact? Am I blowing something out of proportion?"

Mitch dabbed at the remaining water and sank down into a too-small chair. "On the contrary, Stuart, if anything, you're probably downplaying the danger."

Stuart slowly turned and looked at Mitch. "Thanks, that's all I needed. How about elaborating."

"Okay, follow me here. You were almost gassed at the Christian Clinic, right? Our latest Los Angeles donor was found with his microchip still intact, right? All of the others had theirs removed, right?" He waited for a response.

Stuart felt numb and cold. He didn't want the answers . . . but he had to know. "All right," he said. "So what does all of this have to do with anything?"

"My guess is that you were followed from the Christian Clinic and that your being run off the road was no accident—"

"What does that have to do—"

"Let me finish. I think that you know that it was no accident and that you're denying the whole thing because you don't want to believe that B.J. is in danger," Mitch concluded. "I don't think I'm reading too much into the situation."

A long silence followed before Stuart dropped his head in acceptance. "You're right, Mitch. I said it was a bizarre accident because that's what I wanted to believe, but it wasn't. Jesus, what do I do now?" He covered his face with both hands.

"Well, for one thing, remember that you're being followed. Be careful. Hell, for that matter, I'm probably being followed, too. I hadn't thought of that." Mitch slumped back in his chair and stared at Stuart, who was looking at nothing, his eyes darting around like a pinball in a fast game.

* * *

Dr. Nation entered the luxuriant hospital suite on the top floor of Dallas General. "And how are we today, Ms. Vandergriff?" he asked in his most cheerful voice.

"Oh, doctor, I'm so tired of this waiting and waiting and waiting." She paused to catch her breath before continuing. "I can't even make it the short distance to the bathroom without having to stop several times. I'm as weak as a kitten. Will I ever get a donor heart?" she pleaded. Ann Vandergriff lay back on her silk-covered down pillows with a sigh. Her obvious good breeding and wealth were reflected in her surroundings. The suite was large and the only reminder that it was in a hospital and not in a luxury resort was the oversized hospital bed and the medical equipment necessary to keep her alive.

"Well, now. That's why I came to see you this morning—"

She reached for his hand. "They've found me a heart," she said with a gasp.

"Not exactly, my dear. But I think I may be able to help," Dr. Nation said, pulling a velvet chair close to the bed. He lowered his voice to a near whisper and was rewarded by the patient's leaning forward to listen. "This will have to remain strictly confidential, you understand. No one must ever know."

"Please, what do you mean?" she asked, her pleading eyes looking directly into his.

"I belong to an organization that can cut through the red tape when it's necessary. It is, however, extremely expensive to do so," he drawled, then paused for effect. "I have access to a state-of-the-art clinic where the transplant can be performed as soon as twenty-four hours after the money is received."

"I'll do it. I don't care what it costs. Just tell me where to go and who to give it to. My husband will be here soon and he can take me. He'll get whatever amount of money you want. Oh, Dr. Nation, how can I ever thank you?" She looked at him with tears filling her eyes.

"We must first put on a little performance. The nurses cannot think I'm condoning your checking out of Dallas General."

Her eyes widened. "I have an idea," she offered. "I can argue with you about it in front of Gloria. She's my day nurse. Where is she, by the way?"

"I asked her to get you a special treat and told her I would stay with you while she was gone." He chuckled at his own cleverness. "How quickly will you be able to get the money?"

"It's Sunday, so at least by tomorrow. But my husband could write you a check today," she said, grabbing his hand.

"I'm sorry, my dear, but the clinic cannot accept a check. This must be a cash transaction and there will be no receipt. You will be contacted by an associate of mine named Goletti. He'll make the arrangements. Remember, this is not to be discussed with anyone . . . and I repeat, anyone . . . other than your husband," he said gravely.

"Of course. We won't tell a soul. I promise. And I'll have John go to the bank the first thing in the morning and get the money. But, doctor, can I go ahead and check into your little clinic. Then, I'll know for sure that it's about to come true."

He smiled as he patted her shaking hand, knowing it wouldn't be long before he was back at the tables in Vegas.

* * *

Nation ducked into his office after a quick glance down the hall reassured him no one had seen him. Without turning on the light, he made his way to his locked desk. After turning the key, he retrieved a cell phone from the bottom drawer and hit speed dial number one. "Chicago, it should be soon. Remember that the retrieval location must be chosen carefully because the human heart can only last about five hours without blood flow. We'll need to transport it by air. Keep close to Ms. Welborn."

* * *

Stuart sat staring blankly at the telephone, willing it to ring. Damn, where is she? he thought. He knew that if anything happened to B.J., he wouldn't want to go on. She had become the core of his life . . . his present . . . his future. He started when the phone rang, picked up the receiver and asked, "B.J.?"

"Dr. Young?" a strange voice inquired.

Stuart sighed. "Yes, this is Dr. Young. Can I help you?"

"This is Jill French. I'm an R.N. in the Mesquite Community Hospital emergency room. We have a patient of yours, a Mrs. Dorothy Lumlaw, here with a possible closed head injury. She refuses to see the doctor on duty and insists that you be contacted."

"Ah, yes. Mrs. Lumlaw. Please tell her I'm on my way but that she must let your doctor examine her."

Stuart hung up the phone as he reached for his car keys. Closing the door behind him, he didn't hear the phone ring again.

* * *

"The damn answering machine again. I guess I'd better leave a message this time or he'll think I'm dead," B.J. said to Cathy. The two were huddled together in the small telephone booth. The wind caused the rain to leak in around the door of their temporary shelter. As B.J. listened to Stuart's strange message, she frowned and looked at Cathy. "This has got to be some kind of joke," she whispered.

"What is?" Cathy asked. She was attempting to dry the small kitten with the sleeve of her sweatshirt.

"Shh," B.J. admonished. She put her palm to her ear to hear the rest of the message. After the beep she shrugged and said, "Okay, cute man. What grave danger is going to send me running home to you before my vacation is over? Good try, though. You almost scared me. Rest assured that Cathy and I can handle any big, bad Yankee we encounter. We're on our way out of Branson after seeing Tony Orlando. We found out that Branson isn't all country. We'll be spending the night somewhere in either Missouri or Illinois. Unless, of course, we get lost again. And then it could be anyplace. I love you and I don't want you to worry about me. If I get sick, I'll just jump in that ambulance that seems to be taking the same route we are. Call you tomorrow or Tuesday. Love you. Bye."

Chapter 10

Bleary-eyed from waiting up for another call from B.J., Stuart dragged himself out of bed as early as he could manage. After he'd heard B.J.'s nonchalant dismissal of his recording, he had once again changed the greeting on his answering machine to a panicky plea for B.J. and Cathy to stop their northward trek and stay put. He'd never understood B.J.'s aversion to cell phones. Something about radiation. She had always refused to call him on his cell phone and wouldn't have one herself, opting instead to leave a message instead of calling him on the phone he had with him most of the time. It was a thing with her and she'd been that way ever since cell phones had been invented.

Stuart had skipped breakfast, opting instead for coffee and donuts at "Donuts by George" before stopping by B.J.'s to feed her collection of strays. Feeling guilty, he poured out overflowing bowlfuls of food in case it was another three days before he got back.

Later, Stuart absently stuffed the key into the back door of his clinic. As he pushed the door open, someone lunged at him from behind, knocked him headlong into the clinic's back entrance and slammed the door before he could react. His assailant, experienced at the art of surprise attack, easily overpowered Stuart who found himself staring at the carpet with his right arm locked painfully behind his neck in a half nelson.

"Are you Dr. Stuart Young?" the voice of his attacker rasped. Stuart caught a whiff of garlic mixed with the nauseating stench of decaying teeth.

"Yes. What do you want?" Stuart gasped. The weight of his uninvited guest pressed heavily on his lungs until he was sure they would collapse.

"Keep away from the Christian Clinic if you know what's good for you. You poke your head around there one more time and it'll be lights out for both you and your little Ms. Welborn. Got that, doc?" the man said, releasing more toxic breath as he pushed up on Stuart's arm.

Stuart gulped, laboriously trying to suck air into his lungs to keep from blacking out. "I've got it," he blurted.

"Don't you go and forget it, doc. I wouldn't advise it. And here's something else for you to think about . . . your little Ms. Welborn is one push of a button away from becoming a heart donor. Our men are right behind her every step of the way. All I have to do is call them on their car radio and . . ."

* * *

A shrill scream penetrated into Stuart's ebony refuge. He must have been hit with a blackjack. He shook his head and eased his hand painfully from behind his back. The pain from his arm and his head was nothing compared to the stark reality to which he awoke. He stifled a cry and whimpered brokenly.

Debbie rushed over to Stuart and reached for his pulse. At the same time, she opened his eyelid with her other hand.

He blinked. "Well, thank heaven you're not dead. What in the world happened?"

Stuart's head reeled. He struggled to sit up and felt as if a volcano had erupted inside him. The ominous feeling that had been with him for days was gone. In its place was stark terror. He had to find B.J. But how? And what was to stop them from killing B.J. at any moment? What could he do? He couldn't tell Debbie the truth.

"Stuart, I'm calling an ambulance. You're so pale that you look like you're about to faint again," Debbie said. She stood up and dashed for the phone.

"No," Stuart shouted, rubbing his arm. "I'll be fine. I . . . tripped . . . that's all."

"Yeah, right. I'm sure that's what happened. You tripped while patting yourself on the back and fell, wrapping your arm around your neck," Debbie said sarcastically. "You looked like a contortionist lying there. Let me at least get you a cold rag."

"Thanks, I'd like that," Stuart said, stifling a moan. "I'll be in my office. And could you fix some coffee?" Stuart knew he had to do something fast but he had no idea what. He made his way to his office and sank into his chair. He picked up the phone and dialed Hawkins' number. When Hawkins answered, he cried, "I need help, buddy. And I need it fast. I don't know what to do. I'm going crazy."

"Stuart, what's the matter?" Hawkins demanded in staccato. "You sound awful. How can I help? Talk to me."

Still gathering his thoughts, Stuart hesitated.

"Damn it, Stuart," Hawkins yelled. "Say something before I call 911."

"I'm still here. I'm . . . trying to sort all this out. Can we meet for lunch somewhere? Somewhere we can talk without the possibility of being overheard. Wait a minute. I can't leave. It might arouse suspicion. Can you come over here? I'll get Mitch to come over, too. I've just been worked over."

"Worked over?"

"Beat up. Mugged. Worse, they threatened B.J.'s life. It's all tied together somehow . . . the unexplained deaths, the microchips, being run off the tollway. Maybe Conrad Nation is involved, maybe even Debbie. I don't know anything anymore. All I know is I've got to do something to save B.J."

* * *

"I forgot to remind Stuart to feed Fred," B.J. said with a sigh as she cuddled the small kitten. "He's going to let those poor animals starve. I know it . . . I just know it."

"Surely he won't forget. The man has a heart, doesn't he?" Cathy asked. She scanned the highway markers for an indication of how far they were from St. Louis. "Look, here's the exit to Cuba. Want a cigar while we're close?"

"Say the magic word," B.J. quipped, flipping imaginary ashes off her imaginary cigar, "and you'll win a hundred dollars." She waggled her eyebrows as fast as she could.

"Don't do that," Cathy laughed. "You'll make me have a wreck. Thank goodness I still see that ambulance behind us. Kinda makes you feel safe, doesn't it? Sorta cozy and nice . . . like Okie over there."

"Actually," B.J. replied, glancing over her shoulder, "it's beginning to make me nervous."

"Whatever for?" Cathy asked, looking back, too.

B.J. paused and looked back again. "I can't put my finger on it but don't you find it even the tiniest bit strange that an ambulance is taking a tour . . . like we are? No matter where we go, that same ambulance is there."

"Are you sure it's the same ambulance?" Cathy asked.

"Well, my fellow Missouri road-mate, let's find out," B.J. said. She leaned over the seat into the back and searching through her overnight bag. "Voila. Here they are." B.J. looked through the binoculars and focused on the ambulance.

"What can you see?" Cathy asked. She glanced in the rear view mirror only to see the back of B.J.'s head.

"It's a Texas plate," B.J. whispered, lowering the binoculars.

* * *

"Debbie, is that the last patient for this morning?" Stuart asked as he walked back to his office.

"Yes, sir. You're free until one-thirty. That's when Ms. Lumlaw is scheduled for her follow-up. You go on out and have yourself a nice long lunch. I'll mind the shop," Debbie said, handing him Ms. Lumlaw's chart.

"No," he roared, yanking the chart out of Debbie's hand, "you go. I'll stay here."

"My goodness, doctor. Is this going to become a normal mode of communication around this office? If so, you might have to find yourself another nurse," Debbie said with a sniff, then turned, grabbed her purse and left.

Stuart heard her muttering something about missing "Days of Our Lives" as she slammed the door behind her. He hadn't meant to shout. He didn't know for certain if she had any involvement in this mess. Surely, he was only reacting to the uncertainty and to his fraying nerves. He crossed to the window and watched Debbie drive her Volvo out of the parking lot. Stuart studied the nearby streets and alleyways. After a few minutes, he became convinced that nobody was lurking outside ready to follow him wherever he might go. Feeling like he might explode, Stuart ran to the locked medication cabinet, reached into his pocket, retrieved the key and unlocked the cabinet. A cursory check of the contents made it obvious that they were gone. Frantic, he ran to the kitchenette and reached behind the coffee mugs. Damn, he thought, she found those, too. Desperate, he raced to the rest room, yanked off the commode top and sighed. There they were . . . still wrapped in plastic and taped to the underside of the lid. He had never in his life needed one more.

After inhaling deeply, Stuart returned to his office and busied himself with updating patient charts until he heard a quiet knock on the clinic's back door. After checking through a window, he opened the door to a worried-looking Hawkins. Walking up behind Hawkins was Mitch, looking no less concerned.

"God, man. Tell me what is going on?" Hawkins boomed as he entered the clinic. "Why are you looking over my shoulder? What's happening?"

"Yes," Mitch said worriedly, scurrying through the door behind Hawkins. "Tell us before I have heart failure."

"I don't even know where to begin," Stuart said as they sat around the small table in the kitchenette. "This morning I was accosted here at the office by some low-life, bad-breath scum who threatened my life if I didn't stay away from the Christian Clinic. Worse yet . . . he said they were following B.J. and could kill her at any moment by simply pushing a button if I didn't stay away. What do I do? My hands are tied.

If I try to help her, they might kill her. Please, guys . . . talk to me. Tell me what to do."

Hawkins shook his head. "I can't see where you have a choice. You've got to get to the bottom of the whole mess. And the only place we know about is the Christian Clinic. That may be the only place we can find out what's going on."

"But what about B.J.?" Stuart asked. "They said they'd kill her if I went back."

"That's fine. Let them follow you around and Hawkins and I will check out the clinic tonight," Mitch said. He adjusted his bulk on the small chair. "By the way, have you ever thought of getting bigger chairs in here?"

Leaning forward, Stuart said, "No. I'm going with you. I couldn't stand it just waiting around."

"Look, fool," Hawkins bellowed. He rose and glared down at Stuart. "Do you want to put the future Mrs. Doctor Young in even worse danger? You hang tight. Mitch and I can take care of it."

"I swear, guys, I'm too strung out to sit around and do nothing. I have no choice. I'll do it by myself if you won't do it with me," Stuart said, returning Hawkins' glare with equal intensity.

"Look, Stuart," Hawkins said evenly, "Take a Valium. Do whatever it takes. But please don't put B.J. in jeopardy. We . . . can . . . handle . . . it. Comprende?"

"I don't care what you say. I owe it to myself and to B.J. I'm going."

* * *

From their vantage point across the parking lot from Preston Tower, where the Christian Clinic occupied the fourth floor, Stuart, Hawkins and Mitch considered their options. Exercising extreme caution about being followed, the three had waited until dark before leaving for Preston Tower and had crisscrossed and backtracked several times before assuring themselves that they weren't being tailed. They parked in front of the President's Health Club, right next to Preston Tower, where they could observe without being noticed.

Stuart spoke first, pointing. "As best I can tell, the only entrance into the clinic at night is through the front lobby past that night guard. All four exits have automatic self-locking glass doors. They seem to be heavy duty and sturdy but we can try them. Besides, the guard sitting in the entrance can see the back door. We could try the side doors but they have deadbolt locks. We need to get up to the fourth floor where they gave me my physical. I know they occupy at least half the space on that level."

"Yeah," Mitch agreed, "they have the place pretty well buttoned up, all right. How do you propose getting up there?"

"Piece of cake, fellows," Hawkins said with a grin, eyeing Mitch. "We use you as bait."

"Would you mind elaborating on what you mean by bait?" Mitch asked, looking up at the large black man. "By the way, have I told you that I'm glad you're on my side?"

"Thanks," Hawkins said. He glanced around the parking lot. "Okay, Mitch, here's the plan. I want you to create a diversion with the guard while Stuart and I slip inside. You can pretend to have a flat tire or something. Ask for help. Anything. It won't take us long to get through the door once you get him outside. The important thing is that you get the guard to go outside of the building at least ten feet from the door and keep him facing you. Away from the entrance. What do you think? Can you do that?"

Mitch shifted in his seat. "Hey, I once played Robin Hood in high school . . . tights and all. Of course, that was a few pounds ago, but I think I've still got what it takes. One never really loses great acting ability. Count me in. Let's do it."

"Look," Stuart said, pointing toward the entrance, "there's somebody going in the building. When I was here before, I noticed a box labeled Entry Sentry on the outside of the building. It looks like one of those things where you punch in a code to unlock the door after hours."

The three sat in silence and watched a young woman carry in what looked to be a Thanksgiving decoration. She walked to the keyboard, punched several buttons, crossed to the entrance and opened the door.

"One thousand one, one thousand two, one thousand three—"

"What are you doing?" Mitch whispered to Hawkins.

"Shhh. One thousand five, one thousand six. Okay, that's it. The door has a spring-loaded closer. I was counting how long it takes to close and lock. We've got six seconds after the guard comes out before the door closes. It's around thirty-five feet from the side of the building to the entrance. Stuart, I'll have to sprint. You try to keep up. And Mitch, you've got to make a lot of noise. The traffic on Forest will help cover the sound of my running, but I'll need a little more distraction."

"What kind of noise you want me to make? Wait . . . I've got it. I'll drive my car around front and honk, like I'm picking up that cute little girl. But it can't be that girl. Wait. See that podiatrist's office? It's totally dark. I'll tell the guard I'm picking up my girlfriend who's the receptionist there. Hey, man . . . that'll work. I'll get him to open the door so I can go find her," Mitch boasted, mopping his forehead with his ever-handy handkerchief.

"Whatever. Just get him out of the way," Stuart said.

"All right. Give us a few minutes to get around to the side of the building. When you see us in place, go for it.

We're counting on you, Mitch," Hawkins said. He knocked Mitch sideways slapping him on the shoulder.

* * *

Nobody had ever counted on him like this before. He'd die before he'd let Stuart down. The whole thing rested on his shoulders. This would be the performance of his life. It had already been a fifteen-hour day. But no matter, he could do it and he would do it. It was a matter of pride. Mitch watched until Stuart and Hawkins had worked their way to the corner of the building and were in place. He drove slowly to the front of the building, pulled into a handicapped parking space next to the sidewalk and honked his horn three times. The guard glanced out at him before resuming reading his newspaper. Mitch waited a few moments, then honked again. Nervously, he adjusted his tie, opened the car door, threw back his shoulders and strode purposefully toward the entrance.

* * *

It had been a long day. Frank Peterson glanced at his watch again, wishing that nut outside would quit honking his horn. Still three hours left on his shift. He turned to the sports page to read the play-by-play of the Sunday Cowboys' game.

They had trounced the New York Giants. He'd watched the game on TV, but relished each word of the story. Damn, that nut was coming to the door. Frank automatically adjusted his holster as he stood and walked to the glass doors. "What do you need, fellow?" he shouted through the thick glass.

"I'm here to pick up Theresa. We've got a date and she asked me to meet her here at the podiatrist's office. That's where she works. She must not have heard me honk. Can I come in to get her?"

"Sorry, but you're not authorized to enter after hours. Besides, the podiatrist's office has been closed since six and there's no one there," Frank said, watching the overweight man wipe sweat from his forehead. Why's the guy so hot? Frank thought. It's cool outside. He must be nervous about being stood up.

"Are you sure? She told me to be here."

"I'm sure. Better be on your way," Frank said gruffly. He turned, stepped back to his desk, plopped down in front of the spread-out newspaper, and watched as the man lumbered slowly toward his car.

* * *

Damn, Mitch thought as he ambled back to his car. What do I do now? I can't let Stuart and Hawkins down. Desperate for an idea, he patted his coat pocket and felt a familiar small lump. He always carried Tic-Tacs with him. Never could tell when he might run into some cute young thing. Wait a minute. It might work. Turning slightly to the side, he pulled the Tic-Tac box out of his pocket. Quickly, after shaking one into his hand, he threw the container into the periwinkle bed next to the sidewalk. He stuck the lone Tic-Tac back into his pocket and looked back. The guard was watching him. Okay, he thought. Do it now.

* * *

"There's too much light here. I'm afraid we'll be spotted," Stuart whispered. He peered around Hawkins' broad shoulder. "What can you see? What's going on?"

"Hopefully we won't be here more than another second or so. Mitch is at the front entrance now, but it's recessed and I can't see what's going on. He's shouting at the guard. I think he's trying to get the guard to let him in. Wait," Hawkins whispered, "Mitch is leaving. What the—"

237

* * *

Mitch walked a few steps toward his car and then screamed at the top of his lungs, whirled around, grabbed his chest and fell backwards into the flowerbed. "My pill," Mitch shouted hoarsely, "my pill. Somebody get me my pill."

* * *

"Oh, my God. Mitch has collapsed. The excitement must have been too much for him. Maybe it's his heart," Stuart said, starting to run toward Mitch. He was arrested in mid-stride when Hawkins grabbed the neck of his coat and hauled him back. "Let me go. I can help him." Stuart turned in amazement to see Hawkins grinning.

"Good little actor, ain't he?" Hawkins said quietly.

"Yeah," Stuart had to admit. "Too good. I nearly blew it."

"Watch and be ready to go at my signal." The two waited.

* * *

It's working, Mitch thought triumphantly as he watched the guard rush to the front door. Then Mitch saw the guard hesitate a moment, return to his desk and pick up the phone. "Help," Mitch rasped as loudly as he could, "I'm dying. Get me my pill. My pill. My pill." Mitch rolled from side to side in the periwinkles, trashing around like a baby elephant trying to stand for the first time. He risked another glance at the guard, who hesitated before slamming the phone down and rushing outside, the door closing behind him. I did it, Mitch thought, as he increased his groaning and writhing.

* * *

"Go," Hawkins whispered. He sped toward the door, knowing he only had three or four seconds left before the door automatically locked itself. In a burst of speed, he nearly slipped when he rounded the corner to the recessed entrance. Hawkins lunged for the door and stuck his fingers through, just as the door tried to close. He swung it open and Stuart ran in ahead of him. The two of them raced inside without looking back and sprinted to the stairwell.

* * *

"It's in my pocket . . . my suit pocket. Please help me," Mitch implored as the guard knelt beside him.

Frank Peterson lifted the stricken man's head and cradled it in his lap. He glanced back at the empty lobby. The door was closed and locked. There was no sign of life. "Which pocket," he asked.

It was not the first time that Frank Peterson had helped a stranger in trouble. There was that time when he had rounded a curve on a dark highway and nearly ran over a man lying out in the middle of the road next to his overturned car. His quick action in alerting the oncoming traffic and getting someone to go for help more than likely saved the man's life. Frank Peterson was convinced that he had been placed on this earth to help other people. There were the givers and there were the takers. Frank Peterson was a giver. He was a guardian angel to many people.

"Coat pocket. Bottom right side," Mitch gasped. Frank felt around in the dark until he reached Mitch's coat pocket. Sure enough, inside the pocket was a tiny pill. Smiling at again being able to help one of his fellow human beings in trouble, Frank handed Mitch the Tic-Tac which Mitch promptly slipped under his tongue. Soon, Mitch was breathing normally again. He lifted himself off the ground with Frank's help and rose to his feet.

"You are a prince of a man. I can't thank you enough. You saved my life." Mitch shook Frank's hand vigorously.

Beaming, Frank said, "I think you're going to make it. You've had a remarkable recovery judging by your grip." Mitch relaxed his hold on Frank's hand and turned to leave.

"What did you say your name was? I'm going to have to make a report of this. I'm not supposed to leave my post. I could lose my job but you were in terrible trouble and I couldn't just ignore a dying man, now could I?"

"Uh, my name is Frank Robinson."

"What a coincidence. My name is Frank, too. Frank Peterson. Listen, I've got to be going. I have to get back to my desk. Are you going to be okay?" Well, that makes two, Frank thought. Wait until I tell Hazel that I saved another life tonight. She's not going to believe it. My crown will shine brightly. "You sure you're okay, Frank?"

"Oh, yes, Frank. Thanks to you, I'll live to see the sun rise once again. I can't thank you enough." Mitch turned and hurried back to his car. It was still running. He shifted into drive and drove around to the back of the building to wait for Mitch and Hawkins.

* * *

The dimly lit, narrow stairwell seemed to close in on Stuart. The doors on the second and third floors had not been locked. They continued to climb while being as quiet as possible.

"I remember taking the elevator to the fourth floor. That's where we'll find the clinic. That's where I saw Nation," Stuart said, gasping for breath. They rounded the halfway turn between the third and fourth floors. "The fourth floor is more than likely locked. It would have to be very secure. How will we get in?"

Hawkins laughed. "You forget where I grew up, my friend. South Oak Cliff. They didn't call me 'slip lock' for nothing. There wasn't a lock in town I couldn't pick. And probably did."

Stuart felt his way up the banister to the fourth floor in the near darkness. He twisted the knob. It was locked. "Okay, Slip Lock. Show me your stuff." Stuart stepped back. Hawkins reached into his pocket and pulled out a special tool he carried with him at all times. It was his own design which he'd had fabricated years before by a master jeweler. He had made a conscious decision not to patent his invention. Too much explanation would have been necessary. In the wrong hands, it could be devastating. Within seconds, Stuart heard a click. He could feel Hawkins smile. The door opened. Bright light burst through the crack, revealing the naked steel and concrete stairwell. Hawkins blinked at the intensity of the fluorescent lighting in the hallway. Momentarily unable to focus, Hawkins waited. After his eyes adjusted, he inched open the door, making certain they wouldn't be seen. Glancing both ways, he gestured for Stuart to follow. After they entered the hallway, Hawkins eased the door shut, after first making certain that the inside push bar released the lock. They made their way down the hall being as quiet as possible until they came to a closet labeled "Linens and Scrubs."

Stuart nudged Hawkins and pointed. Hawkins nodded in acknowledgment. The two doctors slipped in. Moments later, in surgical scrubs and masks, they reentered the hall and strode purposefully past the nurses' station, seemingly deep in conversation. It worked. No one noticed. They continued their mock conversation until they reached what appeared to be the patient record file cabinet recessed into the wall. Glancing back to make certain they were out of sight, they begin going through the drawers until they reached the W's. Stuart pulled out a file entitled "B.J. Welborn." His hands trembled. He couldn't look. Stuart handed the file to Hawkins with a pleading expression. Hawkins nodded his understanding before opening the folder. "Approved" was stamped in large red letters across the first page. On the second page was a handwritten note. "Excellent candidate - heart - A.V."

"Oh, my God," Hawkins stammered. "Stuart, I'm sorry."

Stuart grabbed the file, glanced at it and felt the blood drain from his head. He closed his eyes tightly, attempting to fend off the onrushing dizziness. Not B.J. His brain reeled, struggling to deny what he had just seen. What could A.V. mean? Stuart looked at Hawkins, who was looking through the file folders. Hawkins shrugged. "No V files," he whispered.

"Wait a minute. We're forgetting something. Let's check to see if any of the twelve unexplained death cases are here. They flipped through the folders but found none of the names.

"Of course," Hawkins said, snapping his fingers. "They wouldn't be in the open files, would they? See if you can find any of them in the closed files. There they are. That drawer on the bottom."

Stuart squatted down for a closer look and pulled on the drawer labeled "Closed." It wouldn't budge. Stuart glanced at Hawkins who withdrew his special tool, squatted down beside him, and inserted the tool into the lock.

The shrill voice came from behind. "Exactly what do you two think you're doing? Those files are closed and locked. No one has access to them except Nation himself."

Hawkins motioned for Stuart to keep quiet. They turned in slow motion to face their questioner. The nurse towered over them, her fists on her hips. Hawkins flashed his toothiest smile and started to rise. "Well now, ma'am, we were only following—"

At that moment, a loud buzzer sounded directly above their heads. The nurse turned and fled toward the nurses' station. "I'll get back to you later," she shouted over her shoulder.

Instantly, Stuart and Hawkins turned back toward the stairwell. They hurried past the nurses' station. It was pandemonium. One of the nurses was studying a monitor. She pressed a button and announced, "Code blue. Code blue. Room 509. Room 509." She immediately left her station.

Hawkins glanced at Stuart. "You okay?"

Stuart nodded numbly.

Hawkins chuckled. "I thought for sure we'd been busted. What do you make of that announcement? You'd think we were in Dallas General's cardiac unit. I've never heard a code blue called in an office building. Reckon it's a terminal paper cut? Maybe we'd better check out of this place. Whatcha think?"

Stuart stopped in the hall and leaned against a wall to regain his composure. He let out a long breath. "Man, I had to stop for a minute. I was about to go into fibrillation. But I think I'm capable of curing a terminal paper cut, even in my state of mind. Come on."

Stuart and Hawkins raced to the stairwell and headed to the fifth floor. Hawkins again took advantage of his street skills and the two slipped through the door. As they made their way down the hall toward the commotion, Stuart stopped abruptly. Finding himself alone, Hawkins spun around. Stuart had flipped on a light and was staring into a room.

"What the hell are you doing?" Hawkins croaked, looking back down the hall.

"Would you look at this," Stuart whispered.

* * *

The sodium vapor lamps cast a yellowish tint over the few remaining vehicles in the parking lot. Mitch glanced at his watch and shifted in the bucket seat. What was taking so long? There had been no indication that they'd been spotted. He leaned forward and looked through the glass back door toward the lighted guard desk where Frank sat, still reading his paper. He could see Frank plainly. Mitch saw him look up and grin. As the elevator door opened, a stout young woman exited and walked up to Frank. Frank jumped up, hurried around his desk and hugged her. Mitch leaned forward. She bears an amazing resemblance to Debbie, he thought. The same red hair. The same demonstrative gesturing. The same voluptuous figure. It could almost be Debbie. He felt a twinge of envy. If only *he* had the guts to hug the real Debbie. He studied the two obvious friends. Frank offered his arm. The woman took it and turned toward the back door. Mitch gasped when she passed under an overhead light. She was smiling. It *was* Debbie. It had to be. He could never mistake those dimples. He dreamed about them every night. Frank held the back door open while Debbie laughed and walked through. Frank made certain the door was locked before he turned around and again offered his arm to Debbie. The two walked straight toward him. Mitch scrunched as low in the seat as he could but he was still visible. He had no choice. He laid down across the center console, the shift lever pressing painfully into his side.

"Yes. Thanks for asking. We had a very productive meeting. The investment counselors were there, too. They want me to put more money into the deal and I'm considering it. Thanks for seeing me to my car, Frank. You're a dear, as always. You can't be too careful these days. Dallas used to be such a safe city but with all the crazies hiding in parked cars or lurking behind trees, I feel safe with a big, strapping man like you by my side." Mitch could visualize the whole scene. But why was she here? At the Preston Tower? This time of night? What investment counselors? What deal?

"You drive safe now, you hear. And lock your doors."

Mitch heard a door slam, a car start and then he heard Frank humming. When it became quiet again, Mitch slowly rose up and looked out the driver's window. He was staring into the muzzle of Frank Robinson's .45 caliber Austrian Gaston Glock.

* * *

"I have never seen the like of it. There must be millions of dollars' worth of equipment in here," Hawkins whispered.

"You got that right. This is a state of the art surgical suite. They even have a dialysis machine and—"

Hawkins finished Stuart's sentence. "—a heart lung machine."

"Organ transplants," they said in unison. The two stared at each other in disbelief.

"What the hell *is* this?" Stuart wondered aloud. "Dallas General is not this well-equipped. Who would believe all of this is in Preston Tower? It's an office building, for God's sake."

"You're right," Hawkins said, shaking his head and looking around in wonder, "but we'd better split before the crisis is over and somebody finds us."

The two edged their way back to the stairwell and slipped through the door. They hurried down to the third level and through the unlocked stairwell door. Finding the hall empty, they doffed their surgical garbs and tossed them into a nearby trash can. After locating the elevator bank, Stuart pressed the down button. They waited.

* * *

"Are you trying to give me another heart attack?" Mitch yelled. "I was sitting here trying to get my strength back before I go home. I fell asleep. So sue me. But, damn it, put that thing away."

"I'm sorry, Frank, but I didn't know it was you. I thought you were a pervert lying in wait for some helpless woman. I should have recognized your car. But why did you drive back here? Are you still waiting for your no-show date?" Frank Robinson laughed at his own joke and put his gun away.

"I'm not that stupid, Frank. I got to feeling funny as I was rounding the building so I stopped. I'm okay now." Mitch turned the key in the ignition, put the car in gear and waved as he drove off wondering how long he should stay away.

* * *

When the elevator doors opened, Stuart and Hawkins strode inside. After reaching the first floor, Stuart stepped out, saying, "How many policies did you sell today, Jim?"

"What? Oh, yes. Three. I sold three today. Pretty good, huh? I only sold two yesterday. And one of the three was a two-million-dollar double-indemnity policy." Hawkins grinned and nodded to the guard as they walked purposefully toward the back entrance.

Outside, Stuart and Hawkins scanned the few remaining cars. No Mitch. They walked around the building. Mitch was nowhere to be found.

"Damn," Stuart said. "Where the hell is Mitch? He'd better get back here and I mean now."

Hawkins laughed nervously. "No sweat. We might have to call for a taxi though."

"But you don't understand. I left my cigarettes in his car."

Hawkins shot Stuart a glance. The two men remained near the rear entrance discussing what they had seen on the fifth floor of a seemingly ordinary office building. When Mitch did show up, he quickly explained what had happened.

Stuart couldn't believe it. "Are you absolutely sure it was Debbie? These strange lights might make someone look like Debbie if they had the same build."

"I'm certain," Mitch said. "I'm absolutely certain. I was no more than six feet from her. I heard her voice right next to my car. I'd know her anywhere."

Stuart was puzzled. "What did she say?"

"I don't remember exactly," Mitch admitted. "Something about thanking Frank for walking her out to her car. Nothing, really. It's not what she said that bothered me."

"Well, what then?" Stuart asked.

Mitch hesitated. "It was the way she obviously knew Frank. The way she talked to him and . . . oh yeah . . . the way they hugged in the lobby. Oh, she knew him all right. Oh, yeah. She comes here a lot. One thing I overheard her tell Frank was about meeting with some investment counselors and some deal she was thinking about putting money into."

Hawkins let out a long, low whistle.

Chapter 11

Mitch averaged seventy on the drive from Preston Tower. It was now after nine o'clock and traffic was sparse. Little was said. All three men were deep in thought trying to make sense of the night's strange occurrences. Stuart had never felt more frustrated in his life. Until now, he had always had a plan for everything that came along. Because he was— and always had been—a natural optimist, few things got the best of him. He had always known that everything would turn out all right. And it always had. Until now. Stuart felt closed in, smothered, surrounded. He had no idea what to do next or how to reach B.J. All he could do was hope that she would contact him before it was too late.

Hawkins looked at his watch and then broke the silence. "Let's go to my office. Maybe we can put together something concrete. And I've got to call Ito soon. It's two hours earlier in Los Angeles. He'll probably still be at his office. He needs to know about this Christian Clinic and what kind of equipment it has. Maybe they have one like it in Los Angeles. Maybe Chicago, too. Who knows? It would make sense that they would have a heart transplant setup in each city because of how critical it is for the donor heart to reach the patient within five hours. Oh, yeah. Speaking of Chicago, I also need to call Legato. When I talked to him Friday night, he agreed to go to the Cook County Courthouse this morning and see if the company is headquartered in Chicago. He needs to know about this latest wrinkle and we need to know what he found out at the courthouse. Since it's this late, I'm sure I'll have to call him at home."

"Hawkins," Stuart said, "somehow we've got to find out who or what A.V. means. It could be a key to saving B.J."

Mitch turned to Stuart. "What did you say?"

"I told Hawkins we had to find out who A.V. is. It might help us find B.J."

"So you did say A.V."

"Yes. I said A.V. I guess we didn't tell you. Those were the initials on B.J.'s chart. It said something about being approved for a heart transplant and it also had the initials 'A.V.' penciled in. Why?"

Mitch mopped his brow with his soiled handkerchief. "Oh my God," he said under his breath. "A.V. could very well be Ann Vandergriff."

"Who is Ann Vandergriff?" Hawkins demanded. "And how do you know her?"

"Ann Vandergriff is a former patient of mine."

"Go on."

"She developed serious heart trouble and I had referred her to Conrad Nation for testing. She turned out to be a perfect candidate for a heart transplant. Even to the point of being scheduled for a donor. I can't believe this."

Hawkins' black eyes narrowed to slits. "I'm confused. Why would this bother you? And what could it possibly have to do with B.J.? Your patients are in Dallas General. So are Nation's. If she's going through the normal route for a transplant, how could it involve Chicago Christian or B.J.?"

Mitch looked down and shook his head. "That's just it."

"Just what?" Hawkins shouted. "If you know something, damn it, spit it out."

"She checked out of Dallas General last night."

Hawkins was stunned. "What? That can't be normal for a transplant candidate. Can it?"

Mitch sighed. "It was completely unexpected. I went to see her this morning on my rounds and she was gone. The nurse told me that Mrs. Vandergriff and Nation had a knock-down-drag-out over her decision but he couldn't talk her out of it. Seems she got cold feet at the last minute and decided to take her chances with her old heart. No one could stop her after she made up her mind. Mr. Vandergriff came and got her and they left."

"You were her doctor. Had she said anything about it to you?" Hawkins asked.

"Not a word. In fact, when I saw her on Friday, she was impatient to get on with the procedure. At that time, as far as she was concerned, it couldn't happen soon enough for her. I don't understand it. Something must have changed her mind."

"So you haven't seen her or discussed it with her?"

"No. I intended to call her. I for sure will, now."

"Tell me what the nurse said. And make sure it's as exactly as you can remember."

"Okay. Let me think. When I came up to see her and found the room empty, I asked the nurse if Mrs. Vandergriff had changed rooms, she told me about the argument with Nation. Nation was against her checking out and tried to talk her out of it. He told her that the decision was hers entirely but that she should think twice before doing something rash. As soon as Nation left, she checked out. Couldn't be talked out of it. Her husband was every bit as determined as she was. I need to talk to him, too because he was all for it until then. Oh, yes, the nurse did say one other thing. She thinks it might have something to do with finances. Maybe money troubles. She overheard Mr. Vandergriff tell his wife that he was sure that they could have the money by Tuesday."

"That's tomorrow," Hawkins said. "What do you think it meant?"

"Well, I don't know what it meant, but I can tell you one thing. The Vandergriffs own one of the most successful trucking companies in the state. They're worth over two hundred million bucks. So money couldn't be the problem."

Stuart finally spoke. "Assuming for the moment that Ann Vandergriff is the A.V. on B.J.'s chart, then she probably has already checked into the Christian Clinic by now. But . . . we didn't find any V's in the patient charts. It doesn't wash. None of it makes any sense."

"Unless she hasn't checked into Chicago Christian, yet," Mitch said.

"Or her chart was in use at the time," Stuart said. "Either way, if Nation is involved in all this and if he talked Ann Vandergriff into having her operation at Chicago Christian instead of Dallas General and if they arranged a little show for the nurses so everybody would think it was her idea to check out . . ."

Hawkins waited but Stuart didn't continue. "Go ahead, Stuart. What are you thinking?"

"Either way, if the Vandergriffs get the money tomorrow, how much time could that leave B.J. before they need her heart? How many days? How many hours?"

Mitch drove west on Loop 635 until he came to the I 35 exit. "You're right," he finally said. "We've got to get to the bottom of this now if we're to help B.J." He glanced over at Stuart who was slumping in the passenger seat of the BMW. "Come on, buddy. We're not licked yet. We can figure this out."

Stuart's eyes were moist when he looked at Mitch. "No. It's over. They've beaten us. I give up. I'll never see B.J. alive again. Even if I called the FBI, what could they do? The bastards can kill her in an instant and probably will, no matter what we do. Just take me home. Somehow I should have figured this out before she left. I should never have let her go. It's all my fault." Stuart's shoulders shook as the tears began rolling down his cheeks. He wept in silence.

Hawkins reached over the seat and squeezed Stuart's shoulder. "Okay, my friend, now we're getting somewhere. You've reached bottom. Now we need to start thinking logically. We can dope this thing out. We're three intelligent, well-educated men. Look how far we've come already. Look how much we've found out. Once we get the information from Legato and Ito, we'll have our direction. I'm sure of it. We'll know what to do. They're not going to beat us and I promise you one thing, Stuart. We'll get B.J. back alive." Alone in the back seat, Hawkins crossed himself.

Mitch turned onto Medical Center Drive and drove toward Hawkins' office. He pulled into the graveled lot and drove up to the front door of the Medical Examiners' building. Lights were on inside. Hawkins unlocked the door and led the way to his inner office.

"Sit, guys. I'll go get the documents and you can be checking them again while I call Phyllis." He left the room briefly and returned with a stack of files, which he laid in front of Stuart. Stuart picked up the top file and began leafing listlessly through it. Mitch reached across the desk and gathered up the remaining folders.

Hawkins sat down, picked up the phone and dialed. "Phyllis, sweetheart," he boomed, "were you able to locate the records on those patients? You know, the ones I asked you to check on to see if they came through Parkland. What's that? Oh, don't you worry your pretty little self about that. I'd never forget our date. Sorry we can't go out before the weekend, but my schedule is crazy right now. Yeah, I'll hold." He swiveled around and turned to Mitch. "We'll know in a minute."

Stuart turned the last page of the file and realized that he had no idea what he had reviewed. He flipped back to the beginning and started over. Nothing. He stood. "Where's a phone I can use to check my messages? I have to know if B.J. called."

"Try the office to your left. Rick should have already gone home by now. You can use his phone," Hawkins said with a worried look. He glanced at Mitch, whose expression mirrored his own. The two shrugged.

Stuart disappeared into Rick's office, called his home number, and queried his answering machine. "Damn," he said aloud after hearing the machine tell him that there had been no new messages. "Nothing. I can't take much more of this waiting." He called his office and got the same report. Exhausted, Stuart leaned forward, crossed his arms on Rick's desk, laid his head down and fell asleep almost instantly.

* * *

"Yes. I'm still here, baby. Nothing? Are you certain? Would you mind if I came over and looked through the files? Maybe something didn't get entered because this is not matching the records we have here. There's a glitch somewhere. Okay, thanks. I'll be right over. Me, too, sugar." Hawkins made a kissing sound into the phone before he hung up and turned to Mitch. When he saw Mitch grinning, he winked. "What can I say? When you got it, you got it. Listen, I have to run over to Parkland to double-check the files. I shouldn't be more than a half-hour. You take care of Stuart and don't let him do anything crazy."

* * *

"Hi, cutie," Hawkins boomed. He bent down and kissed Phyllis on the back of her neck.

"Quit that. Do you want me to lose my job?" Phyllis said with a grin. "I'm not supposed to have anything to do with you doctors. Just go on in there and search to your heart's content. The hickeys will have to wait until Saturday night." She pointed to the records room.

"You're killing me," Hawkins groaned. "You have no heart."

Phyllis laughed. "Get your buns out of here and back where those dusty records are, if you know what's good for you."

"Yes, ma'am," Hawkins said. He saluted before turning toward the storage area. Filing cabinets were lined up as though in formation. A narrow pathway had been left between the rows. The dust showed thick even in the dim light. Hawkins sighed. Where to begin? The files were in chronological order. He pulled a wrinkled list out of his pocket. The chair creaked when he sat in front of the dilapidated desk. He looked at his notes. Luckily, each name had a date of death. At least it was a start. According to Hawkins' records, the jogger was admitted to Parkland on the day he died, which was one week ago tonight. This one shouldn't be too difficult. He walked to the nearest shelves.

* * *

"Where's Stuart?" Hawkins boomed. He glared at Mitch. "He's still here, isn't he? Where—"

"Calm down, big guy. The man's still here. I checked on him a few minutes ago. He's sound asleep in Rick's office. Has been since you left. I thought it would do him good. He's so strung out; I don't know how he's holding on. I also don't know how in the world we're going to help him with this mess. Did you find anything?"

Hawkins shook his head and walked around the desk. "All I know is that none of the twelve came from Parkland. Even the patients whose records said so."

"How can this be?" Mitch asked.

"The ambulance records had to be falsified. There's no other answer. We can find no record where a single victim was taken to any hospital. We can only conclude that the organs were removed at the Christian Clinic. But I still have to make one more call. Are you certain Stuart is still asleep?"

"Yes and from the looks of things, he'll be out for a while," Mitch answered. "Who are you calling?"

"You do know that there's a national organ donor association that lists all potential donors, don't you?"

"I've heard of it, but I don't know the name."

"It's called the United Network of Organ Sharing. UNOS for short. The organization is based in Virginia. Every potential donor gets assigned a number. They'll be able to cross-check the donor numbers from my files against their records. I'll give Phyllis a call. She is so organized that I'm sure she'll have a card for them on her Rolodex." He picked up the phone and jabbed in seven digits. "Hi, doll face. It's me again. What? No, I can't stay away from you. I need to ask you a question. Do you have a number for the United Network of Or—? Right. UNOS. I'll hold." Hawkins covered the mouthpiece and turned to Mitch. He was grinning. "Told you. She's getting the number now. Knew exactly what I was talking about. Even knew—. What baby? It is? Marvelous. So that's the way it works. Okay, got it. Thanks. Bye."

"What's the scoop?"

"Here's what they do. Each organ donor is assigned a number soon after retrieval. This number is coded to provide the day, month, year and chronology of when the organs were retrieved and accepted by an organ bank. It is a tracking device to help prevent black marketing of organs. They never close and I've got the number." Hawkins dialed the number given to him by Phyllis and waited for someone to answer. It didn't take long to verify that the UNOS numbers for the twelve donors were fake. He also discovered that none of the donors had a legitimate UNOS number, even though the records at the Medical Examiner's Office provided such a number. It was a sham. The numbers were real but the names and locations didn't match. Hawkins thanked the lady and turned to see Stuart in the doorway.

"I heard everything," Stuart said. "All of the unexplained death donors had their organs removed at the Christian Clinic, didn't they?"

Hawkins slumped in his chair. "Looks like it."

"Then tell me this? What chance does B.J. have? They'll zap her when she gets to Chicago. Then they'll rush her to the Christian Clinic there in Chicago, take out her heart and give it to somebody else. Or fly it back to Dallas and give it to Ann Vandergriff. Am I right?" Stuart's voice grew louder as he spoke. "Am I right? Answer me," he shouted. "*Someone answer me! Please.*"

"None of this is helping, guys," Hawkins said. "Maybe Ito or Legato can shed some light. That's why we came here in the first place. Remember? Oh boy, look at the time. It's almost eight o'clock in Los Angeles. I should have tried to get hold of Ito earlier. I hope he's still in." He picked up the phone and reached for his Rolodex. Flipping to the I-J listing, he punched in the number. The phone rang five times. As Hawkins was about to hang up, the connection made.

"This is Dr. Charles Ito. May I please to help you?"

"Thank God you're in."

"Excuse, please?"

"I'm sorry. Please forgive me, Dr. Ito. This is Hawkins. I apologize for my lack of manners, but we have a very serious situation here. There may be a life at stake and time is critical." Hawkins grimaced when he realized what he had said. He glanced over at Stuart, who was leaning against the wall with his head down and his eyes tightly shut. Hawkins continued.

"Thank you, sir. I'm most appreciative of your time. I'll try to be brief. It appears as though . . ."

* * *

What was Hawkins saying? Stuart fought to compose himself. After he heard something about a life being at stake, he blanked out. He'd never done that in his life. He knew Hawkins was talking about B.J. He had to get rid of this terrible funk. If *he* didn't help her, no one could. My God. B.J. The thought of her never again hurling herself into his arms was more than he could bear. Stuart shook his head, took a deep breath and straightened his shoulders. He fought to pay attention . . . to listen to Hawkins' conversation with Ito. His whole life depended on it.

* * *

"Yes, sir. It was fake. It was all fake. The numbers that they used were real but none of the names or locations matched. And that's where we stand, sir."

There was silence for a moment while Ito absorbed the new information. He spoke slowly. "I think it would be of wise if I were to duplicate your efforts here in Los Angeles, do you not? That way we would know for sure if we have a very large conspiracy here."

"My thoughts exactly, Dr. Ito. If you hadn't suggested it, I would have."

"I shall take the ball and run with it as they say here in Los Angeles. I will be back with you as soon as I obtain the information. And thank you for the UNOS number."

"Of course. And thank you, sir. You have been most helpful. Please let me know what you find out. Good bye, Dr. Ito," Hawkins said. He glanced at Stuart as he hung up the phone. "Are you okay? Can I get you something? Stuart, answer me."

"I'm fine. I'm okay now. Believe it or not, I'm ready to do something. I don't know what, but I'm ready. What did Ito say?"

Hawkins and Mitch exchanged glances. Hawkins dropped heavily into his desk chair. "All he can do is check it out. He'll let me know if there's a Christian Clinic in Los Angeles and he'll check with the victims' doctors to find out who carried their medical insurance. And he'll check on the donor numbers, too. That's all he can do for now. He'll call back as soon as he knows anything. But don't worry, pal. I'm going to call Legato now at home. It's only a little after ten there. Maybe he'll have a line on whether or not Chicago Christian Insurance Corporation is based in Chicago. Also, I want to tell him about the Christian Clinic. See if he's had any experience with such a clinic. One so well equipped. Then, for sure, we'll know what's what."

Stuart stared as Hawkins spun the Rolodex and punched in the ten-digit number. He waited.

"Legato. Hawkins. Tell me what you found out at the courthouse. Dammit. I forgot. Columbus Day. Okay. I'll call you tomorrow. Better yet, you call me as soon as you know anything. Time is getting short. But first I have to tell you about this Christian Clinic we visited. There's no visible indication but the place was far more than a simple clinic that does insurance physicals. It's housed in an office building, all right. But one complete floor is a totally state-of-the-art surgery unit. Right. Stuart and I invited ourselves in tonight and snuck a look. You won't believe what we saw. It's better equipped for heart transplants than Dallas General. No, it's not advertised as such. Ostensibly it's nothing but a small clinic. The surgical suite is on the floor above the insurance company. By the way, one other thing. Would you call the family doctors of the victims in Chicago? We need to know their insurance carriers. Four out of four that we've checked so far in Dallas have all been insured by . . . guess who? You got it. Right. Exactly what we're thinking. Thanks. Talk to you tomorrow."

Stuart hadn't been saying much. He had been thinking about what Hawkins had told Legato and about B.J.'s phone message. "We're getting nowhere. There's nothing we can do. There's nothing anyone can do."

Chapter 12

Joseph Legato stood impatiently at the entrance to the Cook County Courthouse, a briefcase in one hand and a laptop in the other. He was already a day behind in Hawkins' request for information on Chicago Christian Insurance Corporation. He should have had the information yesterday and would have, except for the Columbus Day holiday that had completely slipped his mind. He glanced at his watch. Already a day behind and they were late opening. Finally, he saw movement behind the glass. A security guard was approaching the door and fumbling with a key ring. Good. It's about time, he thought.

Legato wondered briefly where this mystery was leading him. The large number of unexplained deaths in Dallas, Los Angeles and Chicago had piqued the trait within him that was responsible for his becoming a doctor in the first place—and to enter forensic medicine in particular—to understand the incomprehensible. It was a wonderful time in history to be a doctor. The historic human genome project alone was enough to make it worthwhile. The idea of a road map showing the complete genetic structure of a human being excited him. His footsteps echoed as he walked briskly down the wide, empty hall toward the corporate records room. The stark walls were interrupted intermittently by bulletin boards overlapping with service of citation notices. Occasional benches outside courtrooms were still accompanied by ashtrays, despite the longstanding smoking prohibition. He took no notice of the yellowed map of Chicago next to the photograph of the original Cook County Courthouse. He found the corporate records office at the end of the hall. The door was open.

An hour later, a stunned Legato found what he was looking for and retrieved a hand-held, battery-operated scanner from his briefcase. After making a few practiced wiring connections, he scanned the list of officers and stockholders of Chicago Christian into his computer. The astonished doctor recognized most of the names as being infamous local residents. The name of one of the major stockholders, however, stopped him cold; a company entitled Earth Argon Corporation. He searched the files for more information on Earth Argon. None existed. Puzzled, he asked the clerk for assistance. Same result. Nothing could be found on Earth Argon.

"There must be some mistake in the records. All stockholders must be listed. It's the law," the clerk insisted. "If you wish, I can request a formal investigation. That way we can get to the bottom of it."

Legato glanced at his watch. "How long does that usually take?"

The balding, bespectacled men answered matter-of-factly, "Oh, usually no more than two weeks. I can start the

275

process now if you wish. Let me get the proper paper work." He turned to leave.

"Two weeks? You've got to be kidding. Two *hours* would be too long. I have to have it now."

The startled civil servant turned back around. "But, sir, you've got to under—"

"No, *you've* got to understand," Legato barked. "Lives are at stake, here."

"Sir, we have procedures that we have to follow. I'm sure—"

"Never mind. By the time I explained it to you, it would be too late, anyway."

"But, sir—"

"Go away and let me concentrate. Please."

The rumpled clerk shot Legato a look that said, "The crazy nuts we get in here these days" and shuffled off shaking his head.

Legato turned back to the listing. "Earth Argon Corporation," he repeated. "Earth Argon. Hmm. What is that name trying to tell me?" Legato snapped his fingers. "Maybe that's it." He exited the scanning program and called up his dictionary program. Smiling at his inspiration, he typed in "Earth" and pressed the enter key. Next, he pulled down the "search" menu and selected the fifth option.

* * *

Groggy, Stuart turned over in his bed and glanced at the clock. Nearly noon on Tuesday morning. He sat up quickly and was instantly sorry. Should have known better. Vodka was no solution to his problems. The fifth of Absolut had only succeeded in numbing him for a few hours. He depressed the "play messages" button on his answering machine and was punished by five beeps. No messages. At least he hadn't slept through a call from B.J. He fumbled for a cigarette and his lighter, trying to decide whether to stay home or go to his clinic. He'd already missed his morning patients. Why hadn't Debbie called? He took a long drag, inhaled deeply and picked up the phone and dialed.

"Dr. Young's office. May I help you?" Debbie's voice sounded strained.

"Why didn't you call me?" he snapped. Disgusted with himself, he snuffed out the cigarette.

"Dr. Young. Where are you? Hawkins called as soon as I got in and told me you would be late. He said not to call you. Practically threatened me with bodily harm. What's going on? You missed all of your morning appointments already. Some I rescheduled. Some are still waiting. Should I send them home, too? And do you want me to cancel the rest of today's patients?"

Stuart sighed. "No . . . I'll be there in about an hour. Ask them if they'd mind waiting. Tell them I had an emergency and give them my apologies."

"I already did that. That's what Hawkins told me to do. Are you all right? You sound exhausted."

"I'm fine. I was up late, that's all. See you soon."

Stuart dragged himself into the bathroom and washed down double the recommended dose of Tylenol. Maybe that would help. Stuart knew that he had better keep himself busy until B.J. called or he would go crazy. He shut his eyes tightly to rid himself of the recurring image of B.J. lying in a cold morgue with her heart ripped out. He promised himself that if anything happened to B.J., he would devote the rest of his life to bringing down the people who were behind the diabolical scheme. The thought gave him no comfort. But it helped him to keep going.

For the hundredth time, he considered calling in the FBI and the Highway Patrol. They would be able to locate B.J. through a search of the Dallas car rental agencies. Cathy's father had connections. But no matter how fast they could move, one fact remained. Somebody's finger was merely inches away from a button that could snuff out B.J.'s life in a millisecond. No, there was no one he dared contact. He stepped into the shower.

* * *

Joseph Legato hurried down the hall to a bank of pay phones, his clothes flapping loosely from his thin frame. Scanning the shelves beneath the phones, he finally found one that still contained a set of Chicago phone books. Flipping the pages as fast as he could, he stopped at the city offices listing. Still breathing heavily, he ran a thin finger down the long row of numbers until he found it. "Please still be there," he whispered. He mounted the small stool in front of the phone, dropped in two coins, dialed a number, and hunched over, cupping the receiver with his hand and cursing the lack of privacy with modern pay phones.

The line was busy.

* * *

By twelve forty-five Mitch had completed his morning rounds. Fortunately, all of his hospitalized patients needed only a few minutes of his time. He hurried to a pay phone in the hospital lobby and dialed a familiar number. Hawkins answered.

"Hawkins. Mitch. Got a minute?"

"Of course. Whatcha got?"

"I've been thinking. Shouldn't we somehow be checking to see if Ann Vandergriff is at the Chicago Clinic? If she *is* A.V., don't we need to know it? It might give us some clue as to how much time we have. I brought her file with me this morning. If we can check it against B.J.'s file, it would tell us if they are compatible."

"Mitch, you're brilliant. Fax me the pertinent files. Soon as you do, I'll pay the clinic another little visit and do some more snooping. You got my fax number?"

"Got it. Give me five minutes. Bye."

Proud of himself, Mitch took off for the hospital's business office to look for a fax machine.

* * *

"Morning, Ralph. B.J. Anything new?" B.J. strained to hear over the noise. She plugged her free ear with a finger. She and Cathy had stopped at a station to buy gas. Cathy was taking care of the car. The pay phone hung precariously on a dingy wall outside the station. Cars whizzed by on the highway. An unmanned eighteen-wheeler idled about thirty yards away. Judging by the noise level, she could have been standing right next to it.

"Not a thing. It's like nothing has happened. They can't find any indication that Manning sold out to any of our competition. So, now they're also looking into the possibility that he may have sold out to some foreign government. It may take a while because they're having to bring the CIA in on that one."

"Have you tried asking him?"

"Of course not. That'll be the last thing we do. One thing we did find . . ."

"Yes?" B.J. tried her best to stay calm but Ralph's irritating habit of playing cat and mouse was beginning to get to her.

"Manning took a solo weekend trip to Reno about two months ago. He was at work on Friday and again on Monday. No time off at all."

"Did you say alone?"

"Yeah. Weird, huh?"

"For sure. I've never known him to go anywhere alone. But on the other hand he could have this one time. Listen Ralph, I have an idea. While TI is conducting its investigation, why don't you and I give Dexter the benefit of the doubt? Let's assume that he was feeling crowded one day and decided to go off to Reno by himself and happened to win a million dollars and he doesn't want anybody to know about it."

"Now that's a real stretch."

"I'll give you that. But assuming it is true and assuming you find out that the competition knows nothing about the microchip design details and that he hasn't sold out to some foreign government, we still have some technical decisions to make. Like whether or not we want the microchip GPS to utilize the European RDS standard or go with the American RBDS standard. What is your thinking on that?" She watched as Cathy went into the station to pay for the gasoline. There wasn't much time.

* * *

One of the front office clerks dropped some papers onto Hawkins' desk. "Dr. Hawkins, here's a fax that just came in for you. It's labeled 'urgent.' I thought you might need it right away."

"Thank you, Stella. I was expecting this," Hawkins said. He scooped up the fax from his desk and snatched his coat from the rack in one motion. "I'll be gone for about an hour, maybe longer. Please let Dr. Perwani know. Thanks. You're a doll."

"A Dr. Legato is holding for you on line one. Do you want me to take a message?"

Hawkins stopped short. "No, I'll take it," he said. He hurried back to his desk. Standing in front of it, he grabbed the phone. "Hawkins here."

"Hawkins, Legato. I've got news."

"What did you find? We're desperate here."

"I must warn you. The news is not good. In fact, it's about as bad as it gets. The Board of Directors and Officers of Chicago Christian reads like a *Who's Who* of organized crime in Chicago. You're familiar with the names of Scarface Scaletti, Mario Spinoza and Max Gotti, aren't you?"

"Oh . . . my . . . God. I don't believe it. The only one you *didn't* mention is Al Capone. Are we talking Mafia here?" What are we up against? He thought. How can we possibly tackle the Chicago Mafia? Hawkins rounded his desk and returned to his chair in slow motion. His legs had unexpectedly become too unsteady to support him.

"Hawkins? Are you still there?"

"Yeah, I'm getting cold chills. What can we do?"

"I haven't told you the worst part yet."

"My God, man. What could be worse than the Mafia?"

"This part is almost unbelievable. If I'm right, it could be the biggest scandal in Illinois history."

"Damn it, Joe. Tell me."

"Here's the deal. I'm looking at the list of Chicago Christian directors and I'm freaking out. Like I said, it reads like a Mafia phone book. Then I get to this lone corporate stockholder that I've never heard of, Earth Argon Corporation."

"Earth Argon? Like the gas they use to fill light bulbs?"

"Right. That argon. Only when I look up Earth Argon Corporation, it doesn't exist."

"You sure you didn't overlook it?"

"Positive. I even had the clerk try to find it. No luck. So I keep looking at the name Earth Argon and it keeps trying to tell me something. I guess it's the crazy way my brain works. I don't know. Anyway, so I have this inspiration and I call up my anagram program thinking that the name might be coded somehow."

"And?"

"Bingo. Earth Argon is an anagram for Heart Organ. So I looked and sure enough, there is a corporation in Springfield with that name."

"Who owns it?"

"Douglas Harrison."

"Good God. *The* Douglas Harrison?"

"That's right. The Governor of Illinois. He was there in Dallas last month for medical treatment. He had Conrad Nation do a triple bypass on him. It made a lot of Illinois doctors angry because he insisted on seeing Nation. Now, don't get me wrong. Nation is good, but there must be at least a half-dozen cardiologists in Chicago that are in his league and several that even surpass him in experience and success rates. I wondered about it, too. He got a lot of bad press in Chicago about it but he was unwavering. Nation must have done some kind of sales job on him. He's back on the job now, so I guess everything went okay. But if Earth Argon and Heart Organ are the same, we have a real problem."

Hawkins slumped back in his chair. "That, my friend, is the understatement of the century. How can you find out?"

"I can request an official investigation but it takes two weeks, so I'm going to take a shorter route."

"What's that?"

"I'm going to ask Harrison."

"Are you crazy?"

"No. I've made up my mind. I'm going to ask Harrison. He's in Chicago for the annual governors' conference and according to the paper, he is meeting with the mayor as we speak. I plan to call the mayor's office and see if I can have two minutes with Harrison. The mayor owes me one. I rescheduled one of the DA's autopsies at the mayor's request last month."

"I don't know. Too dangerous."

"I've thought about that. After seeing Harrison, if I think I'm right, I'll go straight to the FBI. They'll want to know all about this, anyway. It has to be done. Hey, man, I know it sounds bad but they've been finding some chinks in the

Mafia's armor in recent months. I think the Feds can handle it. Gotta go."

But that won't help B.J., Hawkins thought. He hung up and dialed a number from memory.

* * *

"He's probably on his way to the office right now, Dr. Hawkins," Debbie said. "I spoke with him about an hour ago. I expect him in any minute now. Is there anything I can help you with?"

"No. I'll try to reach him on his car phone. If I miss him, have him call me the instant he gets there. Do I make myself clear? This is urgent."

"Of course, Dr. Hawkins. I'll . . ." Debbie stared at the dead phone. ". . . be sure and do that," she said, slowly hanging it up.

* * *

His head still pounding, Stuart scanned the neighborhood before unlocking his car door. He'd been too distracted to even think about putting his car in the garage the night before. After opening the door, he eased himself into the driver's seat and fumbled for the ignition key. Before he could insert it, his car phone rang. He jumped. His nerves were brutally sensitive. It's probably Debbie, he thought. He jerked up the receiver. "Yeah, what is it?"

"Not good. More trouble," Hawkins boomed.

Stuart flinched. He couldn't take any more bad news. And Hawkins' voice had reignited the throbbing. "Spill it," he said under his breath as he reached into his coat pocket for a cigarette. He had to know the worst.

"Chicago Christian is owned by the Mafia. It's headquartered in Chicago, like we figured. And Max Gotti is apparently one of the kingpins and the Governor might even be involved. Stuart? You still there?"

"Yeah. Just trying to make some sense of all this. It's worse than I could have imagined. Look, Hawkins, I've been thinking. I can't sit still any longer. I'm going to Chicago. At least I'll be closer to B.J. and I can be there when she gets there. I'll take my cell phone with me and transfer all my calls to it. That way, when B.J. does call, I'll be able to get to her a lot quicker. Maybe I can get that damned chip out of her before they can do anything. At least I've got to try."

"I understand. Is there anything I can do from here?"

"Stay close to your phone and call me with anything else you find out. Anything at all that might help. I'll call you from Chicago."

Stuart hung up and then pressed auto-dial button number one.

"Dr. Young's off—"

"Debbie, cancel all my appointments for today. Better yet, see if Dr. Elwood can fill in for me. If not him, get somebody equally qualified. Do whatever you can. I'll call you later."

* * *

For the second time, Debbie found herself staring at a dead phone. What is he up to? she thought. She hit the switch hook and dialed.

"Dr. Conrad Nation speaking."

* * *

Stuart threw the transmission into reverse and slammed down the accelerator. With a loud screech, the Lexus lurched backward on the short driveway and bounced into the street. He jammed on the brakes, barely missing a neighbor's car, which was parked on the curb across the street. He jerked the transmission into drive and stomped on the accelerator. Without slowing for the stop sign, the car shot across the intersection and sped toward DFW. Stuart picked up the phone and dialed information. When an operator answered, he asked for the phone number of Mustang Travel. He couldn't risk having Debbie make reservations for him as she usually did. Not after Mitch saw her having dinner with Conrad Nation and then spotted her coming out of the Christian Clinic. Maybe he should have confronted her about it. No, too risky. Had to let her believe that everything was normal. Or at least as normal as possible. If she *was* mixed up in all this, he couldn't take a chance on her tipping off Chicago.

Stuart dialed the number given him by the operator. When the receptionist answered, he asked for Jan. There was a short delay. When he heard Jan's familiar voice, he spoke quickly. "Jan, I'm on my way to DFW right now. I'll be there in twenty minutes. I need to be on the next flight to Chicago. Put me on hold while you check it out. And please hurry. It's a medical emergency."

"Dr. Young? Is that you?"

"I'm sorry. Yes, it's me, Jan. Please hurry." Stuart glanced around, aware that he was exceeding eighty miles per hour on I 635. He felt trapped. On the one hand, being stopped by a Dallas cop didn't concern him. On the other, there was precious little time for explanations. Every minute wasted would increase the danger B.J. faced. What could he tell them, anyway? That he was hurrying to Chicago to save his fiancée from the Mafia? Right. As he waited for Jan to return to the line, he checked the traffic. Fortunately, it wasn't heavy by Dallas standards. In a turnabout, Stuart was passing all the traffic instead of making them all pass him. All but an ambulance that was overtaking him rapidly on his right. Instinctively, Stuart pulled over into the far left lane to allow it to pass. Something about the ambulance made him look closer. What was it? What was it about the vehicle that wasn't quite right?

"Dr. Young?" The sudden interruption of his concentration startled him. It was Jan.

"Yes, Jan. What did you find out?"

"Can you be at American Airlines gate thirty in twenty-five minutes? If you can, I can book you on flight 1555 to O'Hare. It leaves at two."

Stuart mouthed a silent prayer of thanks for the flight and for the layout of DFW airport, which allows for parking directly outside each gate. "I'll make it," he said. "Count on it. You're a doll, Jan. Thanks. I owe you dinner for this one."

"Cool. You have a deal. Anyway, the plane will start boarding before you get there. I'll make arrangements for . . ."

Stuart was rapidly approaching the intersection of I 635 and I 35E. He needed to move over into one of the right lanes. And soon. Otherwise, he'd be forced onto I 35E, which would take him miles out of the way. A detour was the last thing he needed. Where was that stupid ambulance? It should have passed him by now. Stuart looked to his right and saw the ambulance pulling up beside him. He could see nothing of its interior because the windows were so darkly tinted, they were almost completely black. Now the ambulance was pacing Stuart's car at the same speed. Stuart slowed to let the vehicle pass. The ambulance slowed also and continued to pace him. It finally dawned on him. That's what was wrong with the ambulance. It must have been going ninety to catch up with him but with no lights or sirens. Stuart dropped his speed even more. The ambulance slowed as well. What the hell was going on? The intersection was now no more than three hundred yards away. Desperate to make sense of it all, Stuart glanced over at the ambulance, again. Its window was being lowered. Too dark inside to make out a face. What was he doing? When the glass was halfway down, the wavering muzzle of a .45-caliber pistol was suddenly thrust toward him. The driver of the ambulance was aiming the gun at Stuart's head, his right hand on the emergency vehicle's steering wheel. A skull-shaped gold ring with brilliant rubies for eyes stared mockingly at him from a fat, hairy finger. Stuart threw on his brakes just as the trigger was squeezed, causing the bullet to smash into his windshield. The shattering glass obliterated Stuart's vision and destroyed what remained of his faculties and the silver Lexus plunged headlong into the crash barrels stacked around the solid concrete overpass pier. The ambulance continued west on I 635, its windows dark again.

* * *

Forty minutes after leaving his office, Hawkins pulled into the Preston Tower parking lot. He chose a space in front of the building but to the side, pulled into it and parked. Then he strode purposefully to the unlocked front door, entered the building and went straight to the elevator bank as though he had done it a thousand times before. As he passed the guard desk, he noticed that it was unoccupied. Interesting. No daytime guard. Hawkins entered the empty elevator without looking around and pressed a button. He was still alone when the machinery whirred to a stop and the doors opened onto the fourth floor. A sign with an arrow to the right greeted him. "Welcome to the Chicago Christian Medical Clinic." Hawkins turned to the left and hurried down the hall.

At the end of the hall, Hawkins opened the exit door and entered the stairwell. He jogged up to the fifth floor, paused at the locked stairwell door and fished around in his pocket. Finally finding what he was after, he turned and bent over the door lock.

"Hey, what do you think you're doing?" The voice came booming through the stairwell. "Hold it right there."

295

Hawkins froze. He could think of no feasible explanation for jimmying the lock of a guarded complex. Trying his best to come up with a story, Hawkins slowly turned, making sure his empty hands showed. His tool was still sticking out of the lock behind him. "Oh, hi," he said, flashing his broadest smile. "I forgot the door locked itself and I came out for a smoke. I was trying to get back in without having to go all the way back down and around to the front. I'm a doctor. I know I shouldn't be smoking and I'm going to quit right after the first of the year. New Year's resolution, you know. Hey, you startled me. I didn't see you. Where were you?"

The guard eyed Hawkins as he descended from the sixth floor landing, his right hand never far from his holster. "I never saw you here before. Besides, none of the doctors are supposed to have stairwell keys."

Hawkins shook his head, still smiling broadly. "You're probably right. That may be why none of my keys would fit. I just started to work today and I thought they gave me a key to this door but I guess they didn't."

"I think I had better check you out. If you're who you say you are, no harm done. Let's go inside and see if anyone is willing to vouch for you."

"Certainly." Hawkins stepped aside to let the guard unlock the door.

The guard fumbled for his key ring while watching Hawkins. When he found the key he was looking for, he turned and reached for the lock. It was then that he saw what was protruding from the keyhole. He whirled back around. "Hey, you're no—"

He didn't get a chance to finish his sentence. With one swift motion, Hawkins grabbed the guard by the shirt with both hands and ducked his head. Then, with two fistfuls of uniform he yanked downward with his powerful arms, bringing the guard's chin crashing down on Hawkins' head. The guard crumpled onto the concrete landing. Rubbing his head, Hawkins pulled the key ring from the guard's hand, retrieved his tool, unlocked the door, opened it a crack and peered through. Satisfied, he gathered up the guard and carried him into the hall over his shoulder. Remembering a broom closet that he had seen the night before, Hawkins deposited the guard's limp form in the small room.

"Here's your keys, buddy. Hope you don't have too big a headache when you wake up. Judging from past experience, I expect you'll be out about thirty minutes. No hard feelings, y'hear? You were just in the wrong place at the wrong time. Bye now and sweet dreams." Hawkins closed the door after making sure it would open from the inside.

After listening for a few seconds, Hawkins continued down the dimly lit hall until he found what he was looking for––the storage closet for linens and scrub suits. Quickly donning one that fit, he walked purposefully to the nurses' station and approached the nurse on duty. He again smiled broadly while reading her name tag. "Good evening, Nurse Barrett. How are you?"

Nurse Barrett looked up distractedly from a chart she was studying. "I'm fine, Doctor—"

She looked at his chest. "Filbert. James Filbert. I must apologize for forgetting my ID badge. I don't know where my mind was this afternoon. I was asked by Dr. Nation to look in on our new patient, Mrs. Vandergriff. Would you be so kind as to direct me to her room?"

"That was quick."

"Pardon?"

The portly nurse lowered her chart and was now giving Hawkins her full attention. "She only checked in a little over an hour ago. Dr. Nation usually sees his patients personally. I was half expecting *him* to show up."

"Oh, he will. He's been delayed and he asked me to cover for him." Hawkins looked expectantly at Nurse Barrett without saying anything further.

"Oh, yes. The room number. It's 502. Right over there." Satisfied, the woman pointed to a room across the hall and went back to her charts.

Hawkins allowed himself an inaudible sigh after he turned away. So far, so good. He crossed the hall to room 502, knocked softly and pushed the door open. The woman lying on the bed reading a magazine looked up. A man, presumably her husband, sat quietly in a chair beside the bed.

"Yes?"

"Mrs. Vandergriff?"

"Yes, I'm Ann Vandergriff."

"How are you? I'm Doctor James Filbert and I wanted to find out if you are properly being taken care of. And is this Mr. Vandergriff?" Hawkins looked over at the man who was now rising to his feet.

When the woman spoke, there was a decidedly grateful tone to her voice. "Oh, my goodness, yes. To both questions. We're both being treated wonderfully. It is so good of Dr. Nation to allow us to cut through the red tape like this. We were beginning to think we'd never—"

"Now dear, remember we aren't allowing ourselves to talk like that anymore. We have been given a golden opportunity and it was meant to be. Let's be grateful for it." Vandergriff turned to Hawkins and extended his hand. "I'm John Vandergriff, Dr. Filbert. I'm glad you dropped by. To answer your question, we only arrived this afternoon at one o'clock but so far we have been treated quite well."

Hawkins thoughts were consumed by the danger posed by every wasted minute. If Nation found him here, no doubt he would end up at the bottom of the Lake Ray Hubbard by nightfall. "Thank you, Mr. Vandergriff. I have to run now but I need to ask you a quick question. Coordination details, you know."

"Certainly. Ask away."

"Has anyone given you an approximate time for the procedure? I must make sure that all the necessary supplies are ordered. Some are very specialized, you know." Hawkins accorded John Vandergriff his best smile and a knowing wink.

Vandergriff frowned at the question. "You know, I'm not sure. We discussed it at the other hospital before we checked out and I think he said that we could expect the, uh, procedure within twenty-four hours of receiving the money. Gracious me, two million dollars is quite a sum of money, and with yesterday being a bank holiday and all, I won't be getting the money until about two o'clock today. Oh, don't misunderstand me, we can well afford—"

"So I can expect the procedure to take place sometime early tomorrow afternoon at the latest, then. Is that correct?" Would you please get on with it, Hawkins thought. My ass is on the line here.

Vandergriff looked at his watch. "That's correct. Or possibly earlier. Gracious me, look at the time. I had better get to the bank right away. I have a lot of papers to sign. I certainly don't want to be the cause of any delay."

"How far away *is* your bank, Mr. Vandergriff?" An idea was beginning to form in Hawkins' spinning brain.

"Oh, it's in downtown Dallas. NationsBank. 901 Main Street. I can be there and back in an hour, not counting the paperwork, of course." Vandergriff rose.

"Of course," Hawkins said. "Is your car close by?"

"Oh, yes. It's parked right outside. I should be leaving now." Vandergriff leaned over and kissed his wife. "Goodbye, dear. I'll see you in a couple of hours." He turned toward the door.

"And I'll see you tomorrow, Mrs. Vandergriff. Mr. Vandergriff, I am a car fancier of sorts and I figure you for the red Jaguar convertible type. Am I right?" Hawkins said while his hand guided Vandergriff's elbow to the door.

"Oh, my gracious, no. You give me entirely too much credit. That would be way too fancy for me. I drive a white

Cadillac DeVille. I would feel too conspicuous in a red convertible, but thank you for the compliment."

"I must go now, Mr. Vandergriff. Thank you for your help." Hawkins turned and stepped briskly down the hall. Vandergriff walked to the elevator bank. As Hawkins passed the broom closet, he thought he heard shuffling sounds. He hurried his pace until he turned the corner. Seeing no one, he ran to the stairwell door, opened it and raced down the stairs. By the time he reached the bottom landing, he was out of his scrubs and also out of breath, as much from anxiety as from the five flights of stairs. Had to beat Vandergriff to his car. After rounding the corner of the building, he spotted the white Cadillac. Walking as fast as he could without being obvious, Hawkins reached Vandergriff's car, bent down and with a motion perfected by practice many years earlier, he slipped what looked like a shortened ice pick into the sidewall of the Cadillac's right front tire. He straightened up, strode briskly to his own car and slipped into it. At the same instant, Vandergriff pushed through the front door of the office building and headed to the Cadillac. Hawkins reached for his cell phone and dialed. No answer. He tried a different number.

* * *

"No, I'm sorry, Dr. Hawkins. I don't know where Dr. Young is. You might try his cell number. He called earlier from it and asked me to cancel all his appointments for today. Let me tell you that it has caused some kind of chaos around . . . What? Chicago? No, he didn't say anything about going to Chicago. Dr. Hawkins, please. You don't have to shout. Dr. Hawkins? Hello? Hello?" Debbie slammed down the phone. "What in the hell is going on around here? Would somebody please tell me?" she said under her breath.

* * *

Hawkins crossed himself, dialed another number and waited without breathing.

Chapter 13

"Mitch. Thank God you're in," Hawkins said, finally exhaling. "We have to talk. I'm on my way to your office now. Whatever you do, stay put. Time is critical. I just left Preston Tower and with any luck, I'll be there in twenty minutes. Good. I'll fill you in as soon as I get there. What? No. Not now. I have to concentrate on my driving. I'm no damn good at driving and talking on the phone at the same time so I'll see you in a few. Okay? Bye."

* * *

Lester Jackson watched in awe as the Lexus plowed into the crash barrels. Jackson had been less than a quarter mile away when it happened and had been passed by both the speeding car and the speeding ambulance. After seeing the Lexus plow into the crash barrels, he pulled over onto the shoulder and watched. Four other cars pulled over at the same time to stop at the accident scene. Several men scrambled out, rushed over and began peering into the interior of the crumpled Lexus. "Look at that," one of the men said. "He drove straight into the barrels. He must have fallen asleep at the wheel." His companion shook his head. "I don't think so. Look at the skid marks. Oh, he was awake for sure. But you're right. He drove straight into the barrels. Why didn't he turn? Look at all that blood. Someone call 911."

Jackson reached to open his door but decided to call for help first. Every second counted. He couldn't wait to tell Dorothy about this. After all, it was Dorothy who gave him the cell phone for his birthday. Up until now, it was an expensive nuisance. Smiling, he lifted the phone from its perch on the console. She'll be proud, he thought.

After reporting the accident, he hurried over to see if there was anything he could do. As he approached the car, he heard someone saying, "Is he still alive? He isn't moving. Wow, would you look at the damage." Jackson shook his head. How could something like this happen in broad daylight and in good weather to boot?

* * *

"This is Joseph Legato. I'm the Cook County Chief Medical Examiner. I need to speak to the Mayor immediately. I wouldn't disturb him but this is an emergency."

"I'm terribly sorry, Dr. Legato. The Mayor is in conference right now with the Governor and he left explicit instructions not to be interrupted."

"But this is an emergency. I must speak to him."

"I heard what you said, but that's quite impossible. It is out of the question."

Legato took a deep breath and tried to sound as calm as possible. "Lives are at stake here. Will you at least pass the Mayor a note for me? You can do that, can't you?"

"I suppose. Let me get a pencil. Hold on."

"No. Don't put me on hold," Legato shouted but it was too late. Already, Frank Sinatra was serenading him—music on hold from the local easy listening station. At least he wasn't singing about Chicago. Legato drummed his fingers on the shelf. As he was about to hang up and redial, the woman returned, presumably with a pencil. He didn't ask. "Write this down verbatim. Do not abbreviate or leave out a single word. It's that important."

"Go ahead."

"Write this exactly. 'Dr. Joseph Legato, the Cook County Medical Examiner, wishes to speak with the Governor for two minutes before he leaves the building. It is imperative. Tell the Governor that he wishes to discuss Earth Argon.'" Legato spelled out the name. "'Dr. Legato is holding for the Governor now on line'—I don't know—whatever line this is. Okay, that's it and this time, do *not* put me on hold. I'll wait for an answer on this *open* line."

"Yes, sir. I'll take it to him now."

"Thank you." Legato wiped his brow with a handkerchief and waited. After what seemed like an hour, he heard a familiar sounding voice.

"Dr. Legato?"

"Yes."

"This is Governor Harrison. I understand you wish to speak with me?"

Legato found himself feeling unexpectedly sycophantically. He wanted desperately to apologize for even suspecting the man of involvement in such a diabolical scheme. He took a deep breath. "Yes, Governor. I have run across some disturbing information and I need to speak with you for a few minutes. I don't think it will take long to clear it up. If—"

"Have you spoken to anyone else about this, Dr. Legato?"

"No," Legato lied.

"Good. Let's keep it that way until we can talk and get this, uh, straightened out." Legato heard the Governor's tone change abruptly. "Well, now. The mayor and I have finished our business and I'm getting a bit hungry. All I've had today is a cup of weak coffee and some dreadful breakfast rolls. Please join me for a bite of late lunch. Are you familiar with Barnfield's Restaurant on Ninety-fifth and Halsted?"

"Yes, I am."

"Good. Can I assume that you're close by?"

"Yes, sir, I am."

"Good. Meet me there in thirty minutes. Park directly in front. I'll have security hold us a couple of parking spaces. What are you driving?"

"A dark blue Mercedes."

"Good. I'll be expecting you. And Legato?"

"Yes?"

"You have stumbled upon some very important and sensitive information. Can I trust you to keep it to yourself until after we talk? After that, you may do with it whatever you choose."

"Of course."

Legato sat on the stool for a full five minutes while he regained his composure. He felt better. Maybe he was wrong. Maybe. The governor sounded straightforward enough. After he'd calmed himself to the point where he was no longer shaking, he dropped in two more coins and dialed his home number. After the second ring, what was surely the most angelic voice in the world answered.

"Hi, sweetheart. How's the most precious person in the world?"

"Joseph. Are you okay? You don't sound like yourself. But I must say, that's the sweetest thing you've said to me in a long time. Where are you? It doesn't sound like you're at the office."

"Actually, I'm downtown at the County Courthouse. I had some records to check on but I'm leaving for a meeting now. Before I go, I wanted to tell you how much I love you. And when you talk to the kids, give them my love, too. Bye, my love."

* * *

"Joseph?" The line was dead. "That's strange."

"What is?"

"That was your father. He called to say he loves us. He hasn't done that since you were little."

* * *

311

"Hi, sweetheart. What are you doing?"

"Oh, Douglas, darling. I am so glad you called. I was about to serve tea to the ladies of the bridge club. Now that you are well, I've started having bridge club at the house on Tuesdays, again. I am so excited our life is getting back to normal, aren't you?"

"I certainly am, my pet and I wish we had time to chat. But alas, my duty and your bridge club both call. Darling, would you do me a big favor? Hang on a moment. Robert, will you raise the glass, please. I wish to have a private conversation with my wife."

The uniformed driver nodded and pressed a button on the stretch limousine's dashboard. The glass partition separating them closed, making it virtually soundproof.

"Now, that's better. Where were we?"

"You were about to ask me for a favor."

"Would it be too much trouble to put me on hold and run to my office?"

"Of course not, darling. It makes me feel so important to do things for you. Hang on. It'll only take a second."

Carolyn Harrison turned and called over her shoulder, "Oh, girls. I'll be right back. Government business, you know." She pressed the hold button and hurried to Douglas' office. Once there, she picked up the extension phone. "Okay, dear. I'm here. Do you want me to connect you up to that machine you told me about?"

"Carolyn, do you remember how?"

"Oh, yes. I've gone over it in my mind many times. I place the telephone receiver in that special cradle you showed me and then all I do is I press the red button. Am I right?"

"That's right, dear. Go ahead and do it now and then you can get back to your bridge game. All right?"

"Okay, here I go." Carolyn carefully placed the receiver into the cradle of the transmitter/receiver. Not satisfied that it was in place correctly, she hesitated, checked once more, then firmly pressed the red button. Pleased with herself, she smiled, turned, and stepped briskly back to her bridge party.

* * *

Harrison heard the characteristic buzz of the encrypting device and pressed a similar button on his receiver. A red light told him that the encryption process was fully engaged. Anyone trying to eavesdrop now would be treated to a series of garbled fax-like sounds. And the telephone company records would reflect only a call to his residence in Springfield. Harrison then pressed a black button on the base of his portable phone. Although no one answered, he waited ten seconds and then said, "Code one one zero. I need to speak with the man."

"Yeah, one one zero here. I copy you. Hang on. I'll get the man."

Harrison grimaced. He detested dealing with lowlife. "Be quick about it. Time is of the essence."

"Yes, *sir*," he heard. Harrison shook his head at the arrogance of one one zero.

After a wait of over two minutes, the man finally arrived. Harrison knew the man was toying with him, showing him who was boss. "Well, if it ain't our esteemed governor. How's the old ticker doing these days?"

"I didn't call to discuss my health. This is quite serious."

"Oh? Just how *quite serious* is it? And by the way, governor, you need to lighten up. You'll live longer." He cackled.

"You told me nobody would be able to trace the ownership of Chicago Christian to me."

"Somebody did?"

"Not just somebody . . . the Cook County Chief Medical Examiner. Now listen and don't interrupt. So far he hasn't told anybody and I am meeting him at Barnfield's Restaurant on the corner of Ninety-fifth and Halsted in exactly twenty-five minutes. He and I will park directly in front of the restaurant. He'll be in a dark blue Mercedes. His name is Joseph Legato. I'm told he's tall, sixtyish, and skinny. I want you to hold two places open. If anyone is already parked there, tow them away. We—"

"Hang on governor." In the background, Harrison heard the man barking out orders. He could picture the scrambling. "Go ahead, governor. We got it under control."

"I'm not finished. This man knows too much. He must be eliminated. I'll keep him in the restaurant for about twenty minutes. This will give you ample time to do whatever you have to do. When he leaves, follow him. Wait until he gets to an area where there's no other traffic and take care of him. I don't want anyone else hurt. Do you understand?"

"Certainly, governor. What about your driver and security? Won't they be outside the restaurant?"

"Of course. Create a diversion or something. I don't care. You know more about that than I do. I shouldn't have to tell you everything."

"Right on, governor."

"And one other thing."

"Yes, governor?"

"Fix those records so nobody else can figure them out. That's an order. I don't want to deal with this again. Is that understood?"

"Yes, governor. I'm truly sorry, governor. It won't happen again, governor."

Harrison slammed the phone down, regretting the day he agreed to circumvent the organ donor red tape. What could he have been thinking? Arrogant bastards. After taking several deep breaths to compose himself, he smiled and then tapped on the glass.

* * *

Leonard Hardtack opened his eyes. Nothing. He blinked. Still nothing. He could tell that he was laying on his back on a hard surface but he couldn't remember how he got there. He shook his head. The darkness prevailed. With his mind reeling, he slowly turned himself over until he was on his hands and knees. Finally, he saw a slit of light over to his left. The bottom of a door? Where in the world was he? He felt around. Small room. Smelled clean like new laundry. Why did his head hurt so? He shook it. Not good. He pulled himself up to his knees and felt around. A doorknob? He turned it. The door opened. The light, although not bright, made him squint. Things were beginning to come back to him. The stairwell. That doctor. He stood up as fast as he dared and staggered into the empty hall. The last thing he remembered was trying to open the door from the stairwell. Everything else was a blank. The doctor, or whoever he was, must have knocked him out. Stupid. Stupid. Stupid. He never should have let his guard down. Now he'd probably lose his job. Better face the music. Feeling foolish, Leonard wandered into the hall and around to the nurses' station.

Nurse Barrett looked up from her papers. "What happened to you, Len? You been drinking on the job or something?" She laughed.

"Never mind that. Has anything happened lately? Have you seen anything strange?"

"Other than you staggering down the hall drunk, no." Nurse Barrett went back to her paperwork.

"What about that stranger? Did you see him?" Leonard peered at the overweight woman.

"Stranger? You must mean that new doctor. He's the only stranger I've seen lately. What about him?"

"Is he legit?"

"Of course he's legit. Dr. Nation sent him over to check on a new patient for him. Why are you asking all these questions, anyway? Go away. I've got work to do. Scram."

"Sure, sure. I'm going. You don't have to be so nasty." Rubbing his head, Leonard wandered back down the hall and into the stairwell where he inspected the lock and found nothing that would even remotely yield a clue about what had happened to him. Maybe if he kept his mouth shut, nothing would come of it. It was worth a shot. Why look for trouble?

* * *

Hawkins forced his ancient Oldsmobile into a broad slide as he turned left too fast onto Walnut Hill Lane and pressed the accelerator to the floorboard. A surprised pedestrian did a balancing act to keep from stepping off the curb in front of the speeding automobile.

"Sorry," Hawkins muttered. "Matter of life and death."

When he reached the Dallas Medical and Professional Offices building—which was two blocks past Dallas General— he aimed the swaying car in the general direction of the parking lot. He skidded the car into a parking place outside Mitch's office, ignored the glares of the two drivers he had cut off, and raced inside. Mitch was waiting for him in the reception area. The two doctors strode quickly to Mitch's inner office without speaking.

After he closed the door, Mitch motioned to a blue leather visitor chair and dropped himself into a matching one next to it. "Take a load off and tell me what's going on. What were you doing back at the Christian Clinic?"

Hawkins gave Mitch a "hold on a minute" signal with his hand and waited open-mouthed until his breath quit coming in short gasps. Mitch fidgeted impatiently.

"Man, I gotta start going to the gym with you and Stuart," Hawkins wheezed. "This rushing around is making me feel like old man."

"Yeah, right. You do that. Now tell me what's going on."

Hawkins nodded. "I don't know where to start. There's so much to tell. First, you call and fax me the information on Ann Vandergriff. Then I head out for the Christian Clinic to do some checking but before I get out the door, Legato calls with the bombshell that Chicago Christian is owned by the Mafia and that maybe even the Governor of Illinois is involved. He's checking further. So I call Stuart to tell him all this and he decides to take off to Chicago to find B.J."

Mitch whistled and shook his head. "How does he plan to find her?"

"He's taking his cell phone with him and having all of his calls forwarded to it. That way, when B.J. does finally get in touch with him, he'll be a lot closer to her."

"Good idea, except for the time he's on the plane. For the three hours he's in the air, he can't get any calls."

"True, but when I talked to him, he was already headed for DFW. He couldn't stand waiting around any longer and he was taking the first plane to Chicago that he could catch." Then, Hawkins told Mitch what had happened at the Christian Clinic. "And, for whatever it's worth, I may have bought us a couple of extra hours by sticking Vandergriff's tire."

Mitch stared at Hawkins while he talked. "Even so, it still means we have no more than a day and a half before they go after B.J. It could be even sooner."

"I hope I haven't thrown a monkey wrench in the works by talking to the Vandergriffs. Once she tells Nation about the Dr. Filbert that visited her this morning, no telling what he'll do."

"What can he do?" Mitch asked. "He might wonder what it was all about but I don't think it'll change anything. At least I don't think we can count on any delay in Mrs. Vandergriff's operation. No, as soon as Vandergriff comes up with the money, B.J.'s a goner unless we can think of something else. And quick."

"Damn," Hawkins howled as he pounded his forehead with the heel of his hand. "You're right. I should have thought of that. Let's go. We'll take your car. Mine's not fast enough." He stood up and started for the door, knocking his chair over backward.

"Thought of what? What am I right about? Where are we going?" Mitch demanded, trying his best to keep up with Hawkins.

"Come on, let's go. I'll explain on the way. Cancel anything you've got," Hawkins barked as he reached the front door.

Mitch followed Hawkins outside. He hollered over his shoulder, "Helen, I'll be on an emergency call. If anything comes up, please either handle it yourself or get Dr. Messinger to take it. Thanks." He turned back to Hawkins without waiting for a response from Helen. "I don't have to cancel anything. I kept the whole day open just in case. My car's over here. Now, where are we going? I need to know since I'm driving."

* * *

Lester Jackson watched as two paramedics carefully lifted the stretcher and its motionless contents into the ambulance. The crowd was beginning to disburse as a wrecker backed up to the badly damaged Lexus. Satisfied that he had done all he could, Jackson returned to his car. He had explained the entire incident to the police officer and was instrumental in helping him complete the accident report. As the star witness, he had cooperated to the fullest, of course. His civic duty. Smiling, he drove from the scene. Wait 'til I tell Dorothy about my day, he thought.

* * *

Legato circled the block until the exact time that he was supposed to meet with Douglas Harrison. Sure enough, when he pulled up to the restaurant, the Governor's limousine was in front with a parking space behind it being held for him by two security guards. One of the guards recognized the Mercedes and motioned for Legato to park. The privileges of rank, he thought. Legato guided the car into the ample space. He and Governor Harrison exited their cars at the same time. The Governor smiled broadly as he approached Legato.

"Dr. Legato?"

"Yes, sir. I'm Joseph Legato. It's a privilege to meet you, sir." The two men shook hands. Harrison gestured toward the restaurant. "Shall we? I'm famished. It's way past my usual lunchtime. You know how windy your mayor is. By the way, they call Chicago the windy city because of the politicians, not the weather." The Governor chuckled at the ancient joke. Legato smiled.

As they entered the restaurant, they were accompanied by a security guard. A table waited in the now-deserted back portion of the serving area where several patrons had been apologetically moved to accommodate the Governor. The guard crossed the room and sat at a corner table with his back to the wall, facing the Governor. Harrison motioned to the smarmy waiter for him to take their orders. That done, Harrison turned to Legato, his smile now gone.

"Okay, Dr. Legato, tell me. What information did you come across and have you talked with anyone about it since we spoke on the phone?"

"No, sir," Legato said truthfully. "Not a soul."

Harrison nodded. There was no discernible expression on his face. "I believe you. I think when you hear what I have to say, you'll understand why the secrecy. Now, tell me. What did you find out?"

"Sir, I was investigating some unexplained deaths in the Chicago area and the information I uncovered led me to an insurance company named Chicago Christian. They sell medical insurance. I suspect that they are somehow connected to the unexplained deaths. In checking the corporate records, I find that the majority of the company is owned by organized crime figures in Chicago."

"Go on. I sense there's more."

"Yes, sir, there is. I hate to have to ask you this, Governor, but do you own the company, Heart Organ Corporation?"

Harrison smiled briefly and looked at the tablecloth. He fingered his silverware. "Yes, I do. Odd name, isn't it. It was my wife's idea because of the heart problems I had for so long until I had my bypass. We set up the company to do fund-raising for heart research." He looked up. A serious scrutiny had replaced the smile. "What led you to Heart Organ?" Harrison knew everything. His face told the whole story.

"Governor, I have a feeling you know the connection. Heart Organ is an anagram for Earth Argon." Legato stared at Harrison. He can't look me in the eye, he thought. The Governor looked relieved when the waiter appeared at the table with their food. Legato nodded imperceptibly. It'll take a lot more than *this* little interruption for you to come up with a reasonable explanation, he thought. You should have thought of this a long time ago.

"Ah, yes. Here's our sandwiches," Harrison said. The waiter, chosen for his expertise and brevity, quickly arranged the food and drinks and then left. Harrison picked up his sandwich and took a bite.

Both men turned to look when a fight broke out right outside the restaurant. Within minutes, the security guards had broken up the fight and it was quiet again. When Harrison finally swallowed his mouthful, he turned and stared hard at Legato.

"Please understand that I did not know what Chicago Christian was in the beginning. They offered a fast solution to my health problems with no questions asked. Purchasing shares through a corporation seemed the easiest and best way to pay for it. They promised me no connection would ever be made. I honestly thought Chicago Christian was only established to move people up the list and to break through the bureaucratic morass that kept slowing things down. I had no idea that . . ."

Legato sighed. Did the Governor actually expect him to swallow this ridiculous palaver as the truth? It hardly seemed possible. "When did you find out?"

"Only last week. I swear I knew nothing before that. Maybe I was turning a blind eye. I don't know. I don't know anything anymore. I only know that if this ever gets out, I'm ruined. Please, I'm begging you. Give me twenty-four hours to come clean in my own way and maybe I can salvage some shred of a career. I hope I don't have to step down. I've worked too hard to get this far to . . ."

Legato stood, his food untouched. "Twenty-four hours, Governor. If you haven't made an official announcement by then, I'm afraid I'll have no choice. I hope you understand."

Harrison nodded. He remained seated. The man looked defeated. Legato almost felt sorry for him. Almost. Legato turned and walked hastily toward the door.

* * *

"We're going to downtown Dallas," Hawkins said. "So get over to Central Expressway. That would be the quickest way this time of day. And drive as fast as you dare. We're going to NationsBank to try and—"

"Intercept Vandergriff before he gets the money," Mitch interjected. "Yeah, I thought about that, too, but what are you going to tell him? Or are you planning to kidnap him?"

Hawkins chewed the inside of his cheek. "Haven't gotten that far with my thinking yet. You got any ideas?"

Mitch kept his eyes glued to the traffic as he sped south on Central Expressway toward downtown Dallas. "Vandergriff knows you as Dr. Something-or-other, right? Maybe you can catch him before he goes in the bank and tell him there's a problem with his wife and that he has to hurry back to the hospital."

Hawkins felt trapped, his mind spinning. Options came tumbling into his head. None, though, seemed to get around the probability of detaining Vandergriff against his will. What he was contemplating was a felony—a serious one. But if he didn't do something, chances were that B.J. would be dead within twenty-four hours. Was there such a thing as justifiable kidnapping?

"Then what?" Hawkins finally asked Mitch. "As soon as he got back to the hospital, Vandergriff would know something was funny. I guess we may have to detain him somehow, on some pretense. But where would we keep him? And how would we get him to stay? We may have to hold him forcibly. If we have to, we will. They won't operate until they get the money and as long as they don't operate, B.J. is safe."

Mitch nodded. "We don't have a choice, do we? We'll think of something. When we—"

"Uh oh," Hawkins interjected.

"What?"

"See that car being towed away?"

"Yeah."

"It's Vandergriff's. And he's not around."

"Is he in the wrecker?"

"Nope. That means I didn't slow him down as much as I thought I did. He must have gotten a taxi or something. Step on it. We can't let him get to the bank before we do."

"Gotcha," Mitch said, pushing the car past eighty.

The two friends rode in silence until Mitch exited onto Live Oak Street and careened toward downtown. "We're getting close, now," Mitch said. "Have you come up with anything yet?"

"Nothing legal," Hawkins shot back. "We'll have to play it by ear. See what happens."

Mitch skillfully maneuvered his Buick through the traffic until he pulled to the curb in front of NationsBank behind an unattended police car. "Damn," he muttered.

"What?" Hawkins said, looking around. "Where's the bank? Is this the right building?"

"Yes. This is NationsBank Plaza. But that's not what I mean. This is a no-parking zone and when the cop that belongs to that car gets back, he'll have me towed. All of downtown Dallas has been a no-tolerance zone ever since the riots that took place after the Dallas Cowboys' victory parade in ninety-three."

"You better wait in the car then. If you see a cop coming, just drive around the block until he's gone. But I still don't see a bank. Where do I go?" Hawkins pleaded, his frustration threatening to overcome his composure.

"Calm down. I know where it is. I used to come here all the time to make payments on my student loan. I know this place like I own it." He pointed to the building. "Go through those glass doors and take the escalator on the opposite side of the building. Don't take the one to your left. Go around the hanging metal sculpture and the escalator is past all of the elevator banks. It'll be to your right. You'll be able to see the bank directly in front of you. It's just past the Chinese restaurant."

"Thanks," Hawkins said as he opened the car door. "We either got here before him or we didn't. If he beat us, it was through no fault of yours. I never knew you could drive like that, good buddy."

"Neither did I," Mitch confessed, mopping his brow with the ever-present handkerchief. "Good luck."

Hawkins jumped out of the car, barely noting the red metal sculpture that looked as though it had fallen off the roof and implanted itself in the concrete outside the building. He cursed when he realized that he was trying to open the heavy, button-activated handicap entrance door. He pushed harder just as someone exiting the building hit the button. The force impelled him through the door and he almost collided with a knockout gorgeous woman with long dreadlocks. Another time, Hawkins thought absently. He glanced around, spotted the hanging welded objet d'art and quickly skirted the round opening through which the artistic freeform hung between the ground floor and the lower level. There was the escalator. He strode down it taking two steps at a time and raced forward. The bank of tellers was to his left. He stopped short and glanced toward the glass-enclosed garden. Any other time he would be tempted to explore the ponds and greenery that looked so out of place underground. He turned to his right and was rewarded by the sight of bank officials seated at widely spaced desks. At the farthest desk he spotted Dr. Vandergriff hunched over a batch of documents. He was flipping pages. A uniformed police officer stood a respectful distance away while two men in business suits pointed to various places on the documents. A third man, obviously also a bank official, held an oversized briefcase. Hawkins quickly retraced his steps and slipped back into the Buick.

"Didn't see him?"

"Unfortunately I *did* see him . . . in the bank surrounded by official looking people. It looked like they were in the process of signing a lot of papers. Damn. How did he get here so quick?"

Mitch shook his head. "The bank must have had everything ready for him."

"Yeah and he must have called for a cab when he had the flat on Central. I guess he didn't get to be worth hundreds of millions by being slow getting things done. Now we'll have to wait until he's finished. It's okay. I'll talk to him as soon as he comes out and we'll get him to let us take him back to Preston Tower."

"Well, where do we take him?"

"Don't know yet. I'll think of something. I expect it'll be a while before they're done signing papers. He told me the clinic is charging him two million dollars for the operation and even somebody as rich as Vandergriff doesn't keep that kind of change lying around."

Mitch let out a low whistle. "Two million bucks," he said.

Twenty minutes later, Hawkins elbowed Mitch. "Here he comes. Get ready. I still don't know what to do. I'm just going to wing it. Oh, no! I can't believe I didn't think of that. Damn. Take off." Hawkins slid low in his seat. "Go, go."

* * *

Across the one-way street and inside a black Lincoln Town Car, two men sat low in the front seat. One nudged the other. "Heads up. He's coming out." Both men watched as Legato exited the restaurant, nodded to the security guards, slipped into his Mercedes and roared off in a cloud of diesel smoke. "Look at that air pollution. Think we ought to do something about it?"

"What the hell are you talking about, Manny? Oh, yeah. That's funny. Let's do our civic duty and ice the bastard. Teach him a lesson. Go. Don't lose him."

"Have you ever known me to lose anybody?"

"No, and I don't want to see you start now."

"Well I ain't going to. So shut up about it, Willy."

The Town Car followed with two cars between it and the Mercedes until the traffic began to thin. After that, it dropped back to about three hundred yards.

Willie stared at the Mercedes, a smile of anticipation beginning to form at the corner of his twitching mouth. "Say when."

"Now."

"You got it."

Willie turned to glare at Manny. "I said do it now."

"I did. I pushed the button but nothing happened."

"We must be too far back. I'll pull a little closer."

"Don't get too close."

"Don't tell me my business."

* * *

Legato continued to analyze his strange conversation with the Governor. Did he do the right thing in allowing Harrison an additional twenty-four hours? For what? Was he stalling for some reason? The more he mulled it over, the more convinced he was that he had done the wrong thing. Twenty-four hours could further endanger Dr. Young's fiancée. Finally, he changed his mind. No matter that he had given his word to Governor Harrison, he had to turn the whole thing over to the FBI. And he had to do it now. Innocent lives were at stake. Legato swerved suddenly into the far right lane, narrowly missing a tanker truck. The driver let go a blast with his air horns to vent his displeasure. Legato barely noticed.

* * *

"Wait. Not now. He must have spotted us. He pulled over next to that gasoline truck. If you push the button now, the blast'll get us, too."

"Yeah, and half of Chicago. Back off a little and we'll see what happens. Look. He's getting off at this exit. Keep on his tail. All right. Looks like the truck is going straight. It won't be long, now."

* * *

I'll go down to the federal building, Legato thought. The FBI ought to be in there somewhere. It would be his last mortal thought. The blast blew out all four tires and shattered all of the glass, which only added to the violent eruption. It ripped through the car with lightening swiftness, vaporizing his blood and spreading it over a hundred-yard radius. The Mercedes was hurled tumbling and twisting some fifteen feet into the air. It skidded and slid to a fiery rest halfway down the exit ramp.

* * *

Mitch obediently started the car, dropped it into drive and pulled into the traffic. "What is it, Hawkins? What happened? Why did we leave?"

"I should have thought of that possibility. It never occurred to me that Vandergriff would have a police escort to

Preston Tower, but it makes sense, carrying two million in cash."

Mitch nodded. "I didn't think of it either but it makes perfect sense. *I'd* want an escort for sure carrying around that much money. What do we do now?"

Hawkins rubbed his face with both hands. "My friend, I honestly don't know. I'm stumped. Let's go back to your office. Maybe we'll think of something. Better yet, let's go to Stuart's office. I need to look at B.J.'s chart to see her vitals. I looked at Mrs. Vandergriff's and I want to see if they match."

"You think there's a chance in hell that they won't?" Mitch asked.

"Not likely. But it's worth a shot. You got any better ideas?"

Mitch steered the Buick onto the Central Expressway on-ramp. "Nope," he said, "but if Debbie *is* involved, do you think it might tip her off?"

Hawkins grimaced. "It might, but I think we have to chance it. I'll tell Debbie that Stuart asked me to look at her chart for something or other. I'll come up with a good reason."

Chapter 14

"Thank God you haven't left," Hawkins thundered.

"Well, look who's here," Debbie said with undisguised sarcasm. She eyed Hawkins and Mitch as they entered Stuart's office. "And why wouldn't I still be here?"

"Because it's well after five o'clock. I expected you to be gone already."

"The office may close at five but I never leave before six. Now maybe you two can answer some questions. I'd like to know what's going on around here. How about it?"

Hawkins tried his best to look clueless. "How about what?" he asked.

Debbie's hands flew immediately to her hips. She said, "Don't give me that wide-eyed innocent crap, Hawkins. First, you call me and tell me that Dr. Young will probably be late but not to call and wake him up. So I don't and he misses all his morning appointments. And when he does call, he sounds all hung-over and then he gets mad at me for *not* waking him up. Next, you call back looking for him and you hang up on me after I tell you he's on his way. Then, he calls me from his car phone and tells me to cancel everything he has for the day and then *he* hangs up on me. And if that wasn't enough, his travel agent calls and says that she was talking to him when he hung up on *her*. Something about catching a plane to Chicago this morning. To Chicago. Why Chicago? I'm beginning to get a complex and you say, 'How about what?' Give me a break. Don't you think you owe me even a teensy bit of an explanation? I am trying to do my job, you know."

Hawkins looked at Mitch, who shook his head and frowned as if to say, "Uh, uh. Don't look at me. You do it."

"Well," Hawkins started, "Mitch did say he wanted me to come over here and look through B.J.'s folder to see if I might spot something. I think he's worried about her health. That can make a guy crazy, sometimes, you know."

"Yeah, but can it make everybody else around him crazy, too? All right. If you can't or won't tell me what's going on, hang on and I'll get you B.J.'s file. Anything to help shed some light. Hers is not with the rest of the files. It's in Dr. Young's office on his desk. I'll be right back." She turned and disappeared down the hall.

"What do you make of Stuart hanging up on his travel agent?" Mitch whispered when Debbie was out of earshot.

"Maybe he drove into one of those covered parking areas at DFW and lost his signal," Hawkins said, shrugging. "Who knows?"

Mitch cocked his head and frowned in concentration. "Yeah, I guess that makes sense," he said. "Shhh, here she comes."

* * *

The door closed behind the stocky, well-dressed man. He turned and smiled broadly. "I understand you have the, uh, fee, Mr. Vandergriff," he said.

John Vandergriff's hands shook as he handed over the briefcase. "Yes, I do, Mr. Goletti. It's all there. I'm sorry it took so long. I had a flat. I haven't had a flat in thirty years. Ever since I switched to those—"

"The money, Mr. Vandergriff."

"Yes, the money. They counted it twice at the bank and let me tell you they had lots of questions about it. They even—"

"What did you tell them?" Goletti snapped.

"I did what you told me to do. I told them it's personal and that I'd rather not discuss it."

Goletti seemed pleased. "You did just fine. Now, just in case the bank made an error, I'll have our, uh, accounting office look at it." He disappeared into the inner office, returning ten minutes later. "It's all there, Mr. Vandergriff. We can start cutting through the red tape. It won't be long, now. By the way, we understand that a doctor visited you this afternoon before you left. What was his name again?"

* * *

Debbie returned from Stuart's office carrying B.J.'s folder. She slapped it into Hawkins' outstretched hand with a glare. "You gentlemen do understand that, by reading B.J.'s file, you are violating the doctor-patient privilege? That record is confidential."

"Debbie, this could possibly be a medical emergency. Stuart has asked me to consult with him on B.J.'s medical care. I'll get a signed consult form for the file as soon as Stuart gets back from Chicago," Hawkins said. He opened the folder.

"You guys are acting strange," she muttered and then went back to her desk and started rifling through paperwork. "What kind of medical emergency anyway? You're not going to tell me what's going on, are you?"

"If we knew, we would," Hawkins said as he studied the papers. He found the page he was searching for and gave Mitch a nod. B.J. and Mrs. Vandergriff were perfectly compatible. No real surprise there. But what now? Where did they go from here? Hawkins was about to suggest to Mitch that they head out when the phone rang. Something made Hawkins wait.

Debbie answered with her usual cheerfulness. Then her face went chalk white. "Oh, my God," she said in a whisper. "What's the prognosis? I see. Thank you for calling."

Hawkins looked up from his folder. "What is it, Debbie? What's wrong?"

Debbie slowly replaced the receiver in its cradle. She turned to Hawkins and Mitch. "That was Dallas General."

"And?" Hawkins said impatiently.

"Dr. Young is not in Chicago, after all. He's still here in Dallas."

"Go on."

"He was admitted to ICU after his car smashed into a concrete abutment on 635."

* * *

The darkness subsided at a snail-like pace at first, like a faint ray of light penetrating a black cave. His head throbbed unmercifully. The nightmare's finally ending, he thought. Boy, was it a doozie. They weren't usually so tenacious, though. He shook his head and immediately regretted it. What was wrong? Still couldn't see. Had to be patient. It would go away in time. Crazy dream. What was it? There was an ambulance. A gun. B.J. Chicago. Stuart sat bolt upright, not wincing at or even caring about the searing pain. His focus was returning but it seemed interminable. He blinked again and again, trying to squeeze away the blur. After what seemed like an eon, the smoky forms began to take shape. He was in a room. A hotel room? What hotel? Where? No, not a hotel room. Definitely a hospital room. The decor looked familiar. My God, I'm in the Dallas General ICU, he thought. How many times had he been there? Dozens, maybe even hundreds--but never from this side of the bed.

Stuart swung his legs over the side of the bed and looked around as his senses returned. Nothing seemed broken. Everything appeared to be in working order. His inventory complete, Stuart hastily started unhooking himself from his electronic prison.

"Dr. Young. What in the world are you doing? You lay right back down." The nurse had just entered the room carrying a tray of dressings and antiseptics. She dropped her tray on the serving table and eased Stuart back onto the bed. "You gave us a scare," she said.

The nurse was now in full focus although his head still throbbed. "Doris, what happened to me? How did I get here? How bad is it?"

"Well, now that you are awake, I think you'll probably live. With a coma you never know. According to your chart, you had a nasty car wreck."

Stuart looked for his watch. It wasn't on his arm. "A coma? How long was I out?" he asked. "What time is it? What day is it? I have to get to Chicago."

The slender, attractive nurse smiled. "Relax, Dr. Young. Chicago can wait. You won't be going anywhere for a while at least. Judging from the paramedic's report and by how long you've been here, you were out for about four hours, but Dr. Jamison will be back in a few minutes and he'll give you a complete report. He went down the hall to answer a page. It's almost six o'clock, by the way."

Hawkins stared at Debbie. "Stuart's in ICU? Good God. How is he?"

"He's stable but unconscious. I can't believe it. Nobody drives slower than Stuart. How could something like that have happened?"

Hawkins looked at Mitch. Nothing surprised him anymore. Not after all they had found out. "Let's go, buddy. We have to get to Stuart."

"I'm right behind you," Mitch said, leaping to his feet.

The phone rang. Again Hawkins paused. "Not yet," he whispered and motioned for Mitch to wait until they found out who was calling.

Hands shaking, Debbie answered the phone. "B.J.," she said.

Hawkins crossed the room in two strides and jerked the receiver from Debbie's hand. "Give me that," he demanded.

Startled, Debbie stepped back in shock.

"B.J., whatever you do, don't hang up. This is Hawkins. Where are you?"

"Hawkins? What's wrong? Debbie sounded strange. So do you."

"Don't say a word. Just listen to me. And whatever you do, look and act normal. You're being watched at this moment. I want you to smile. Are you smiling?" Hawkins demanded.

"Hawkins, you're scaring me. What's wrong?"

"I'm not kidding. Smile, damn it. Now I'll ask you again. Are you smiling?"

"Yes."

"Good. Now continue to smile occasionally and look normal. They must not suspect that you know anything. Okay?"

"I *don't* know anything. And who is *they*? Who is watching us? Is it someone in that ambulance? We've seen an ambulance that seems to be following us. It's beginning to get spooky."

"Are you smiling?"

"Yes."

"Good. Now listen carefully and try to concentrate on what I'm saying. The ambulance is definitely following you. Your insurance company, Chicago Christian, is in reality a front for an illegal human body parts ring operated by the Mafia."

"My God."

"Smile. During your physical, you were implanted with a microchip capable of not only tracking you with a radio signal but killing you with one as well. Keep smiling. They're following you in that ambulance so they can whisk you off to one of their clinics in Chicago to remove your heart and fly it back to Dallas to be transplanted in a patient who is waiting here for it." Hawkins could hear the gasp clearly. He winced at having to put it to B.J. so bluntly.

"Now wait a minute, Hawkins. If you are talking about what I think you're talking about, I know all about that program and it damn sure isn't used like that. What in the world makes you think—"

"Never mind *how* I know. I just know. Right now we have to get you to a place where we can remove the microchip. Don't forget to smile. Do you have a pen and paper?"

"Uh, yes. In my purse. I have it with me. But why don't I just try to escape to someplace shielded where the signal won't reach me? Like a metal building."

"Too risky. If you start running now, they'll know you know. They can zap you anytime they think something's gone wrong. Long before you can make it to safety. Do you have it yet?"

"What?"

"The pen and paper."

"Oh . . . yes, I have it. Go ahead. I'm ready."

"Are you smiling?"

"Yes, and I'm also shaking."

"That's okay. But try not to let it show. Now, exactly where are you right now?"

"Springfield."

"Missouri?"

"No, Illinois."

"How far is that from Chicago?"

"Uh, I think it's about two hundred miles south of Chicago. I'm not sure."

Hawkins glanced at his watch. "It's all right. That'll work. Here's what I want you to do. Keep going north toward the intersection of I-57 and I-80 in Chicago. You got that? Pace yourself to be there at about eleven or eleven-thirty tonight. At that intersection, there is an all-night eatery called the Windy City Restaurant. It's an upscale hamburger place. I-57 and I-80. Write that down. Are you smiling? Have a late dinner there and linger over it. What time do you have by your watch?"

"It's almost six o'clock. Five fifty-eight. Why?"

"Hang on a second." Hawkins slipped the digital watch off his wrist and pressed the buttons until it registered exactly six o'clock and holding. He looked up to see a stunned Debbie and a ghost-white Mitch hanging onto his every word. He sighed. Nothing he could do about it now. If Debbie was involved, he had blown it. Hawkins shot a glance to Mitch and let it slide off to Debbie, hoping that Mitch would understand to watch Debbie closely. He was rewarded with an almost imperceptible nod. Hawkins turned back to the phone. "Does your watch have a second hand?"

"Yes."

"Good. Now I want you to say 'go' the instant your watch reads exactly six o'clock. Understand?"

"Of course I understand. Don't patronize me. It will be six in about, uh, fifteen seconds."

"I'm sorry, B.J. I didn't mean to patronize you. Are you smiling?"

"Yes, I'm smiling." Hawkins could feel the irritation in B.J.'s voice. There was a short silence before B.J. continued. "Get ready. Get set. Go."

Hawkins depressed one of the buttons on his watch. "Okay, we're synchronized. Here's what I want you to do. At precisely midnight, get up from your table and go alone to the women's rest room. I will be there and I'll remove that microchip. It will be in your scalp, somewhere near your hairline."

"Damn."

"What?"

"That's what that was. Hawkins, now it's my turn to apologize. It's all falling, or I should say, crashing into place now. I had a sore spot just above my hairline that was tender for a few days after my insurance exam that I thought was a mosquito bite or something. I don't feel it now."

"I'm sure that's it."

"Hawkins, just how widespread is this network?"

"We're not sure. We think it's at least in Los Angeles and Chicago as well as Dallas. We uncovered it at our national Medical Examiners conference in Chicago last week."

"That's right. I remember Stuart telling me you were going there."

"We have the ME's in those two cities helping us, a Dr. Legato in Chicago and Dr. Ito in Los Angeles."

"Ito. As in Judge Ito of the O.J. trial?"

"Exactly. Don't know if they're kin or not."

"Is Chicago the headquarters for Chicago Christian Insurance? I remember wondering that when I was filling out the application."

"Yes it is. You wouldn't believe who all is involved. But I'll tell you about it tonight."

"Hawkins, is it wise for me to go on into Chicago if the headquarters for the operation is there?"

"It's probably as safe a place as any. We have to meet somewhere and since you're already close to Chicago and I can get a direct flight to O'Hare, let's go ahead and meet at the all-night hamburger place. Now, one other thing."

"What?"

"You can't tell your friend."

"Cathy? Why not?"

"Because you both have to act natural. And the best way for her to do that is for her to know nothing."

"I'm not so sure."

"Why?"

"She'll suspect. She knows me too well. There's no way I can fool her."

"Listen to me. You have to fool her. I didn't want to tell you this but those thugs in that ambulance are cold-blooded killers. If they know you're on to them, they wouldn't hesitate to zap you on the spot. And then what do you think they would do to Cathy?"

"I . . . I see what you mean."

"Good. Now, if she suspects something's wrong, tell her you're getting a headache or something. Tell her you had another fight with Stuart on the phone. Tell her anything that would explain your sudden mood swing, okay? Promise me. Your life and Cathy's life depends on it."

"Well, since you put it that way—"

"Good. I've got to go now. I have a plane to catch. Smile."

"Wait. I want to talk to Stuart."

"Sorry. Stuart's at the hospital right now. I told him I'd talk to you if you called. He's been frantic to make sure you were safe. I'll give him your love. See you at midnight. And let this be your last call. We don't want them to get suspicious. But don't worry. Everything is going to be okay. We'll take care of it. Just be there."

"Will Stuart be coming with you?"

Ouch. Hawkins was afraid she would ask that one. No way could he tell her the truth. "No, B.J., he can't. He has to take care of things from this end, things that only he can take care of."

"Hawkins?"

"Yes?"

"Are you telling me everything?"

"Scout's honor. Listen, gotta go if I'm going to make that plane."

"Hawkins?"

"Yes?"

"Thanks."

"Of course. Now—"

"One more thing, Hawkins. How in the world did you come up with all this information? You're a medical examiner, for God's sake."

"It's a long story and I promise to tell you everything tonight but believe it or not, it all started with an autopsy."

"Amazing."

"Quite. Now don't forget to act normal or—"

"Yeah, I know. Zap. I'm dead. And Hawkins?"

"Yes?"

"I'm smiling. Are you? Bye."

Exhausted and feeling as though all the strength had been drained from his body, Hawkins looked up and saw tears filling Debbie's eyes. Forcing as much smile as he could muster, he placed the receiver into her trembling hands.

After several fumbling attempts, Debbie returned the phone to its cradle. "Hawkins, I'm so sorry I gave you such a hard time. Poor Stuart. I had no idea," she said. "How did you—"

"I believe you, Debbie, but I'll have to fill you in later. First we have to book me on the next flight to Chicago and then we'll check on Stuart. If those bastards have—"

The phone interrupted Hawkins. All three sat mesmerized until Debbie reached for it. "I'm almost afraid to answer it," she said. "Hello, Dr. Young's office. Stuart! Is it really you? How are—? Yes, I know exactly where he is. You couldn't get ahold of him because he's right here in front of me. Hang on. Here he is." She thrust the phone back to Hawkins.

"Stuart, what happened? I was on my way to see you. The hospital called. They told us you were unconscious."

"I was until a few minutes ago. I was on my way to DFW when someone in an ambulance—I couldn't tell who it was—opened fire on me. The bullet smashed my windshield and I couldn't see a thing. That's all I remember until I woke up about fifteen minutes ago. Dr. Jamison checked me over and said that, aside from a concussion, I seem to be okay. Quite a few cuts and bruises, but that's all. I've—"

"'Scuse me for cutting you off, old buddy, but you need to know this. I talked to B.J. not three minutes ago."

"Thank God. Is she okay? What did she say? What did you tell her?"

"First, she's fine. Now, here's the plan. B.J. and her friend are getting close to Chicago. They suspect that an ambulance is following them. She's sure of it after talking to me."

"Oh God. They're capable of anything."

"It's okay. I told her to go on as if nothing had happened. In fact, B.J. is not even going to tell her girlfriend, what's-her-name."

"Cathy."

"Right . . . Cathy. She's not going to tell Cathy anything about it. I'm flying to Chicago as soon as I can get out of here. There's this restaurant up in Chicago that I know about. It's an all-night hamburger place. I've told B.J. where it is and we're going to meet there at exactly midnight so I can take out that damned microchip. We synchronized our watches. It'll work." It has to, Hawkins thought.

There was a pause before Stuart answered. "Hawkins, come get me. Now. I can be out of here in no time. Dr.

Jamison wants to take some precautionary X-rays before he'll release me. But never mind that. I'll just leave. I'm okay."

"Hang on a minute, Stuart. Debbie, get on the other line and book two seats to Chicago on the next available flight. Stuart is going with me." He watched Debbie hurry toward the other office. "Okay, I'm back."

"Don't come to ICU. Wait for me out front. I'll be right down."

"Are you sure you're up to—"

"Yes, I'm sure. I've never been so sure of anything in my life. Do you honestly think I could stay here and do nothing? I'd go crazy. Now that I know B.J. is still alive and that we have a plan, I'll be all right. Really, I'll be fine. I won't slow you down."

Hawkins suddenly jerked and dropped the phone. "What the hell?"

Mitch was obviously startled. "What is it? What happened? What's wrong?"

Hawkins grinned sheepishly. "Nothing. It's just my beeper. It's set to vibrate when I get a call. It'll be my answering service."

"Good. I thought you were having a heart attack."

"So did I for a second."

"Welcome to the wonderful world of technology. The medical term for what you suffered is beepilepsy. By the way, when did you get a beeper?"

"Yesterday. I was missing too many calls." Hawkins called his answering service. "Thanks," he said after writing down the message. He hit the switch hook and dialed. "Dr. Ito. Hawkins."

"Hello, Dr. Hawkins. I believe you will be most interested in the results of my labors."

"Dr. Ito, I apologize ahead of time for asking you to make this quick but I am heading out the door right now. Stuart and I have to make the next plane to Chicago."

"Ah so, Dr. Hawkins. I will make my report brief. We have come to the same conclusions as our esteemed Dallas colleagues. Our records also appear to have been falsified. We cannot correlate even one. We do have a branch of the Christian Clinic here in Los Angeles although we have not yet investigated it. That is everything in—I believe you call it—a nutshell. I trust everything at your end is all right?"

"Not really, I'm afraid. And again I must apologize for making this brief. Someone tried to kill Dr. Young this afternoon. He's okay. Only a concussion. But we now have a plan to rescue Dr. Young's fiancée. I talked to her only moments ago. She is definitely carrying a microchip under her scalp. That we know for a fact. We also know that an ambulance is following her. They are stalking her every step of the way and monitoring her every move. We have to be careful so as not to arouse their suspicions. We believe they would kill her on the spot if they thought we were on to them."

"My, my. That is certainly a most dangerous situation. You must be very careful. What is your plan if I may inquire?"

"This is the tricky part. I plan to meet her in the ladies' rest room at a Chicago restaurant at exactly midnight to remove the microchip."

"That is certainly an ambitious strategy. Can you get there by midnight?"

"We have to. Dr. Young's secretary is making the flight arrangements as we speak. You may have heard Dr. Legato mention the restaurant where we will be meeting B.J. The Windy City Restaurant?"

"Ah, yes. The Windy City Restaurant. This must be where the Italian restaurant used to be. Her name is B.J.?"

"She goes by her initials. I have to run now, Dr. Ito."

"Yes, of course and God speed, Dr. Hawkins."

"Thanks, Dr. Ito. Bye." Hawkins' gaze jumped from the wall to Debbie when she came bursting through the door.

* * *

B.J. waited at the pay phone until she was able to regain some semblance of composure. She tentatively felt for the bump at her hairline but jerked her hand back down when she realized what she had done. They're watching, she thought. There had been no soreness recently. All that remained was a small raised area. They had done a good job. The finest surgeons money could buy, she thought and managed a hollow laugh. Good girl, you're getting your sense of humor back. Mustn't look rattled. Must look as normal as possible. B.J.

took a deep breath, stood up tall, and walked back to the car. Cathy had returned from the food mart with a bagful of munchies and had managed to get a good start with them. She looked up when B.J. opened the car door and opened her mouth to say something. Her smile vanished.

"What's wrong? You're as pale as a ghost. I mean it. Did someone die? I'd say it was your best friend but I'm still alive."

That's it, B.J. thought. The idea calmed her and for the first time since she heard what Hawkins had to tell her, she allowed a tear to escape.

Cathy took B.J.'s trembling hand. "I knew it. You got some bad news. What happened, honey? Share it with me, please."

B.J. forced a smile. "Fred got loose when Stuart went over to the apartment to feed the animals. He ran out into the street and someone ran over him and kept on going. They didn't even stop." She needed to cry. She wanted to cry. Couldn't allow herself that luxury.

"B.J., I'm so sorry. I know I joke a lot about your menagerie but I also know how much you love those animals. Do you want to turn around and go back home?"

B.J. managed a weak smile and said, "Oh, no. Stuart has already taken care of Fred for me."

"Stuart must feel terrible about what happened. He probably thinks he was responsible."

"Actually I didn't talk directly to Stuart. I guess he was over at the hospital with a patient. I talked with a friend of Stuart's, a Dr. Hawkins. He told me about it."

"Well, my friend, let's do something exciting, something to help you feel better. Whatcha say? What would take your mind off your troubles?"

"Let's keep on driving north. Dr. Hawkins told me about this all night hamburger place in Chicago where they have these incredible midnight specials every night. He was up here a few days ago and he made me promise to check it out tonight. I guess he thought it would take my mind off Fred. I promised I would, so let's head out."

Cathy started the car. "Well, if that's what you want to do, Chicago here we come."

B.J. felt relieved. It had gone better than she could have hoped. Cathy hadn't suspected a thing. She reached into her purse for an Excedrin. The whole episode had given her a splitting headache. She slipped the small, white tablet under her tongue and smiled faintly. Stuart could never understand how she could do that. It always gagged him. Why did everything make her think of Stuart? She ached for him now. Something made her look out her side window as Cathy turned left and merged with the northbound traffic. Her sigh turned to a gasp. Parked across the street at a supermarket was an ambulance with a Texas license plate. She watched as it pulled into traffic three cars behind them.

Chapter 15

Debbie looked at Hawkins as she hung up the phone. "You and Stuart are booked on American flight 2340 to Chicago. It boards at seven forty, leaves at eight o'clock and arrives at ten fourteen. As of now, the flight is on schedule so give yourselves plenty of time. You know how busy DFW can be."

"Thank you, Debbie. That ought to give us plenty of time to arrive at the restaurant by midnight. I'm out of here." Hawkins turned to Mitch. "Wish us luck. Please stay available, my friend. We may need you." He stepped over and gave Mitch a bear hug.

"Wait a minute, Hawkins," Debbie said. "Let me get Stuart's medical bag for you. I think you'll need it. And by the way, I'm staying right here. All night if necessary. You may need me for something. I won't forward the calls to the answering service. I'll be available myself. And please call me no matter what. I have to know."

Hawkins glanced at Mitch. "Sure, Debbie. I'll give you a call." He watched as Debbie disappeared into Stuart's office. "Mitch, you'd better stay with her. Watch her closely. Try to listen to every phone call she makes. Figure out who she's talking to if you can. Here she comes."

"Hawkins, why don't I stay here with Debbie? That way, if you need either one of us, we'll be here. Debbie, don't you have the refrigerator stocked?" Debbie nodded. "Good. Then we don't even have to leave."

Hawkins hesitated and then walked to the door. "I hope I'm doing the right thing taking Stuart with me."

"Dr. Hawkins, don't forget this," Debbie said, handing him Stuart's black bag.

"I must be rattled to forget the most important thing, even after you reminded me. Nothing like trying to perform a delicate operation with a pocketknife. Thanks." He took the small bag.

"Sure. Now, get out of here, and Hawkins?"

"Yes?"

"Good luck."

"Thanks. We'll need it." Giving Mitch a thumbs-up and a knowing nod, Hawkins turned and strode purposefully to his car. He hoped he had appeared more confident than he felt. Alone in his car, Hawkins mouthed a prayer of supplication.

* * *

"Just what do you think you're doing?" the portly doctor asked.

"Well, Doc, I'm leaving. I have a plane to catch. I know you're not going to agree with this but you can't talk me out of it." Stuart was dressed and ready to leave.

"You're in no shape to fly anywhere. You had a concussion and you know as well as I do that you could have some internal hemorrhaging. We aren't done with the tests yet." The doctor looked over the top of his reading glasses. Only fifty-eight, he was entirely too young to wear bifocals— or so he thought. They made him look way beyond his years so he opted instead for constantly switching between two pairs, one for reading and one for distance.

"It wouldn't matter. There's no prognosis that would keep me from going to Chicago." For the first time since Stuart found out about the chip, he was optimistic about being able to save B.J. At least they had a plan. As long as they could get to the restaurant by midnight, there was a chance. It was infinitely more hope than he had when he woke up this morning.

"You have one hellova hard head, my friend, both literally and figuratively. When will you be back? We need to complete the MRI and the CAT scan as soon as possible. Other than your concussion, some external bruises and lacerations, you seem all right. Your X-rays didn't show anything. But I do have one other piece of advice."

"Oh?"

"Give up those cigarettes. They'll kill you."

"I plan to."

"When?"

"Midnight tonight."

"Strange notion but I approve. Now, get out of here if you must. But you're leaving against my better judgment and that's going on the record."

Stuart glanced at his watch. Hawkins would be outside in five minutes. "Thanks, Doc," he blurted out and bolted for the door.

Dr. Jamison shook his head and stared at the empty doorway. "Why is everyone in such a hurry these days?" he said to Doris.

Doris shrugged. "He has to get to Chicago."

"What could possibly be so important in Chicago that it couldn't wait until tomorrow or the next day?"

"Nothing that I know of, although he acted like it was some kind of an emergency."

"I don't know about this new crop of young doctors. Everything is an emergency. They should slow down."

"You're right about that."

* * *

"It looks like it's going to be a long night. I'll put on a pot of coffee. Make yourself at home in the reception area. It's the only place I know where we can be comfortable and still hear the phone. Tell me what you think about it. I decorated it myself."

Sure, Mitch thought. Get off by yourself and lace my coffee with barbiturates and put me to sleep? I may be dumb but I'm not stupid. Fat chance I'll let you alert your Mafia buddies. We'll do it my way. He said, "Why don't I give you a hand, Debbie? I can be pretty useful in the kitchen."

"That's what Stuart tells me. He says you're quite a gourmet cook. Problem is, the fridge is only stocked with Healthy Choice, bologna and Velveeta. I don't think even someone as talented as you could whip up a creation with those ingredients," Debbie said, turning and flashing her dimples at

Mitch. "I could go to Kroger's and pick up some stuff if you'd like."

"No," Mitch said abruptly before consciously softening his tone. "I can create a masterpiece out of nothing but bologna and some spices. I'm sure you have everything that we would need. No sense going out. I might need you here." As if I'd let you get by with that little ruse, you cute little traitor, Mitch thought. You're staying right here with me. And if you think your dimples will help you out with me, you're wrong, missy. You may be beautiful but you're dangerous.

* * *

Stuart took another long drag on his cigarette as he paced and peered up the street. Where was Hawkins? He glanced at his watch. Plenty of time yet, he told himself. There was no hurry. The calmer he stayed, the better he'd think. Still, it wouldn't hurt to get on out to DFW early. Finally, he recognized the Oldsmobile. How long was Hawkins going to keep that old thing? Surely he could afford something better by now. Hawkins pulled to a stop. Stuart opened the door and piled into the front seat.

"This rattletrap can't possibly help you pick up women," Stuart said, slamming the door for the third time and finally getting it to hold. "You must have incredible charm. Oh, well, any port in a storm, I suppose. I'd suggest taking my car to the airport but it's in the shop for a minor tune-up."

Hawkins grinned and shook his friend's hand. "You don't look too bad for somebody who nearly got himself killed this morning. How do you feel?"

"Other than the feeling of having been run over by a cement truck, I'm fine. Nothing was broken but I was woozy for a few hours." Stuart looked over his shoulder as Hawkins pulled out from the curb. "I'll tell you what, though. I'll never feel the same about ambulances again. That was some scary feeling to see that thing pull up beside me and then have a gun pointed at my head. I find myself looking around for them right now."

Hawkins nodded. "It wouldn't hurt to keep our eyes peeled all the way to DFW. If they know they didn't kill you, they're liable to come gunning for you again. Matter of fact, after what I did today, it wouldn't surprise me to see them come after me, too. I didn't tell you about that, did I?"

Hawkins told Stuart about his latest trip to the clinic. "And don't you know they're wondering who the hell Dr. Filbert is and what he was doing there? It wouldn't be so bad except for that guard I had to knock out. I wonder if they've figured out who I am yet."

"They can't have much to go on. I think it'll take them a while to figure it out. But by now they probably know about my surviving the accident so you can bet I'm going to be watching for them." Stuart again turned to look back. "So far so good," he said. "I don't see anything suspicious but be ready. If I tell you to exit, don't ask why. Just do it."

"Give me as much warning as you can. This baby doesn't corner as well as she used to. Guess some new shocks wouldn't hurt."

Stuart was silent for a time. "How did B.J. sound?" he asked. "And what exactly did you tell her?"

Hawkins related his conversation with B.J. in as much detail as he could remember. "She's not expecting you to show up. I hope she doesn't give anything away when she sees you. I hadn't thought of that. Maybe it would be better for me to go in the restaurant first and find out if I can slip you in without her seeing you."

"Even if you can't, I'm sure she knows how important it is to not attract any attention." Stuart looked behind again but saw nothing suspicious. "We're getting close to the airport entrance" he said.

* * *

Nation entered the room with a practiced flair. "And how are you today, Mrs. Vandergriff? I'm sorry I'm late. I had a very important press conference. You know how those reporters can be."

"Oh, yes, Dr. Nation. We've seen you many times on the television. It makes us proud that you are my doctor. Why, I was just telling John that I thank my lucky stars that Dr. Mitchell turned me over to your care."

Nation beamed at the compliment. "Why thank you, Mrs. Vandergriff. How nice of you to say so. I'm sure everything will work out nicely. And how are you today, Mr. Vandergriff?"

John Vandergriff rose to his feet and extended his hand. Nation nodded and accepted the gesture. "Just fine, Dr. Nation. I got the money, sir. Your accountant has approved the transaction. I had a bit of trouble, I don't mind telling you."

"Oh, I hadn't heard. What kind of trouble? With the bank?"

"Goodness gracious, no. Nothing like that. No, I had a flat tire on the way to the bank. I am definitely switching back to those tires that—"

"I see. Well, I'm glad everything worked out for you. We wouldn't have wanted any delays, now would we? And, yes, I did check with my accountant about the fee. I'm happy to report that everything is complete on that end. Now, getting down to the business at hand, I've gone over all of Mrs. Vandergriff's test results and everything looks perfect." Nation turned to Ann Vandergriff. "Physically and medically speaking, you are ready. We can schedule the procedure for as early as tomorrow morning. How does that sound to you?"

"It can't be too soon for us, Dr. Nation. I'm ready to get it behind me so we can get on with our lives. This thing has been dragging me down long enough."

"That's a wonderful attitude, Mrs. Vandergriff. I wish all my patients had your outlook. With our system connections always at the ready, we should have your new heart here at the clinic by no later than six o'clock in the morning. We'll begin then. I'll be back tonight to check on you one more time before the procedure. We can't be too careful, you know. By the way, I trust the staff are treating you well. We hire only the best, you know."

Mrs. Vandergriff laughed. "You doctors must all think alike."

Nation cocked his head. "How so, Mrs. Vandergriff?"

"That's the same thing Dr. Filbert said when he came in earlier today."

* * *

"Who would have thought that my decorative spice rack would have come in so handy? These sandwiches are delicious. I thought you were kidding when you said you could make a great meal out of bologna and spices," Debbie said. She leaned forward and helped herself to another finger sandwich off of the paper plate. "It wouldn't do for me to eat your creations on a regular basis. I'd be the size of a blimp."

"Not to be a braggart but I'll have to agree with you. I really am somewhat of a genius . . . at least with food," Mitch said. "But you're a genius with coffee, I can tell. You'll have to let me in on your secrets. Nothing complements a good meal like good coffee." He took another sip and glanced around the reception area. The large room contained the couch where Debbie sat, his chair, several other scattered easy chairs and a coffee table. An oversized antique armoire stood majestically against the wall next to the main entrance. It must have been originally built for a church because there were two crosses engraved in the rich, dark wood. The focal point of the piece was a mirror, slightly darkened with age and framed with brass coat hooks. He could picture an usher helping his grandmother with her coat before she entered the chapel. She would have peered into the mirror to make certain her hat was straight.

Mitch wondered if the paintings on the walls were copies. If so, they were the best he had ever seen. The comfortable overstuffed leather chair reminded him of the one in a hotel room in New Orleans. That thing had caused him to miss half of the meetings at the medical convention. Add a view of Bourbon Street and Mitch could easily be there. The chair, the antique and the paintings must have cost a small fortune. Even for those few items. "Debbie, I've never paid attention to them before, but some of these pieces are exquisite. Who is your decorator?"

Debbie laughed. "You're looking at her and I thank you for the compliment. I did my best with the money Dr. Young allowed me when we first opened the clinic. I'll have to confess, though, that the antique vestibule piece, the coffee table and the paintings are mine. Also that chair you're enjoying. I bought them last week and had them delivered here. The room definitely needed something. At least it's a start. We still have a mixture of early K-Mart and vintage grandeur; don't you think? I can't wait for B.J. to see the changes. Can I warm up your coffee?" Without waiting for a reply, Debbie left the room with Mitch's cup.

Mitch's curiosity got the better of him and he reluctantly surrendered his chair to more closely examine the paintings that he knew to be the work of the local artist, Betty Jackson. To his surprise, they were all originals that must have cost at least five thousand dollars apiece. He recognized that none were from Betty's "starving artist" period, but were fairly recent. The ringing phone startled him. He heard Debbie pick up the extension in the kitchen. He eased closer and listened.

* * *

"Did you say, 'Dr. Filbert?'"

"Why, yes, I did. I know his last name was Filbert. I believe he said his first name was James. Dear, didn't the nice young doctor say his name was James Filbert?"

John Vandergriff's brows knitted in concentration. "I do believe you are right, my dear. Your memory is so much better than mine about names but I do believe you're right. He said something about ordering supplies so that everything would be ready in time for the operation. Some things have to be ordered ahead, you know."

"Yes, I know. He must be new on the staff. What did this Dr. Filbert look like?"

* * *

Mitch listened as Debbie answered the phone. "Dr. Young's office. Hello, Mr. Timmons. No. Dr. Young's not here. He's on his way to Chicago right now. Is there anything I can help you with? I don't expect him to call in until after his plane lands a little after ten."

Why was she telling him all that? Who is Timmons? Mitch wondered. A patient would have no business knowing where Stuart was at this time of evening.

"If you'd like, I'll give you the number of Dr. Elwood, who is covering for Dr. Young while he's out of town. He wouldn't mind. Or you could speak with Dr. Mitchell. He's here at the clinic with me right now. He's a close friend of Dr. Young's. No? All right. I'm glad you called. If you change your mind about needing to speak with a doctor, let me know."

That was no patient. That was Debbie's contact person. Maybe even Nation. Now they knew everything. He hurried back to his chair before Debbie returned from the kitchen. They now knew Stuart was on his way to Chicago . . . hell, they even knew what time his plane would land. What could he do? How could he warn Stuart and Hawkins? She hadn't told them that Hawkins was with Stuart. Maybe that was a point in our favor. Hawkins was a big man, but against the Mafia? Wait a minute, he thought. Now they know I'm here with Debbie. They could be coming after me.

"That was one of Dr. Young's patients. The phone startled me though. I nearly spilled your coffee. I must be more on edge than I thought." Debbie set the cup on the coffee table within Mitch's reach before sitting on the couch.

* * *

Nation dialed a long distance number. "We've got trouble," he said as soon as someone picked up the receiver.

"What now?"

"Someone was snooping around the clinic today posing as a doctor. He even questioned one of our recipients. I don't know how much he knows or how much he learned. Hell, I don't even know how he got in the area. We have very tight security."

"Obviously not tight enough. It wasn't Young this time for sure. Vinny put him out of his misery. He won't be bothering us no more."

"No, this man was described as black and quite large. And very friendly."

"Probably a cohort of Young's. When did it happen?"

"As best I can tell, it was around two o'clock."

"Something is beginning to smell funny about this. Have you or anyone else checked to make sure Vinny finished the job? It might be good for you to do a little snooping around."

Nation raised his voice. "I'm sure I don't have the time to chase after your thugs to see if they did their job adequately or not."

The shout in response to his remark made Nation jerk the phone away from his ear in pain. "Look Nation," he heard, "You'll do as you are told. Doctors like you are a dime a dozen. We have six waiting right now to take your place. You're the one with the hospital contacts. Now get your ass on the phone and find out if anything went wrong if you know what's good for you and do it now." Nation heard a click. There was no way they could replace him and he knew it. But these people were not going to be jerked around. He knew that, too. He hit the switch hook and pressed speed dial number three.

*　*　*

Hawkins slowed long enough to snatch a ticket from the automatic ticket dispenser, then sped toward the American Airlines terminal. "We're almost there. What gate?"

"Thirty-five." Stuart had the gate number memorized.

"Got it." Hawkins maneuvered his car into the left lane and down the ramp to the covered parking lot. He wanted to get as close to gate thirty-five as he could. "We're in luck," he said and pulled into a parking space across from the gate. He grabbed Stuart's black bag and both he and Stuart jumped out. So far, so good.

Stuart took off in a trot. He raced up the concrete stairs that led from the parking area to the ticket counter. Impatiently waiting for the automatic doors to open, he looked back at Hawkins lumbering after him. "The plane boards in fifteen minutes. Believe it or not, we're on time. By the way, you'll probably have to show some identification for that bag. Matter of fact, these days you have to show identification to board a plane." The doors finally opened and Stuart squeezed through before they had a chance to part completely. The two men elbowed and shoved their way through the maze of humanity and made it to the counter. Three passengers stood in line. Stuart had an almost overpowering urge to declare himself on an emergency mission and step in front. He caught himself. "Calm down. There's plenty of time. Take a deep breath," he told himself. The three customers in front were quickly dispatched and the two doctors were through, tickets in hand, in less than five minutes. A quick glance at the monitor showed that the flight was still on time. Even so, they hurried over to security and sidled past the passengers who were placing their bags on the conveyer belt and then waited for their turn to enter. A portly man was sweating heavily and removing his belt after his third unsuccessful attempt through the archway without sounding the alarm. Finally, the security guard completed his manual wand search and, with a nod of his head, motioned for the passenger to go on to his gate. The embarrassed man shrugged at Stuart in apology while he buckled his belt. He hurriedly gathered his keys and pocket change and took off, disappearing into the crowd.

Hawkins grinned at Stuart. "That guy must have a metal plate somewhere," he whispered. "He never did make it through without a buzz." Turning back to the guard and opening the black bag, Hawkins thrust it out for inspection and, at the same time, held up his physician identification card for the man to study.

Finally, they made it to gate thirty-five. The door to the Jet way was still roped off. Stuart peered outside through the picture window. The jet was waiting. "At least the plane isn't late," he said. "It's already here." He squinted at the departure monitor. "And the flight is on time. We're doing good. Maybe we can relax for a moment."

Hawkins plopped into the nearest chair. "Wow, I didn't realize how bushed I was. It's been a long day. This feels good."

Stuart sank into the adjoining chair and buried his head in his hands.

"Hey, you okay?"

"A little dizzy, that's all. It'll pass. The old body can take only so much trauma before it begins to protest. I just need a few minutes."

"Hate to say this, my friend. Nothing personal, but you don't look too good. If you want to know the truth, you don't look much better than many of my usual patients. Got anything in here that'll help?" Hawkins offered Stuart his black bag but Stuart motioned for Hawkins to keep it. "Yes, but I'm going to hold off taking anything until I absolutely have to. I don't want to be out of it come midnight." He looked up. "Say, isn't it about time to board? What's the holdup, anyway?"

"I'll check." Hawkins made his way past the line of passengers confirming their seat assignments and motioned to one of the agents behind the counter. "Pardon me, miss, but has there been a delay in the flight."

The harried agent didn't look up. "There has been a stack up of traffic at O'Hare," she said. "We're not allowed to take off, yet. Our best guess is that we'll have at least a thirty-minute delay."

* * *

"Dr. Jamison did what? Let me speak to him this instant. Did you hear me? I said now and I don't care that he is indisposed. You tell him that Dr. Conrad Nation wishes to speak to him immediately. Is that clear?"

"Yes sir."

"Good. Now do it." There was no way that it could be true. Someone was either lying or very much misinformed. Maybe there was even a cover-up going on. That was it. A cover-up. That would explain everything. Young was dead on arrival and the hospital was stalling for time so that—

A voice interrupted his thoughts. "Conrad, is this important? I was with a patient that needs—"

"Of course this is important. Do you think I would interrupt you if it wasn't? A colleague of ours has been seriously injured or maybe even killed and you ask if it is important? That impertinent nurse of yours tells me that Stuart Young has been released with a concussion."

"That's true. He has. About six o'clock. He was released under his own care at his own request. He *is* a doctor, after all. Why is it a concern of yours?"

"Never mind why it's my concern. It simply is. Where did he go? What did he say? Anything you can tell me will help."

* * *

"What's that?"

"What's what?"

"Quiet," Mitch whispered. He cocked his head. "I thought I heard something. Wait. I did. It's the back door. Did you lock it?"

"Of course. Don't worry. It's only the janitorial service. They come in every evening after closing," Debbie said, standing. "I'd better let them know we're here. Sometimes they turn the radio on too loud. And sometimes a janitor brings his girlfriend along."

Mitch was frozen. That was no janitorial service. They had sent someone to do away with him. Maybe he should try to make it out the front door. No. That wouldn't work. He was a goner for sure. And Debbie was so cold about it. She was either a very good actress or she really didn't give a damn about what happened to him. He mopped his forehead. His handkerchief, already drenched, helped little. Now he knew how B.J. felt. He flinched at the sound of dual footsteps. She was bringing the hit man back to get him. When he saw the pushcart come around the corner, Mitch instinctively threw his hands in front of his face.

"What in the world are you doing, Mitch? You look like something is about to attack you. We don't have bats here. By the way, this is my friend, Tony Capetti. Tony, this is Dr. Mitchell."

What? No kiss on the cheek? Just a simple introduction to finger me? he thought. She wasn't fooling him. Mitch was not about to let down his guard. He studied Capetti. Capetti was no janitor. Not with those Bruno Magli shoes and that Pierre Cordin leather jacket. He looked more like Gary Busey in one of the *Lethal Weapon* movies . . . the epitome of a hit man.

"You're probably thinking I don't look like a janitor," Capetti said with a grin. He leaned across the coffee table to offer his hand.

Mitch reached out to shake hands with his executioner. How civil, he thought. "You're right. You can't be a janitor. What are you?"

"I'll show you what I am," Capetti said. He reached with his right hand into his left jacket pocket. Mitch ducked, squeezed his eyes shut, cowered in the chair and awaited his fate.

* * *

Nation dialed the long distance number for the second time in ten minutes. "We got trouble," he growled when it was answered.

"How bad?"

"Bad. Real bad. Young not only survived your so-called hit but he is on his way to Chicago."

"So? Don't have a stroke, doc. Some people are lucky. It happens. He won't be so lucky the next time. How is he getting to Chicago?"

"American Airlines flight 2340. It was supposed to board at seven forty and leave at eight but it's been delayed at least thirty minutes. Young is confirmed. He has already checked in and he's waiting to board as we speak."

"How do you know all that?"

"I called the airlines. Doctors have privileges. Didn't you know that?"

"You have any idea what happens to smart ass doctors? Of course I knew. I forgot. Is the black dude on the plane with him? The one that was snooping around the clinic?"

"I didn't ask."

"I didn't think so. It would be good if he is. We could kill two birds with one stone. Never mind. Let's see. That gives me fifty minutes to get Vinny and Al on the plane with them. They'll follow them to Chicago and we'll have a lively reception waiting for them when they arrive. No problem."

"What if the plane is full?"

"Don't worry. You'd be surprised how little it takes to buy a couple of seats."

"You'll take care of it, then?"

"I'll take care of it."

* * *

His satellite transceiver sounded. He picked up the mike. "Yeah?"

"Vinny?"

"Yeah."

"You told me you iced that doctor."

"So?"

"He's on his way to Chicago with a friend."

"What? How could he have survived the—"

"Shut up, Vinny. Never mind how he survived. He did. Get on out to DFW now. I want you and Al on the plane with him. Follow them every step they take and make sure they don't get past you. This time I'll have you some help waiting in Chicago to finish the job. You and Al both leave your pieces in the car. Your blades, too. Don't even take fingernail clippers with you. We can't take any chances with security these days. By the way, did he get a look at either one of you?"

"No. That I'm sure of."

"Good. Okay, listen up. Here's what I want you to do."

* * *

"What time is it?"

"That's the fourth time you've asked me that in the last thirty minutes. Are we suddenly on a time clock, or something?"

B.J. shuddered. "I'm sorry. I guess I'm preoccupied. Am I making a pest of myself?"

"Ever since you made that phone call, you've been as antsy as I've ever seen you. Is there something besides the dog that's bothering you? You were on the phone a long time. Are you sure everything's all right?" Cathy took her eyes off the road long enough to study her friend. "It's a little after eight. It's time for your pill."

"My pill?"

"It's a joke. Lighten up, girlfriend."

B.J. shook her head as if the cobwebs would magically go away if she did. Eight o'clock. Four more hours. Could she hold out? How far from Chicago were they? She pulled the Illinois road map from the door's side pocket. "Okay, now. Let's see where we are. That was Lexington we just passed. When we get to Pontiac, we'll be about a hundred miles from Chicago."

"It's getting late. You want to spend the night there?"

"*No!*"

B.J.'s response made Cathy jump. She shot B.J. a glance. "All right, already. I had no idea you felt that way about Pontiac. Just tell me where you want to stay and we'll do it."

"I know I'm acting weird. Please don't ask me why. Here's what I want to do. And please, no questions. Agreed?"

Cathy eyed B.J. and shook her head. "Agreed . . . for now."

B.J. looked at her lap, unable to face Cathy. She hated doing this to her best friend. "All right, I'll tell you, then. Here's what I want to do. I want to go to that all-night hamburger place Hawkins told me about. I want to get there by eleven thirty and have a hamburger there at midnight. Is that asking too much?"

"Of course not. We're on this trip to do what we want to when we want to. But I swear, someday I'll worm it out of you. I promise."

One way or another, you'll know soon, B.J. thought.

* * *

"But I'm a doctor and I have an emergency in Chicago." Stuart tried to keep his voice in check but he felt frustration and anger beginning to rise deep within him.

The attendant looked harried. "I'm sorry, sir. We're doing the best we can. If we board at eight forty, we'll only be an hour late. There's nothing we can do about the stackup at O'Hare. Please be patient."

"Are there any other flights leaving before this one? On any other airline?"

"No, sir. I've already checked for you. There are no other flights leaving before this one. Even if there were, they would be facing the same delay."

His anger now beginning to boil over into rage, Stuart whirled around to face Hawkins, who was standing behind him. "What else can we do? We can't just stand here and watch the time pass. I'm going crazy. We'll—"

Hawkins grabbed Stuart by the shoulders and squeezed. He pulled Stuart's face to within inches of his own. "Stuart. Listen to me. Get ahold of yourself. You'll be of no use to B.J. if you lose it. Now calm down." The awaiting passengers were watching the scene with growing restlessness. Some had begun whispering among themselves. Hawkins led Stuart away from the crowd. "She said that we should be loading soon. It's eight thirty, now. If we board by eight forty, we'll still have plenty of time to get to the restaurant by midnight."

"And what if we don't board by eight forty? That's ten minutes from now."

"Then we'll have to think of something else." Hawkins looked up to see an attendant motioning to him.

* * *

"Debbie, I can always come back when your friend feels better."

"Hang on a minute, Tony. Mitch, what in the world are you doing? You're acting like Tony is going to hit you or something. Quit that. Mitch, look at me."

Mitch opened his eyes and saw Capetti standing in front of him holding a business card—not a gun. He suddenly felt foolish. "Sorry, I had a chill. Must be coming down with something."

"Mitch, that's pretty lame. You're going to have to do better than that," Debbie said, frowning.

"Look, folks," Capetti said. "Let me clean the other suites first. I'll leave you two alone and come back later. Debbie, can I talk to you privately for a moment?"

"Of course. I'll walk you to the back door. Mitch, you stay put. I'll be right back," Debbie said.

Mitch watched as Debbie and Capetti, pushing his cart, walked toward the back door. Before they disappeared, Debbie looked back at Mitch and frowned again.

What can I say to her? Mitch thought. How was he to know that Capetti was the owner of a janitorial service and not a Mafia hit man? No way did he look like one. So he wasn't a Mafia hit man. So what? She still had those connections with Nation and the Christian Clinic. Maybe even the Mafia. How in the world was he going to explain his strange behavior without tipping her off that he knew? He'd have to play it by ear. But it was too bad about Debbie. She was everything he had ever wanted in a woman. Where would he find another one like her? If one existed, that is. Damn shameful waste.

"All right, Mitch. Let's talk." He looked up to see Debbie standing in the doorway with her hands on her hips. "There's something strange going on. Maybe even stranger than what is happening with Dr. Young and B.J." She walked over to stand directly in front of him. "Can I get you something? A sedative? A glass of wine? I have an excellent bottle of Chianti in the kitchen. I bought it to celebrate Dr. Young's engagement but we ended up going out that night."

She looks as though she really cares, he thought. "I could do with a glass of Chianti. Thank you."

Debbie left the room while Mitch stared into space. He wiped his forehead with his shirtsleeve. When the cork popped, he jumped. Got to compose myself, he thought. He should never have let her go into the kitchen alone—especially to fix him a drink. "Debbie," he called, "do you need any help with the wine?"

"No, thank you. You relax. I'll be right there."

Oh, well. He was tired of worrying about dying. If she spiked the wine, he didn't care anymore. Belatedly remembering his manners, he stood as Debbie came back into the room with two glasses of wine. He took the glass that

Debbie offered. Their fingers touched. It was a shame that things hadn't turned out differently. Trying to put on a good front, Mitch smiled and raised his glass. "To the safe return of B.J., Stuart and Hawkins," he said and touched his glass to hers. To his amazement, Debbie broke into loud sobs. She put her glass down and covered her face with her hands. Mitch felt helpless. "Here, here," he said and gently patted her shoulder.

Debbie sank onto the couch and began rocking back and forth. Her sobs grew louder. Mitch sat next to Debbie and took her into his arms. He held her while she cried.

* * *

"Let's go."

The attendant took the two doctors aboard the plane and gestured to the front row of first class. She nodded. "This way, you'll be the first ones off the plane. We'll get the other passengers loaded as quickly as possible." She rushed back to the waiting area where the other attendant had already begun the call for preboarding.

Stuart eyed the open door to the cockpit. As best he could tell, the crew had already begun preflight preparations.

He closed his eyes and sighed. Almost under his breath, he said, "I've never before had the urge to hijack a plane but I have a powerful one right now." Before Hawkins could react, Stuart had jumped up and bolted inside the crew compartment.

The captain looked up. "Yes, can I help you?"

Stuart knew how wild-eyed he must look. He smiled broadly and offered his hand. "I'm Dr. Stuart Young and I have one very important question to ask you."

The captain's expression turned from one of concern to genuine relief. He accepted the proffered hand, shaking it firmly. "I'm Captain Turner. I'll answer your question if I can. What do you want to know?"

"Captain, how much latitude do you have concerning our arrival time? The reason I'm asking is that Dr. Hawkins and I are on a medical emergency and we must get to Chicago as soon as possible. Lives are at stake."

"Epidemic?"

"Something like that, yes. We're carrying the antidote with us." Stuart gestured to the black bag in Hawkins' lap. Getting the message, Hawkins lifted the bag for the pilot to see.

"If we don't get to Chicago well before midnight, I'm not sure what's going to happen."

The pilot's smile faded as he listened to the story. "In answer to your question, I can do quite a lot, actually. You've given me the right to request priority clearance for takeoff and landing. I can also check the various altitudes for best possible wind speed. Within limits, of course."

"Of course. I wouldn't presume to tell you how to run your business, but please do all you can to get us there in the shortest possible time. I assure you it couldn't be more vital."

"I understand. Now where are you sitting? With your friend?"

"Yes, we'll be right behind you."

"That will make it handy. Now, you sit back down and let us get to work on it. We'll do everything in our power. I'll keep you posted."

"Thank you," Stuart said calmly, even as his raw emotions urged him to scream and shout. "Thank you." Stuart turned back to his seat, surprised at his own equanimity.

"Looks like that went well," Hawkins said. "I thought you were about to hijack the plane before anybody else got on."

Stuart dropped heavily into the roomy and comfortable first-class seat. He barely even noticed. "Nobody hijacks a plane to Chicago," he said.

"Well, I don't know. The way you've been acting . . ."

"Yeah, you're absolutely correct. I'm probably capable of anything right now."

"I can't blame you. Look, they're boarding."

Stuart glanced at his watch and bit his lip. It was eight forty. He had to restrain himself to keep from leaping up and herding the passengers toward their seats. Anything to keep them moving. He had never seen people move with such seemingly deliberate lack of vigor. Stuart could never remember feeling so helpless. He surely must be turning blue.

Finally, all passengers were settled, their bags stowed and their belts buckled. Only four of the eight seats in first class were occupied. Two passengers had come in at the last minute, glanced at Stuart, looked at each other and then settled into the two seats across from Stuart and Hawkins. Neither of the doctors noticed. They were watching the flight attendants close and latch the passenger door and busy themselves with preparations for takeoff. The attendants smiled and nodded to Stuart and Hawkins when they passed. They knew. The captain glanced at Stuart and gave him a thumbs-up as he closed the crew compartment door. So far, so good. The jet began to move backward as it was pulled from its gate. Shortly, it was in the clear. The powerful jet engines screamed when they were directed to move the big airliner forward. To Stuart's numbed mind, it sounded like a band of heavenly angels singing the Hallelujah Chorus. Slowly, the jumbo jet began to pick up speed and taxi toward the runway. From his window seat, Stuart could see five planes lined up and waiting for them to pass. He looked at his watch again. It was nine o'clock. Even if they weren't able to gain any time in the air, they would still arrive in Chicago by eleven fifteen. It was still doable. But if they were able to gain a few minutes, it would give them some precious margin. For the first time, Stuart leaned back and closed his eyes. But there would be no sleep.

Chapter 16

"It has something to do with that ambulance, doesn't it?"

"What?" The question had taken B.J. by surprise. Her reaction infuriated her. How was she going to keep up the charade until midnight if she kept letting her guard down so easily?

"You heard me, B.J. Welborn. When was the last time you were able to keep a secret from me? When have you ever been able to? I've been watching you carefully and you must have glanced back at it at least a hundred times in the last hour. I know that there's something you don't want me to know. I haven't a clue as to what it is but what I can't figure out is why you won't let me in on it. How long have we been best friends? I think you know something about that ambulance that you're not telling me. Something you learned during that long phone call back in Springfield. I'll tell you another thing. I don't think your damn dog's dead, either. It simply wouldn't upset you like this and I know how much you love the dog, okay? Are you listening to me? Are you hearing what I'm saying? Am I getting through? Hello? Anybody home? Look at me, B.J. I said look at me."

B.J. slowly looked up. She stared straight ahead, saying nothing. It was dark. Cathy was driving. They were stopped in traffic in a little town named Dwight. B.J. had insisted on cutting over to I-57 on the slowest route to keep from getting to Chicago too soon. They had long ago turned off the radio and had been traveling in silence for over an hour, which is why Cathy's question had taken B.J. so much by surprise. The red light seemed interminably long. The silence was heavy and hung over the two like a blanket. When the light turned green, in her peripheral vision, B.J. saw Cathy shake her head before accelerating from the intersection faster than usual. She couldn't blame Cathy. She'd feel the same if it were Cathy acting so strange. Should she tell Cathy? Could she justify putting her in that much danger? Only two more hours. She wasn't sure she could make it. She looked back. The ambulance was a half block behind. She felt faint. Absently, B.J. wondered if her blood pressure was approaching a dangerous level. The irony almost made her laugh.

* * *

"I'm sorry, Mitch. I didn't mean to break down like that. It's just . . . everything has been so mixed up . . . so turned upside down. I've been so tense and I'm having trouble handling it all."

Mitch found himself enjoying comforting Debbie in spite of the potential danger. It was becoming harder and harder to picture her connected to such shady characters. Reluctantly, he released his hold on her and leaned back. "It's all right," he said. "Everyone is having a hard time coping with all that has happened lately. Don't worry. Everything will be okay."

Debbie picked up her goblet and sipped the red liquid in slow motion, swirling the wine between sips and studying the patterns that it made on the glass below the rim. She looked puzzled about something and deep in thought. Mitch said nothing but watched her. Finally, she spoke. "Mitch?"

"Yes, Debbie?" Here it came.

"This may sound like a crazy question in light of all the other weird things that are going on, but something is bothering me. Why would Dr. Stuart make his own reservations to Chicago for this morning's flight?"

"Why do you ask?"

"Because I always make reservations for him. As far as I know, he doesn't even know how. He doesn't know the phone number of his travel agent and it isn't programmed on his cell phone. He would've had to call information to get it. Why would he go to all that trouble when all he had to do was call me and I'd have taken care of it for him? I was here the whole time."

Mitch was puzzled. Debbie was not sounding at all like a person with something to hide. She wasn't acting like one, either. It was risky but he decided to take a chance. "Debbie, I don't know how to tell you this . . . but Stuart doesn't trust you."

Debbie looked at Mitch as if he had slapped her. "I don't think I heard you right."

"You heard me right."

"I couldn't have."

"He doesn't trust you."

"Good God, Mitch. That's awful. Why would you say such a terrible thing?"

Mitch watched Debbie's reaction. She seemed sincere. "Because it's true."

"I'm . . . I'm confused. You had better explain yourself, Dr. Mitchell. You evidently know something that I don't."

"I'll be up front. It has to do with your association with some pretty unsavory characters."

"Like who, for God's sake. I don't know any—as you put it—unsavory characters. Who?"

"Like Conrad Nation, for instance." Mitch waited for her response.

"*What*? Uncle Connie? What on earth are you talking about? What about him?"

"Uncle Connie? Conrad Nation is your uncle?"

"Yes he is. He's my great-uncle actually, my grandmother's youngest brother. So what? And what do you mean by referring to one of the country's most respected doctors as an unsavory character?"

* * *

The captain suddenly appeared in front of Stuart. Stuart had been so lost in thought that he hadn't even seen the cockpit door open. He tried to jump to his feet but the seat belt held him fast. Irritated, he unlatched it and stood up. As soon as he saw the pilot's face, he knew. It was bad news. "What's wrong? I thought we were making good time. Are we having a problem? I'm not sure I want to hear about it if we are."

"Actually, we're making excellent time. We've picked up at least fifteen minutes which could put us on the ground by eleven o'clock."

The captain's face did not reflect the encouragement that his statement implied. The obvious dichotomy rattled Stuart. Puzzled, he looked at his watch. "That's only thirty minutes from now. I seem to be missing something, Captain. If we're doing so well on time, why do you look so worried? What's the problem?"

The pilot's visage continued to express concern. "The problem now is the weather in Chicago. There are some bad-looking thunderstorms developing in the area. They're advising us that we may not be able to land after we get there."

Stuart dropped back into his seat. He looked up at the captain. "When will we know?" he said, almost in a whisper.

"Don't lose hope. It's not definite, yet. Right now it's just building up. I'll keep you posted." He turned and disappeared into the cockpit.

"Thanks," Stuart whispered long after the pilot had gone. He looked at Hawkins who shrugged and shook his head in response.

"Is it really so urgent that we get to B.J. by midnight? Surely thirty minutes won't make any difference," Stuart said.

413

"You're forgetting that Mrs. Vandergriff will be ready for her surgery tomorrow morning. It'll take them three to four hours to transport an organ back to Dallas for the transplant procedure. My guess is they'll be ready for it shortly after midnight. Since I told B.J. I'd be there at midnight, if I don't show, she could become hysterical and run. I'd probably do the same thing. She thinks if she can get to a metal building, she'll be safe. Any sudden panic on her part could trigger the transmission right then. Listen, I know the weather thing doesn't look good but I've been doing some thinking," Hawkins said, "and I believe I've come up with a backup plan in the event we get delayed by the weather."

* * *

Mitch was flabbergasted. He knew he had made a big mistake. Conrad Nation was Debbie's uncle. That would explain her "date" with Nation but it wouldn't begin to explain her association with the Christian Clinic. He had to know more.

"I'm sorry about that, Debbie. Really I am. It was uncalled for and I apologize."

"But why would you even make such a ridiculous statement? What did you mean by it?"

"First, let me ask you about the Christian Clinic. Let's simply say that you were seen there recently."

"I have no idea what you're talking about. What in the world is a Christian Clinic? Wait a minute. Christian Clinic. Where have I heard that name before? That's it. When Hawkins was talking to B.J., he mentioned it. But I know that's not the only time I've heard that name."

"Does Preston Tower ring a bell?" Mitch asked, looking straight into Debbie's eyes.

"Of course it does. My best friend has her office at Preston Tower. She's an attorney. I go there quite often to see her. I was there night before last. What is this? An inquisition? I haven't done anything wrong. Certainly nothing that would cause me to lose Dr. Young's trust. Please explain yourself," Debbie said, glaring at Mitch.

"Who is your friend?"

"What business is it of yours?"

"Because I saw you hugging Frank Peterson. That's why?"

"You saw *what*? You're crazy. I don't even know a Frank Peterson?"

"Debbie, don't take me for a fool. I was there. I saw you myself. He walked you to your car not six feet from mine. It was you. I would know you in my sleep," Mitch said.

"Pardon me. Just what do you mean by that? And where is this supposed to have taken place?"

"I told you. Preston Tower. After dark."

Debbie frowned. "Frank? The security guard? He walks me to my car, for God's sake. Sharon insists on it. She's known Frank for years. You find that sinister? You have a twisted mind," Debbie yelled, jumping to her feet. "And I'll tell you another thing, Dr. Mitchell. Frank will walk me to my car the next time I visit Sharon. And I'll probably give him another hug. He's a nice guy. So what."

"But Christian Clinic is in Preston Tower and that's where they're doing the illegal heart transplants. I thought that's where you were," Mitch said. He stood to face Debbie.

"Then what were *you* doing there? Should I be suspicious of *you*?"

* * *

"What if I give Joseph Legato a call," Hawkins said, "and have him go out to the restaurant and stand by in case we don't get there by midnight? I could ask him to take his instruments and be ready in case we don't show up in time. He knows where the restaurant is. He's the one who took me there in the first place. He knows all about the chip and where they implant it. He's a doctor. He could easily do it."

"That's great. Do it. Give him a call now. Give him B.J.'s description and have him there waiting for us. If we show up, fine. If we don't, bingo. He goes into the bathroom after B.J., explains everything and removes the chip. B.J. doesn't even have to know about it ahead of time. I think it'll work. It has to. Seriously, Hawkins. It's a great idea and it would make me feel a lot better knowing we had an alternative plan. Give him a call right now. Here, use this phone right in front of us." Stuart snatched the in-flight phone from its mount on the bulkhead and shoved it into Hawkins' hand. "Wait a minute. B.J. doesn't know Legato. She may think he's one of them. She could panic and no telling what would happen."

"I told B.J. about Legato and about Ito. When he says who he is, she'll put it together. Don't worry," Hawkins said, reaching for his credit card. He activated the phone and dialed the number from memory.

* * *

"Why would you possibly suspect me?" Mitch yelled. "I'm Stuart's best friend and I'd never do anything to jeopardize his happiness. He loves B.J. Wait. I know what you're doing. You're trying to change the subject. Well, I'll change the subject for you. Explain these Betty Jackson originals. Explain that obviously expensive antique. Explain your Volvo."

"My Volvo? You want me to explain my Volvo? You have finally lost it, doctor. I don't have to explain a thing to you. My inheritance and my possessions are none of your concern. Furthermore, you may leave right now," Debbie said, pointing to the door.

"This is getting us nowhere. I give up. I don't care about your artistic taste or the car you drive," Mitch said with a groan. He slumped into the chair. "I have to be here in case they call. Hawkins asked me to and he may need me. I'm not leaving."

Debbie sighed. "Okay. I'm here to help, too and I'm not leaving either. Let's just forget this entire conversation. But tell me one thing. Why did you say what you did about my uncle being an unsavory character? There's not an unsavory bone in his body. He's the most wonderful man in the world as well as a brilliant doctor."

"All of that may be so, but he's still the one doing the illegal heart transplants."

"No, he's not. He practices at Dallas General. He's one of the most renowned transplant surgeons in Texas, if not in the world. Why would he be mixed up in something like that? Something illegal?"

"I don't know but Stuart and Hawkins both have confirmed that he is involved." Mitch looked up at Debbie. The poor kid really doesn't know, he thought. She has no idea. "I'm sorry, Debbie. I really am, but it's true." Mitch watched as Debbie blinked to hold back the tears. He had an overwhelming urge to hold her again—to comfort her. No. He wanted to be more than a comfort to Debbie.

* * *

"It's ringing. Hello? Yes, this is Dr. Hawkins from the Dallas Medical Examiner's office. I'd like to speak with Dr. Legato, please. Yes, I'll hold. Hello, Rose. This is Dr. Hawkins. Whoever answered the phone must have misunderstood. I had asked to speak with Joseph. I don't mean to be abrupt but I have an emergency. What? Sergeant who? Why are the police there? Is something wrong? Rose. Are you okay? Are you all right? Hello? Yes, this is Dr. Hawkins. Who is this? Yes, I'm a colleague of Dr. Legato and I have to talk to him. When did I do what? Why is that important? All right, all right. The last time I talked to Dr. Legato was today. He called me sometime before noon. No, I'm sorry, that's confidential. I can't tell you what we discussed. Not without his permission. What do you mean I'll have to? Please listen carefully. I must speak to Dr. Legato immediately. It's a matter of grave urgency. Please put him on the phone. Now. I have to—"

Stuart had been staring at Hawkins as the bizarre conversation unfolded. The more he listened, the more panicked he became. Something was horribly wrong. Hawkins' eyes mirrored sheer terror. "What? What is it? Hawkins, answer me." At this point, Stuart was certain he didn't want to know what Hawkins was hearing. He shook his head and buried his face in his hands as though by doing so, the whole ugly episode would disappear and the world would magically be made right again.

Hawkins continued. "Oh, my God. Oh, no. When did it happen? I see. Yes, I'm on my way to Chicago, now. I'll contact you tomorrow and give you a complete report. Yes, I'll do that. I'll help any way I can. Thank you. Goodbye." Hawkins turned to Stuart. He had tears in his eyes and his lip was quivering. "I don't know how to say this—"

"What? Tell me what happened? Say it, man. Spit it out."

"Legato was murdered this afternoon, apparently not too long after I talked to him. I can't believe it."

"How did it happen? Was he shot? What?"

"Car bomb."

"My God. Mafia."

"That's what it looks like. Remote control. He was on the freeway. Blown to bits. He must have died instantly."

"I'm so sorry, Hawkins. I know the two of you had become very close. You must be hurting. Is there anything I can do?" Stuart asked.

"Thanks, friend. Nothing. But we have to come up with another alternative."

"Do you have any other ideas?"

"None. What time is it anyway?"

"Ten of eleven. What's happening? Do you feel that?"

"Feel what?"

"Damn."

"What?"

"We're circling. We're not descending. We're circling. They're not allowing us to land. Think of something, Hawkins. We're running out of time."

Hawkins squeezed Stuart's shoulder. "I'm sorry, buddy. Right now I'm fresh out of ideas."

* * *

"Where are we, now?"

"This is Manteno."

"Manteno?"

"Yes, Manteno."

"Then how far are we from our, uh, destination?"

"If you're referring to the hamburger place, about thirty miles."

"Then that should put us there at about the right time, right?"

"About eleven thirty, yes."

"Where are we staying tonight? That is if it isn't asking too much for you to tell me."

"I don't know. It may not even matter."

"Damn you, B.J. I wish you would stop talking in riddles. First you go weird on me and then you top it off by talking like a crazy person. I don't know what to think."

"You'll know soon enough. Maybe too soon."

"What is that supposed to mean?"

* * *

"Hawkins, I can't believe we're still circling. I'm afraid to look. What time is it?"

"Buddy, time is running mighty short. It's eleven fifteen."

"It may already be too late. How long did you say it took to get to the restaurant from the airport?"

"It's thirty-seven miles. I remember precisely because when we drove to the restaurant, I was watching Legato's odometer like a hawk because I was so hungry. It took forty-five minutes in good traffic. I could probably make it myself in thirty or thirty-five if I drove. I know. We could call ahead for a police escort."

"No. We can't do that. The paramedics would know something was up."

"You're right. That would never work. Too dangerous."

Stuart cradled his forehead in his hands and rubbed his eyes. Without warning, he jerked open his seat restraint. "That's it. We have to land now. I'm going to talk to the pilot."

Just as Stuart rose, the cockpit door opened and Captain Turner appeared. He looked ashen and paused before he spoke. "I'm sorry. I did everything I could. The air traffic controller simply refused to allow me to land the plane."

Stuart grasped the captain's arms. "Don't they understand that lives are at stake here?" he pleaded.

Captain Turner nodded. "Yes, they do, but they're not willing to put the lives of my passengers at risk. Surely you understand."

"That's it?"

"I'm afraid so. The storms are expected to abate in about fifteen minutes. That would put us down at approximately eleven forty. Can you make it to where you need to be in twenty minutes?"

Stuart looked at Hawkins. Hawkins shook his head. "Not a chance. Not even *I* could do it in that short a time."

The captain turned to leave. "I'm truly sorry," he said.

Hawkins put his beefy arm around Stuart's shoulder. "I think we had better notify the police, don't you? I'll call that inspector back that was at the Legato home and get him to go. I'm sure I can explain it to him the quickest."

"But what could he do? He can't take the microchip out. All he would succeed in doing would be to alert the paramedics and they'd kill B.J. I can't chance it."

"But Stuart, B.J. is in Chicago, now. They're liable to take her any minute anyway, don't you think? Maybe the police could arrange for us to have a helicopter and a pilot waiting. We could get there in about twenty minutes."

"And you think a helicopter landing at the restaurant wouldn't tip them off? Give me a break. I'm sorry, Hawkins. That was uncalled for." Stuart sighed deeply. He felt defeated . . . ready to give up. "I honestly can't think of anything else.

I've never felt so helpless. If we call B.J. at the restaurant, it will surely alert them. If we do nothing, B.J. might panic when you don't show up. Is there nothing we can do?"

"Of everything we have thought of, I think the best thing to do is to alert B.J. and let her decide what she wants to do. It's dangerous I know but what else is left? You better let me make the call. If *you* call her at the restaurant, she's liable to get excited and blow her cover."

"You're right. You better do it."

Hawkins retrieved his credit card, activated the flight phone and dialed 312-555-1212. When the Chicago information operator answered, Hawkins said, "Yes, operator. This is an emergency. Please give me the number for—"

Captain Turner burst spiritedly through the cockpit door. Hawkins and Stuart looked up. This time his face appeared flushed. "We still can't land at O'Hare but the flight controller has given me permission to make an emergency landing at Midway. Would that help? We could be on the ground at eleven thirty-five if you give me the word."

Stuart was stunned. He turned to look at Hawkins. "I have no idea where Midway is. Do you?"

Hawkins didn't hesitate. "Yes. Do it, Captain," he boomed. "Do it now. I know where Midway is. We passed the entrance to Midway on the way to eat. It's only about half as far from the restaurant as O'Hare is. We should be able to make it there in twenty minutes. We still have a chance." Hawkins deactivated the phone.

"Right." Captain Turner spun around and retreated into the flight crew cabin.

Almost immediately, they heard the announcement. "Ladies and gentlemen, because of the weather conditions in Chicago, the captain has made arrangements for a landing and temporary layover at Chicago's Midway Airport. Please fasten your seat belts and place your tray tables and seat backs in their upright and locked positions. We should be landing in just a few minutes."

Stuart pursed his lips and let out a long sigh. He looked at the ceiling and stretched his stiff neck first to the left and then to the right. He glanced at the passenger across the aisle from Hawkins. Something caught his eye. The man had a pack of cigarettes in his shirt pocket. Maybe he could bum one to smoke after they landed. He needed one badly. All at once Stuart froze. A red flash. The passenger had reached up with his left hand to adjust his overhead air vent and the cabin light had reflected off a brilliant ruby in his ring. Slowly, Stuart turned to Hawkins. He whispered, "Don't look around. Don't make any unusual moves. Don't say a thing. Do exactly as I tell you. I am going to get up and walk to the back of the plane like I'm stretching my legs. Wait about ten seconds and follow me. Go into the kitchen area where we can talk without being overheard."

Stuart unbuckled his seat belt, stretched and wandered toward the rear of the plane. After a few seconds, Hawkins followed. When they reached the food service area, a flight attendant stopped them. "Dr. Young, you'll have to return to your seat for landing."

Stuart nodded. "Thank you, I know. This won't take but a second." He turned to Hawkins. "We've been followed."

"How do you know?"

"The man sitting directly across the aisle from you is the one who tried to kill me this morning."

"Are you sure?"

"I'm certain. There can't be two left-handed people in the world with a ring like that. He was the one driving and even though I couldn't see his face when he shot at me, I'll never forget that left hand sticking awkwardly out the window with a gun in it. And those hairy, fat fingers and that skull ring with the ruby eyes. I'm positive. And I'm afraid he heard everything we've been talking about. What can we do?"

"Has he used the in-flight telephone at all?"

"I have no idea. Watching the other passengers was the last thing on my mind."

"All right. The first thing we have to do is assume that he's dumb enough not to be able to put it all together even if he heard everything we said. These goons are trained to observe but they don't usually give them any more information than they have to for them to get the job done. He probably has no idea what we've been talking about. If I'm right about that, then he hasn't alerted anybody. If that's true, the rest is easy. Just follow my lead once we get off the plane. I'm sure he's here to finish the job but I've got a few tricks up my sleeve, too. He won't try anything in the terminal so we'll have a slight edge since he doesn't know that we're on to him. One more thing. We also have to assume that the guy sitting next to him is his accomplice since they don't put first class passengers next to each other unless they're traveling together. Not when there's only a few first-class passengers."

"But how did they know we were here?"

"Who knows?"

Stuart felt a hand on his shoulder. "Dr. Young?"

"Yes, of course. We were just headed back to our seats." Stuart motioned for Hawkins to follow and the two made their way back to the first class section. Maybe this is God's way of trying to tell me something, Stuart thought. If so, I get the message loud and clear. Here I was lusting after a cigarette that turned out to belong to none other than the man who tried to kill me today. Help me save B.J. and I promise I will never light up again.

When they reached their seats, Stuart resisted the urge to stare at the mobster. Instead, he dropped onto his seat, buckled up and stared out the window.

* * *

The runway lights glowed in the fog. The high winds buffeted the plane as it made its final approach. Captain Turner glanced at his co-pilot. "Ray, do me a favor. Tell Dr. Young that I've arranged with airport security for a car and a driver to take them wherever they need to go. The driver's name is Sam. He'll be right outside the main entrance in a white Ford Taurus."

* * *

"Well, finally, here it is. I only hope it's half as good as you say it is. Why do you keep looking at your watch? Hey, look. Here's somebody backing out and leaving us a good parking place right in front. Let's go on in and get it over with. And another thing. Quit yakking so much. You're making me nervous." Cathy maneuvered the rental car into the newly vacated parking space. She turned and stared at B.J.

The crushing pressure of being moments from death and utterly helpless finally caught up with B.J. Unable to control her emotions any longer, the dam burst. B.J. became furious. Why wouldn't Cathy leave her alone? Couldn't she see that what was needed right now was patience, not lectures? B.J. lashed out with unvented fury. She screamed at Cathy. "Just back off and give me a little space, all right? I still have some things to sort out." After seeing the expression on Cathy's face, she immediately regretted her outburst. "I'm sorry. It's not your fault. I shouldn't snap at you like that. Maybe I'll feel better after I get something in my stomach."

Incredibly, Cathy maintained her composure. "True," she said with a calm that took B.J. aback. "We are eating a little late. Okay, then. Let's do it." She opened her door to get out when B.J. grabbed her arm. Cathy stopped in mid-motion and watched her troubled friend.

B.J. couldn't do this. Cathy deserved better. Not even if it did turn out to be the last hour of her life. Her emotions finally overflowed and B.J. welled up. Tears threatened. Suddenly remembering Hawkins' admonition to act natural, B.J. stiffened and forced the tears to stop. They may be watching. She smiled, took a deep breath, and wiped her face with a tissue. "You're right," she said, ignoring Cathy's stunned look. "Let's eat." She threw open the door and hopped out with enthusiasm. Nobody was going to see her act any way but normal. No way. As she walked toward the restaurant entrance, using her peripheral vision, B.J. watched the ambulance pull into an empty parking space at the building next door.

Chapter 17

A cheerful table server greeted B.J. and Cathy as soon as they entered the front door of the restaurant door. "How many in your party?"

"Two," Cathy answered.

"Would you prefer smoking or non-smoking?" she asked.

"Non-smoking."

"Certainly. This way, please."

This won't do at all, B.J. thought. Not only could she not see the front door, but Cathy could see anyone that went into the ladies' rest room. She pointed to a table that would give her a clear view of the front door. Also, if she sat Cathy in the opposite direction, it would block Cathy's view. "Would it be all right if we take that one over there?" she asked, pointing to another section of the restaurant.

"Of course, but that table is in smoking."

"That's perfect."

The server turned to lead the way to the table B.J. had selected. As B.J. followed, she could feel Cathy's look of incredulity. "I know I'm acting weird," she whispered. "Bear with me. I'll explain a little later. Please." Cathy responded by sighing and rolling her eyes. "You sit here," B.J. said when they reached their table. Cathy complied without a word. "I'll be right back. I'm going to the bathroom."

"I'll go with you," Cathy said pushing back her chair.

"No. I mean I need to be alone for a minute."

"Go," Cathy said resignedly. "I'll stay here by myself."

"I'll take your order when you're ready," the server said with a hint of apprehension. "What can I bring you to drink?"

"Water will be fine," B.J. said. "Cathy, I'll be right back."

B.J. heard Cathy mutter something unintelligible as she walked to the rest room. Quickly entering the room, she found it empty. No Hawkins yet. She paused, took a deep breath and washed her face.

* * *

Mitch crossed the room to where Debbie was sitting on the couch. He approached her from behind and began gently massaging her shoulders and lower neck. "I wish they would give us a call or something. Anything. This waiting is driving us both nuts. How does that feel?"

"Please don't stop. It feels wonderful."

"Debbie?"

"Yes?"

"Someday after this is all over . . ."

"Yes?"

"Maybe we could . . . do something."

"Do something?"

"Yeah, like maybe go out or something."

"You mean like a date?"

"Yeah . . . or something."

"I'd like that."

"Really?"

"Really. I'd like that. No, please don't stop."

* * *

Shawn Purdon was as excited as he had ever been in his eighteen short years. He had finally finished his cherished two-year-long project; a customized Lincoln that he was sure would have made George Barris, arguably the greatest car customizer ever, proud. His dad hadn't seen it yet. He had been on a business trip for over a week. Painstakingly and lovingly, Shawn had completed most of the work himself in junior and senior auto mechanics classes. The last step, the inch-deep black lacquer paint job, had been left to the professionals at the local paint and body shop. It was the only compromise he could afford. Barris, of course, would have chosen a '51 Mercury instead of the '51 Lincoln. It was the car of choice for professional customizers. That was the rub. He had really wanted Mercury, but supply and demand had put the Mercury out of Shawn's reach. But that didn't matter now. His was the most beautiful car in whole Chicago area and likely one of the best looking in the world. It was nosed, decked, chopped, channeled, had a louvered hood, electric doors, pleated and rolled interior and a pair of black and white furry dice hanging from the rear view mirror. He had found his prized two-door sedan in the garage of an old house in Deerfield. The owner, a widow no longer able to live alone, was selling her house and furnishings and moving to an assisted living facility. The car had been purchased new by her husband and was a genuine cream puff. It only had thirty-eight thousand miles on the odometer. The V-8 engine and automatic transmission were in great shape and needed no work at all. Shawn had learned of the car from a friend and had managed to talk the woman into selling it to him for only three hundred dollars. He told his friends that he had to beg on his hands and knees to get her to do it.

"What time is it, Sonny?" Shawn asked his friend who had come along for the ride. Sonny was still awkward, skinny and pimply faced even though most of the kids in his class had already begun to outgrow the phase. Shawn, by contrast, had matured into a tall, good-looking athlete.

"It doesn't matter. You're going to be late if you don't step on it," Sonny replied. Your dad's plane has landed by now and he's probably already in baggage claim. He's not gonna like it if he has to wait for you."

"Yeah, you're right but I don't want to get no ticket."

Sonny burst into laughter. "Do you remember the fifty's song about the hot rod Lincoln?"

"I think so, why?"

"Because your dad hasn't seen your car, yet."

"So?"

"I heard it today on the radio. In the song, the dad tells the kid, 'You're going to drive me to drinking if you don't stop driving that hot rod Lincoln.'"

* * *

"We're down. What time is it?" Stuart asked. Unwilling to wait for the jetliner to slow from its landing speed, he unbuckled his seat belt and stepped over by the exit door.

Hawkins stood up, stretched, retrieved the black bag from the overhead, stepped over beside Stuart and whispered. "I understand what you must be going through, good buddy, and what you must be thinking," he said. "It has to be hell. It's already eleven thirty-five and we can't get out until the plane stops at the gate, but don't forget about our two friends behind us. We can hurry down the ramp but we shouldn't start running until we get clear of the boarding area. Then we can take off and run like scalded dogs. If we can fake them out, we can gain a small advantage. These guys weren't hired for their thinking ability. If we can get inside Sam's Taurus and take off, we'll have it made. Especially if he lets me drive."

Stuart sighed. His eyes were wild looking. "Damn. I forgot about the security guy. I'm glad you're along. My brain has turned to mush. I can't think any more. Are you sure you know how to get from Midway to the restaurant? Tell me again. We can't afford any slip-ups at this point."

Hawkins nodded. "Hopefully, Sam knows his way around town. But even if he doesn't, the captain told me that all we have to do is go south on highway 50 and stay on it until we reach I 57 and then turn right. At that point, we're practically there. We'll be almost on top of I 80."

"Excuse me, Dr. Young. We're almost stopped, now. If you'll move aside, I'll get that door open for you. I know how anxious you are to get going."

Stuart and Hawkins wasted no time moving to the side. "Thank You," Stuart said. "You've been most kind. And thank you for arranging these seats for us."

"You're most welcome. We hope you'll think 'American' the next time you fly," the blond flight attendant said. Stuart briefly noticed how pretty she was. Up until now, he had taken absolutely no note of her and wouldn't have recognized her the next time he saw her.

"Of course," he said absently.

Hawkins leaned close to her and whispered, "Do you think you could do us one more small favor?"

"I believe I can manage that. What can I do?"

"No questions?"

"No questions."

"I need for you to delay the other two first class passengers as long as you can."

"I believe I can handle that," she said as she swung the door open with a practiced motion and stepped aside.

"Brilliant," Stuart said. He took off in a fast walk.

"Oh, sir," they heard behind them, "Excuse me. I have to do something. Please step aside for a moment."

When Hawkins rounded the first turn in the Jet way and was no longer in sight of the plane, he broke into a run. "Let's go," he said.

"I'm right behind you," Stuart said.

Behind them they heard a loud clunk and a muffled shout, "What are you doing? Get the hell out of my way. Open this thing up."

"Can you believe that? I think she closed the door on them," Hawkins yelled.

"Which way to ground transportation?" Stuart yelled to a bored gate attendant who woodenly pointed to a sign. "Thanks, I see it." Pushing through passengers who were lined up to preboard another plane, the two runners leaped over stacks of luggage and a barrier rope and sped down the wide corridor leading to the down escalator some three hundred yards away. Taking the steps between the up and down escalators three at a time, Hawkins reached the ground level and following the signs, wound his way through the baggage claim area and burst through the glass exit doors and into the night with Stuart right behind him. He scanned the loading area. There was no white Taurus in sight.

"Where is Sam?" Hawkins yelled, looking around in all directions.

"There must be another exit," Stuart said, gasping for breath and bent over, his hands on his knees.

"Too late to look for another exit," Hawkins yelled.

"What do we do, now?"

As if in answer to Stuart's question, Vinny and Al burst through the double glass doors looking around wildly. Vinny spotted Stuart and instinctively reached inside his jacket to his shoulder holster. Finding it empty, he let out a loud curse. Several people in the loading area looked around and frowned in disapproval.

"Quick, this way," Hawkins said, gesturing for Stuart to follow. With Stuart right behind him, Hawkins raced over to where a sharply dressed older man was loading baggage into a brand new white Lincoln Town Car rented moments earlier from Hertz. The man had carefully placed the first of his six pieces of obviously expensive luggage into the cavernous trunk. The Lincoln was parked in the loading area with its engine running and the driver's door swung open. "Go around," Hawkins yelled.

Stuart didn't bother replying. He tore around behind the man and leaped into the passenger side of the Lincoln, slamming the door behind him. He looked up to see Vinny and Al running toward them. Stuart searched the car's armrest for a door lock button.

The man had bent down to pick up the second piece of his luggage and had turned around to place it carefully beside the first one when someone ran past him hollering something.

He paused with the suitcase in midair. Hawkins, still carrying the medical bag, held it up as he raced past the bent-over man. "Medical emergency," Hawkins yelled to the startled man. "I need to borrow your car for a few minutes. I can't explain now." He jumped into the driver's seat, slammed the door, tried to shift into drive and at the same time, mashed the accelerator to the floorboard. The car remained in neutral and the engine screamed but the car went nowhere.

Vinny made it to the car just as Stuart started frantically pressing buttons on the door's armrest. Vinny tried to jerk open the driver's door but not before Stuart had managed to hit the door lock button. Vinny banged on the window with both fists. "Al, go around to the other side," he yelled. "Do something. Break a window. Something. Anything."

"What's wrong with this car?" Hawkins hollered above the roar of the engine. "It won't shift."

"Step on the brake," Stuart yelled.

"What?"

"The brake. Step on the brake before you shift. Do it."

Hawkins complied. The Lincoln, with its trunk lid still open, shot forward in a smoking, squealing fishtail. Al, who had made it around to the passenger side, jumped backward when the car took off. Vinny pounded one more time on the window in frustration as the car sped away into the darkness. The man, still holding his suitcase, fell backwards onto the other four pieces of luggage. The acceleration surge caused the car's massive trunk lid to slam itself shut. "Hey, how about that," Hawkins said, looking at Stuart and grinning.

"Nice trick, but watch where you're going."

"Don't you worry about that. This here's like riding a bicycle. You don't ever forget how to do it."

"You used to drive like this?"

"All the time."

"I'm glad I didn't know you back then."

"How come I had to step on the brake before it would shift?"

"Safety feature on some of the newer cars. If you didn't drive such an antique, you'd know."

"Amazing. You learn something every day if you pay attention. Okay, navigator. Look for a sign to Highway 50. Never mind. I see it now."

* * *

"Wow. Sonny, did you see that? Cool." Shawn pulled over to the left curb and stopped behind the dazed man sitting on his pile of luggage. "I think we better find out if the old guy needs any help. He looks pretty shook up."

"Wouldn't you be if someone just stole your car?"

"Hell, yes I would. Let's go." Shawn shifted into park and pressed the release buttons for the two electric latches. He and Sonny shoved open the heavy car doors at the same time. Shawn had no more than swung his leg out when a powerful hand grabbed his arm and he found himself jerked out of his car and skidding across the concrete sidewalk on his back. Sonny was jerked out in similar fashion and thrown into the street. The surprise was total. Neither boy was able to react. For Vinny and Al, it was business as usual. This wasn't the first time they had pulled off this particular carjacking stunt.

While both boys were still sprawling on the pavement, Vinny and Al slid onto the front bench seat of the customized Lincoln and slammed their doors shut. Vinny dropped the car into drive, turned hard to the right and tore off after Stuart and Hawkins.

* * *

"I'll drive and you watch the car," Vinny growled. "We gotta catch them."

Al ducked low to be able to see out of the chopped vehicle. "The roof on this thing's so low I can hardly see out much less watch for that car," Al complained. "This windshield can't be more than six inches high. Why would anybody do something stupid like this to a car?"

"If you know what's good for you, you'll keep your mouth shut and your eye on that white Lincoln," Al said. "Hey, this old crate will really move."

"Keep your shirt on, Vinny. I ain't going to lose them. You know you can trust me. Get in the right lane. Looks like they're turning. Hey Vinny, you ain't got no heat. How you gonna ice him?"

Vinny shot Al a venomous look. "Never you mind. I'll figure that out when we catch up to them. You just keep tabs on them. I'll do the thinking. If we hadn't landed at Midway, we'd have had a welcoming party for them and they'd be dead already. Wish I had my satellite phone."

* * *

"Uh oh."

"Uh oh what?" Stuart asked.

"We've got company."

Stuart looked back. Sure enough, headlights were gaining on them about three hundred yards back. "What are you going to do?"

"It didn't take them long to borrow some wheels. Pedal to the metal time. Hang on." Already exceeding eighty-five, Hawkins pushed the luxury sedan up to ninety-five. Still, their pursuers were gaining. "I'm having to give this my full attention. Be sure to watch for signs to Highway 57. We definitely don't want to miss it."

"Roger. That is one sign I won't miss, I promise you. I don't care how fast you drive." Stuart turned to look over his shoulder. "They're still gaining. I don't know what to expect. They don't have any guns. I saw one of them reach for his and come up empty. Otherwise we'd already be using the instruments you brought to pick lead out of our butts."

"For sure. Thank God for security systems. But I wish there was more traffic this time of night. It sure would help," Hawkins said, checking in his rear view mirror. "Uh oh. That's what I get for wishing. A squad car passing in the opposite direction just spotted us. I saw the lights come on."

"We've got to beat them to the restaurant. If we don't, the sirens will spook the thugs in the ambulance."

"Hang on."

* * *

"You almost got them dead to rights, Vinny. We can't be more than a hundred yards behind them. Figured out what you're going to do yet?"

"You stick to your business and I'll handle the thinking. Watch them carefully. I intend to finish what I started. Whatever you do, don't blink. Uh oh. Cops."

"Don't worry. They're going in the opposite direction. We'll be out of sight by the time they get turned around." Vinny had the old Lincoln going as fast as it could. He had long ago topped out at one hundred ten miles per hour. Smoke was now pouring from the exhaust pipe and the engine was starting to clatter noisily. Vinny didn't notice. His one-track focus blocked out everything from his mind save one— restoring his stature as a capable and reliable killer. His reputation was at stake, now. If he blew it this time, they may not give him another shot and he knew it.

* * *

"Hawkins?"

"Yeah?"

"They are really getting close. There's the sign for highway I 57. You're going to turn right. At that point, we'll be almost on top of I 80 according to Captain Turner."

"Brace yourself. I've never done this at over a hundred before."

"Hawkins, you're passing up the exit."

* * *

Vinny eased up alongside the white Lincoln. "Hang on. And watch this. You might learn something," he said. The hot rod held rock steady. Vinny waited to make his move until the white car was almost even with the huge light pole that illuminated the exit. Like a viper, he struck. With all his might, Vinny forced the steering wheel as hard and as fast as he could to the right.

* * *

"Brace yourself."

At the same instant that Vinny turned, Hawkins turned to his right, knocking a chunk of concrete from the light pole stanchion with his left front bumper. After righting the swaying machine, he rocketed down the off ramp and onto I 57. Having anticipated Vinny's move, Hawkins had timed his move to allow the hot rod to pull up beside them and to exit at the last possible instant to keep Vinny from following them down the exit.

"That was beautiful," Stuart yelled, beating on the dashboard with his palms. "It was fantastic. We're going to make it."

"Now, look for I 80."

* * *

Vinny's hot rod shot past the careening rent car, missing the light pole. He slammed on the brakes and attempted to maintain a controlled broadslide at the same time. "They turned, you idiot. You were supposed to warn me."

"How was I supposed to know they were going to turn?"

A '51 Lincoln did not come equipped with antilock brakes. The suddenness of Vinny's maneuver at speeds the old car had never before seen caused it to do four double axles. After spinning out of control using all five traffic lanes plus both shoulders for more than three hundred feet, Vinny finally stopped the vehicle in a cloud of blue smoke. Miraculously, the old car's engine was still running. Vinny found himself facing the direction he had come from and quickly accelerated. Two oncoming cars had to swerve to avoid the strange looking car streaking down the freeway the wrong way. Three other cars honked loud and long.

"Shut up and get the hell out of my way," Vinny shouted, shaking his fist in defiance at the offending drivers.

After making his way through the honking traffic and back to his exit, he deftly executed a sliding hundred and eighty degree turn and sped down the ramp to follow his quarry. "Did you see which way they went?"

"I think so."

"You *think* so? You lost them. You'd better find them if you know what's good for you."

* * *

"They're not giving up, I assure you. I think it was them coming down the ramp just as we went over the last hill. At least it looked like them," Stuart said.

"Bet on it. What time is it, anyway? And watch out for the I 80 signs."

"There it is. I 80 next exit. It's eleven fifty-nine, by the way. Better step on it."

"You got it. Hang on. We're coming in."

"Is that the restaurant up ahead?" Stuart asked, pointing to a well-lit building that appeared to be on a corner at the next intersection.

"That's it. We're going to make it. No time to spare."

* * *

"There they are," Al said. "See. Told you we wouldn't lose them."

"They're stopping. What the hell? They're pulling into a restaurant. I can't believe they're going to eat. Hey, look over there. Isn't that one of our meat wagons?"

"Yeah. You're right. Wonder what it's doing here. Drive over to it. I'll find out." Vinny drove over to the ambulance. Al jumped out and banged on the driver's window.

Startled, Pony jerked around, furious that he had allowed someone to sneak up on him. "Al! What the hell are you doing here?"

"What are *you* doing here? You were in Dallas when we left."

"That doctor that was snooping around the clinic survived the wreck we arranged for him, so me and Vinny here got on the plane and followed him from Dallas to this place. That's him over there in the white shirt. Why did he come here, you think?"

"Holy hell. Something's bad wrong. Hang on. I better do something." Pony grabbed for the dash mike. "Chicago. Something's coming down. Al and Vinny just drove up behind that doctor that was snooping around the clinic back in Dallas. Him and somebody else we don't recognize are about to go in the restaurant to warn Welborn. Should you take her out now?"

"Hell, yes. I'll take her out now. Okay. Signal confirmed. She's dead. Go pick her up and bring her on in. I'll alert the clinic that you're coming in early so they can get the patient ready."

"What about the doctor and his friend and what do we do with the girl that's traveling with Welborn? She'll make trouble."

"Tell Vinny and Al to take out the doctor and whoever's with him. I don't care how. You two take care of Welborn's friend. Do whatever you have to do but bring her in with you. Got that? We'll take it from there."

* * *

"What time is it?" Stuart asked, pausing to peer through the front glass of the restaurant.

"Exactly twelve oh-four. Do you see B.J.?"

"No. But I see Cathy. She's sitting at a table by herself. That's her over there with her back to us." Stuart pointed toward the table and looked at Hawkins. "Where's my bag?"

"Right here." Hawkins handed Stuart the small bag. "You go in and take care of B.J. I'll stay out here in case they try to come in. Stuart pushed open the front door of the eatery. He walked briskly toward the ladies' room. Without knocking, he opened the door and slipped into the small room, closing it behind him. He saw B.J. lying on the floor, blood staining her forehead and a man bending over her. He was too late. "You son of a bitch," Stuart screamed. "Get the hell away from her. I swear I'll kill you if you've hurt her."

Stuart, overtaken by pure instinct, dropped his medical bag, grabbed the surprisingly light man, slammed him against the wall and dropped to B.J.'s side. He held her limp form and cradled her head in his arm.

"Baby," he said softly, "you're going to be all right, now." Not daring to believe his own words but hoping nevertheless, he laid B.J. on the tile floor, still cradling her head with his arm. He looked down at the still form. An anguished groan erupted from deep within him. "Please, God," he moaned. Stuart carefully laid her head on the floor so that he could better feel her neck for a pulse. Yes. A faint one but it was a pulse. He was certain. Wasn't it? No. He couldn't tell. With his hands shaking so violently, he couldn't be sure.

"Pardon me. I believe this is what you are looking for."

"What?" Stuart's head slowly turned until he finally focused on the small man in the room with them. He was holding out a bloody scalpel. "What?"

"Please allow me to apologize for the lack of sterile conditions. However, if we treat the wound with antiseptic from either your bag or mine, I believe it will have the desired effect."

"What?" Stuart's foggy mind wasn't grasping reality, whatever that was. He felt B.J. stir. His gaze returned to her face. She was smiling faintly. "My God. You're alive." He gently drew B.J. into an embrace and again focused on the man, who lowered the scalpel for Stuart to inspect. On its tip was a tiny microchip with a trailing antenna and a probe wire that—until moments ago—had pierced B.J.'s skull awaiting its deadly signal. A wisp of smoke still curled up from the tiny device.

"Who are you?" Stuart managed to ask in a hoarse whisper.

"He's Dr. Ito," B.J. said.

"But how in . . . why—"

The blare of approaching sirens broke the silence. Stuart finally allowed himself to breathe. He wanted to pull B.J. close to him and spend the next hour holding her and stroking her and loving her. A long sigh escaped his lips. "I think the cops have caught up with Hawkins," he said laughing. They had won but he was too exhausted to move, too emotional to say anything else and too shaky to stand.

With a trickle of blood trailing down her forehead, B.J. looked over at Stuart and said with a weak smile, "Dr. Young, you have got a lot of explaining to do, but not now."

Outside the restaurant, two officers with guns drawn held Hawkins prisoner. Another officer had guns trained on Vinny and Al after Hawkins had insisted that they were implicated. Also, at Hawkins' insistence, a second squad car called in for backup had taken off in pursuit of Pony and Aretti in the ambulance.

Epilogue

Dr. Ito rose and bowed. "May I have your attention, please? Much important news tonight, my friends. First, I would like to thank our host for the magnificent repast that he prepared. My compliments, Dr. Mitchell. Second, I am honored to dine with my esteemed colleague, Dr. G.P. Hawkins. Without his brilliant insight into forensic medicine, we would not have solved the mystery of the unexplained death phenomenon. I have recommended to his superiors that they honor him as well. Dr. Hawkins, please address this distinguished audience on your own behalf."

"Thank you, Dr. Ito. It's way more than I deserve. I played a small role, actually. There is one very important accomplishment that I would like to acknowledge. Due to B.J.'s efforts to make the world safer, we no longer have to worry about the same thing happening again with this technology. As of last week, any key personnel of any company that is a DOD-authorized user of the GPS system must undergo a rigorous security investigation. It will also be retroactive for all who presently are authorized. Since B.J. is taking the lead role in the GPS expansion program, even Stuart will have to go through it. Family members must be cleared, too. And speaking of being cleared, Dr. Ito, I have to laugh every time I think of the grilling that you, Stuart, B.J., Cathy and I had to go through at the hands of the Chicago FBI. It took a lot of fast talking to convince them that we were not carjackers or mobsters, didn't it? Thank you." Hawkins grinned and sat down.

Ito stood again. "Spoken with characteristic humility. Thank you, Dr. Hawkins. I now have the distinct honor of announcing the engagement of Dr. Clarence John Mitchell to the lovely Miss Deborah Justine Smith." Dr. Ito raised his wineglass. "Much happiness to you both."

Debbie unconsciously touched her diamond engagement ring and wedding ring pair and leaned toward Mitch. "Clarence?" she whispered.

"Deborah Justine?" Mitch responded. He smiled, leaned over, kissed her dimpled cheek, then stood and pushed back his chair. "Thank you, Dr. Ito. For the compliments and for your good wishes. I think I have found what I need for happiness. Like my good friend here. We all know how close Stuart came to losing everything. The look on his face tonight is reward enough to those who had some small part in B.J.'s rescue." He paused. "Dr. Ito, I don't quite know how to express the gratitude that all of us feel for what you did for B.J. and Stuart. If it hadn't been for your foresight and your flight to Chicago on the outside chance that Hawkins and Stuart might not arrive in time, B.J. wouldn't be celebrating with us tonight."

Stuart's arm tightened protectively around B.J.'s shoulder as he listened to Mitch. Never again would he let her away from him.

B.J. turned to Stuart and smiled through tears. "I love you," she whispered.

Stuart cleared his throat, picked up his wineglass and stood. He looked around the table and saw Hawkins, the friend who had been with him and beside him throughout the nightmare. To Hawkins' right sat the flight attendant who helped ease the interminable flight to Chicago and who gave them those precious moments of lead time in the airport. She smiled and looked down. On Hawkins' left sat Joseph Legato's widow, Rose. She still wore black in honor of her husband, her composure regal. He watched her lean toward Dr. Ito, seated to her left, and whisper something to him. Dr. Ito. The man he almost killed in an insane rage. The man responsible for saving B.J.'s life. He could never repay that gift.

Cathy, B.J.'s lifelong friend, now one of Stuart's favorite people. She had been so calm that damnable night so long ago. Had it only been four months? Cathy had brought a date. B.J. hoped he might be Cathy's soul mate, like he was B.J.'s. Stuart's arm still rested on B.J.'s shoulder. The comfort it gave him could not be described.

And Debbie. How could he have doubted Debbie? Fiercely loyal since the day she came to work for him. He would never know why she left Dallas General to be his office nurse but he'd forever be grateful. Debbie and Mitch belonged together. Stuart winced at the thought of the pain Debbie had suffered throughout the indictment of her uncle, Conrad Nation, for his role in the Christian Clinic operation.

Mitch. His professional clone who had been helpful in so many ways when he couldn't locate B.J. and nearly went nuts because of it. Thank you, Mitch, he thought. Stuart's gaze once more rested on Hawkins.

Stuart began to speak. "Friends. I almost lost my reason for living." His hand tightened on B.J.'s shoulder. "When I thought they would take her from me and give her heart to someone else, I turned into something that I'm not proud of. I can never explain that time in my life. I needed your help and you were there for me. I can only say 'thank you' to all of you for your patience and understanding. Rose, I know that Joseph's investigation cost him his life. I'm so sorry. But please take pride in knowing that he alone was responsible for bringing down the vile and hideous organ transplant operation. I'm only sorry that the evidence necessary to indict Dexter Manning disappeared from the files at TI before they could gather it up. Manning, himself can no longer be located, not even for questioning as a witness. The case against him has been put on hold and TI has finally given up the idea of a civil suit. They did, however, spread the word around the industry about Manning. He's through in electronics. But because of Joseph Legato, Earth Argon, Christian Clinic and Chicago Christian Insurance Company are no more and the governor of Illinois is under indictment. Joseph deserves every accolade bestowed on him. Dr. Ito. Hawkins. Debbie. Mitch . . ." Stuart couldn't continue.

Dr. Ito stood again. He gazed fondly at Stuart and B.J. and raised his glass. "Gentlemen and ladies, it appears that the honor has once more fallen to me. May I please to announce the forthcoming birth of a child to our dearest friends, Doctor and Mrs. Stuart Young?"

* * *

Manning stared at the piles of paper spread out on the king-size bed in a specific order meaningful only to him. His room service dishes were stacked haphazardly on their tray next to the double locked door with the chair back jammed under its handle. All drapes were tightly drawn. He had paid for the room for two days in advance. Cash. They'd made him put up a $25.00 deposit since he wasn't paying by card. Guess they thought he might steal something from the honor bar. So much for honor.

"Yes, operator. I'm still here. Does anyone on that end speak English? Good, because my Chinese is rather poor." He laughed nervously. "I'm placing a person-to-person call to Mr. Kahn Fung. Yes, that's right. Fung. In Beijing. Peoples Republic of China." He held the card closer to the lamp. "The country code is 86 and the number is 55-598-00. Yes. He's the minister of technology there and he's expecting my call. Mr. Fung? Yes, I am here. Is the interpreter on the line? Good. Are you ready to hear my proposal?"

THE END

ACKNOWLEDGEMENTS

First, a disclaimer: This novel is purely a book of fiction. Names, characters, places and incidents are the product of the author's imagination or are used fictitiously. Any resemblance to actual events, locales or persons living or dead is coincidental (or used fictitiously).

Next, the author would like to thank the following people who helped more than they know:

-First and foremost, my incredible wife, Pat. Anyone who knows Pat knows that she is the consummate encourager. And I get to enjoy that all the time.

-Melinda Gossage, who took the proverbial bull by the horns and made it her personal goal to get this book published. Moe, you're the greatest.

-My sister, Jeanne Royston, who typed every word of the original manuscript since, at the time, I hadn't learned to type. She also was an incredible idea person.

-Dr. Dan Spivey, my expert on the medical and anatomical aspects of the book. Thanks Dan.

-Mark Johnson, for your help in working through the intricacies of book publishing.

-Floyd (Spock) Marsellos, for your thoughts, encouragement and friendship over the years.

-Jack Kilby, for inventing the integrated circuit (microchip) and incredibly, agreeing to review the manuscript and make comments.

BACKGROUND OF 'THE BLACK CHIP'

MY AEROSPACE ODYSSEY

by

Chuck Royston

Talk about lucky . . . I was born at the perfect time, in the perfect place, went to the perfect school, married the perfect woman and had the perfect career. My journey began around

7:30 in the evening on October 4, 1957. Where were you at that time? Give you a hint . . . it was on a Friday.

If you guessed Russia orbiting SPUTNIK I, you win the prize. SPUTNIK I was about twenty-three inches in diameter and weighed a hundred and eighty-three pounds and it was circling overhead every hour and a half and could be seen from just about anywhere.

To put it all into perspective, at the time, it had been only eleven years since we dropped the atomic bomb on Hiroshima. Think of it. Only eleven years. It has now been more than two decades since 9/11 and you see how vivid **those** events *STILL* are in our minds.

It petrified the nation with this thing zooming overhead at more than 17,000 miles an hour only five hundred miles up. It was visible all around the earth and its radio beacon transmitted on 20 and 40 megahertz, detectible on ham radios around the world. Scary. Very scary.

Only eight months after that, Texas Instruments (TI) hired a young engineer named Jack Kilby to work on a problem that the industry was facing. Transistors had been invented about 20 years before but were relatively bulky. To create a machine that would make the number of calculations per second that were becoming necessary, the millions of transistors that would be required would result in a gigantic machine. Kilby was hired because he had a theory that resistors, capacitors, switches and inductors (the basic components of an electrical circuit) could be made from the same material and manufactured with no wires, making the circuits infinitely smaller.

Kilby was hired in June 1958 when most of the TI employees were on a company-wide vacation. So Kilby was allowed to play around in the silicon lab alone during those two weeks. By the time everyone came back from vacation, he had a working model of a chip, a microcircuit.

On May 10, 1961, JFK spoke to a joint session of congress and challenged them to fund a program to land a man on the moon and return him safely to earth before the decade was out. This could not have been accomplished without the microchip.

Nine days later I graduated from college with a bachelor's degree in electrical engineering. Six weeks after that, Pat and I began our life in Seattle where we both worked on Boeing's Minuteman Missile program.

In May 1963 I requested a transfer to South Dakota so that I could get experience with installation and checkout of the Minuteman missiles into their underground silos.

In September of that year I requested a transfer to New Orleans where work was underway on the largest, most powerful, rocket ever attempted, the Saturn V, the most powerful rocket ever built, 363 feet tall in the Apollo configuration and able to lift seven million pounds off the launch pad. It produced seven and a half million pounds of thrust and for over fifty years, remained the most powerful rocket ever built. It is surpassed only by the Artemis moon rocket, which produces eight point eight million pounds of thrust.

In December 1964 I was hired by NASA to work on the Apollo communications systems design. I never got a chance to witness an Apollo launch because I had to be at Mission Control in the Mission Evaluation Room (MER) during every mission. We had three shifts and were present every minute of the flight. By chance, I was in the MER at 8:06 in the evening on April 13, 1970 when the Apollo 13 explosion rocked our world. I heard in real time, "Houston, we have a problem."

All personnel involved in the incredible Apollo 13 rescue received the Presidential Medal of Freedom award for our role in the rescue. It was a proud time for NASA.

The last seven years of my aerospace experience was in Sunnyvale California supervising the manufacturing and upgrading of the TRIDENT submarine missile launchers. Talk about an engineering marvel. The idea was to launch intercontinental ballistic missiles from a submerged TRIDENT submarine without getting the missile wet. It was a hoot "launching" test missiles in San Francisco Bay.

After retiring from aerospace engineering, I was able to finally see a launch. Only it wasn't an Apollo launch, it was the final Space Shuttle launch (STS 135). It was everything I had imagined it to be. My nephew, Eddie Gossage, and I sat in the VIP viewing area about three miles from the launch pad and watched as the vehicle rose majestically into the air through a hole in the cloud cover which magically appeared at just the right time. It was as close as anyone could get to the launch who wasn't actually involved in the launch itself. It was, in a word, awesome. Through Eddie, I had previously met Doug Hurley, the Shuttle pilot for STS 135. That made the experience very personal.

In August of 1998, it was announced that Jack Kilby would finally get the recognition he deserved by winning the Nobel Prize in Physics for inventing the integrated circuit. On a whim, I wrote to Kilby at TI to congratulate him on winning the Nobel Prize. In the letter, I told him that he ruined my life. All my college education was about vacuum tubes and transistors. In my junior year of college, he ups and invents the microchip, which is all I saw after I graduated. I was obsolete the day I started work as an engineer. It was all in fun, of course.

A week or so later, Pat and I were watching TV in the den when the phone rang. I answered. A deep, booming, thundering voice asked, "Is this Chuck Royston?"

"Yes, it is," I answered, not recognizing the voice. "I just called to apologize for ruining your life." WOW! To an electrical engineer, it was like getting a call from Thomas Edison. We had a great visit and I told him about a novel I had drafted entitled, 'The Chip.' Would he be so kind as to review it for me and give me his comments if I sent him a manuscript? He told me he would be proud to. He followed up the call with a letter saying that the book sounded very interesting and clearly different from anything he had seen and that he wasn't much of a literary critic but would be glad to look at the manuscript. He again apologized for making me obsolete.

I wasted no time getting the manuscript to him. About a month later, Jack (note the first name basis) called back with his comments. He said he loved the book and thought it was very well done and apologized for taking so long. He said that because of nature of the story, the book should be entitled, 'The Black Chip.'

So there you have it. Hope you enjoyed 'The Black Chip.'

The author & wife Pat at the

beach

The author & STS-135 Shuttle Pilot

Doug Hurley